A Biography of a Chance Miracle

Tanja Maljartschuk

FG-UA0001L
ISBN: 978-4-908793-41-7

Cover: Joe Reimer

Cadmus Press
CADMUSMEDIA.ORG

A Biography of a Chance Miracle

Tanja Maljartschuk

Translated from the Ukrainian
by
Zenia Tompkins

Cadmus Press
2018

Ein Hund, der stirbt
und der weiß, dass er stirbt wie ein Hund,
und der sagen kann, dass er weiß dass er stirbt wie ein Hund,
ist ein Mensch.

A dog who is dying,
and who knows that he's dying like a dog,
and who can say that he knows that he's dying like a dog,
is a man.

Erich Fried

Contents

1   WHAT SHE CALLED HERSELF
       AND OTHERS

Lena was born in San Francisco and called herself Lena.

San Francisco is a little Ukrainian city, more to the west than to the east of the country. It was named in memory of those who left for the United States in the early twentieth century in search of the land of their dreams. Those who stayed behind said, "This here is our America." And they named their city San Francisco.

After World War II, the Communists renamed it, of course, but Lena continued to call her home city by its American name and even said that the real American San Francisco was far less real than the Ukrainian one.

Lena always referred to herself as Lena and nothing else. She could've been an Olena or an Olenka, but she hated these two variants more than the Russian Lena. And she hated the "Russian" as much as most of the residents of Western Ukraine, with all her might.

The Russian had most likely attached itself to her name out of spite, and she was never able to get away from it. That's what always happens with something that you hate. It never lets you go.

When she was little, Lena was forced to memorize a poem from her reader about little Olenka, and its first line went like this: "Little Olenka, why are you so *splendid?*" And this Olenka replies, "Because my family makes me so!"

Lena's relatives would clap in delight and were always

asking her to recite this poem. Lena would blush and beg not to, but it was obvious that the relatives wouldn't budge. So, in the end, she would get up from behind the table and shout loudly, "Little Olenka, why are you so *stupid?* Because my family makes me so!" Later Lena would have unpleasantness to deal with: They would stick her in a corner or simply wouldn't talk to her for a day or two.

Lena associated the name Olenka with stupidity, and being stupid was the one thing that she spent her whole life trying to avoid but never evaded.

As a child she was afraid of losing something, of missing something, and of being stupid as a result. She later understood that there was no way to escape this and that wisdom didn't depend on the number of books you'd read. Wisdom, Lena would say, depends on having the courage to admit what and how you think. You have to have your own opinions and then, maybe, wisdom will come. But it's imperative to have opinions. At the same time, you also have to carefully listen to other people and decide if you're in agreement with their opinions or if you're standing by your own. It's important to be honest with yourself. It's important to adopt the opinions of others if they're better than yours.

Lena wasn't actually to blame for the fact that she hated everything Russian. For one, she was born in a place where not liking Russia was a matter of historical justice. Second, Lena entered preschool right at the time when the teachers and nannies were tearing down Lenin's portrait from the assembly hall wall. It was evident that they hated him wholeheartedly. They explained to Lena many times in preschool that Ukraine had suffered greatly at the hands of Lenin, and at the hands of the Communists, and at the hands of a lot of other Russians. And that's why there was no need to like Russia. Before the Communists, there was the Russian Empire, which called Ukraine "Little Russia" and banned the Ukrainian language. The kids were told about the prisons in which Ukrainians sat and died and about that Siberia to which Ukrainians were exiled to a certain death amid snows, tundras and polar bears. She was taught to sing songs in which young Ukrainian boys went off to war to defend their native land, typically leaving behind a pregnant fiancée at home. Lena always felt very sorry for this fiancée.

Lena knew the biography of the nineteenth-century Ukrainian poet Taras Hryhorovych Shevchenko in detail and always cried at the point when the little serf Taras wants to study, but his landowner's drunken clerk is beating him and forcing him to fetch water from the river barefoot in winter. It's unclear whether or not Lena had been told that the drunken clerk was a Russian. Lena didn't like the Poles either, but that's another story.

Precisely then, while in preschool, Lena underwent a psychological trauma related to the Russian language.

She had a lot of teachers, all middle-aged biddies with fake clip-on buns on their heads and a boundless love for their homeland. There was nothing else memorable about them. But one teacher was fundamentally different from the others. She was older. She had long gray hair, which she always wound into a hefty lump at the nape of her neck. This lump was bigger than her actual head. And the teacher didn't love her homeland.

To tell the truth, Lena didn't discuss the homeland with her, but it was obvious that the teacher didn't love it. Unlike the other teachers, she never uttered a single word about the homeland. She talked to the kids in Russian, which was very conspicuous in the ultra-patriotic preschool. In the assembly hall, where Lenin's portrait had once been, there now hung a full-length Shevchenko that was somewhat reminiscent of his predecessor, and everyone gazed at him with reverence and fear, as if gazing at an icon.

This one teacher alone behaved differently. Maybe she didn't know who Shevchenko was, or maybe she just didn't consider him worthy of taking The Leader's place.

The teacher had spent her whole life in San Francisco

but never did learn to talk like a normal person, be it because she didn't want to or because she couldn't. Her Russian sounded comical — with a distinct Ukrainian accent and peppered with Ukrainian words that she, as a rule, inserted in all the wrong places. The teacher had probably had a rough life because you can't get too far with that kind of language among strangers.

Lena called her Big Lump.

Big Lump loved children, especially Lena. She would teach her songs and always said that great people would come crawling out of Lena. It was unclear from where exactly these great people were supposed to emerge, from which specific part of Lena's body, but then Lena would grow awfully proud of herself and would sing so loudly that the panes in the windows would rattle.

Big Lump would also tell Lena that she would grow up to be a good-looking woman and have a good-looking husband and good-looking children. That was obviously a lie. Lena had a chubby torso and short hair, cut unevenly with blunt scissors. The teacher would tell Lena that it wasn't worth getting too worked up over her torso and hair right now because all people were ugly as children. And that was also a lie because all around her Lena could see other little girls with long blond braids, in sumptuous dresses, with almost doll-like faces.

But Lena sang the loudest, and Big Lump had said in Russian that she'd grow up to be great people.

One day the headmistress of the preschool called in the teacher and ordered her to talk to the children only in Ukrainian. The teacher promised to do so. For a month or two she tried, as best she was able, giving it all she had, but these attempts sounded pitiful. Her tongue just wouldn't cooperate. It would get stuck mid-word. Instead of "Hello, kids," she would say "Hello, keedz." The "keedz" would cackle, and Big Lump would cry. During nap time, Lena would try to chat with her to calm her down a bit. To pay her back for the great people.

"But you do understand," Lena would say, "Russia is a very bad and evil country. A lot of Ukrainians died because of it. In Siberia and at the White Sea too."

The teacher's face would be flushed and swollen from crying. She would sit in silence, and this silence would give Lena no peace.

Lena would push on: "Tell me, are you Russian? Because if you're Russian, then you might be my enemy."

"I'm Russian," Big Lump would reply bravely, it was unclear in which language.

"Well, then, you must be a good Russian. Even good Russians are possible."

Lena had had enough and went to talk to the headmistress.

This headmistress was very stern. Kids would break into a cold sweat at one glance from her, but Lena convinced herself that for the sake of a good cause she would survive.

She knocked softly on the door of her office and, without waiting for a response, poked her head inside. The headmistress was sitting at her desk in her inevitable white lab coat, which she for some reason wore in the preschool as if it were a hospital.

"What is it?" she shouted nervously.

Lena slithered into the office like a weasel, which she had been told was able to slither through the smallest of microscopic crevices, stretching out and flattening its body as it pleased. And now Lena, like a weasel, slithered through the cracked door and chirped in a trembling voice, "I want to request, sir — Headmistress Vasylivna — that you let her talk to us in Russian. Or at least to me. Because I understand it all. It's not hard for me."

The headmistress looked sternly at Lena. Lena went on muttering something, and this muttering was seamlessly transitioning into weeping. The headmistress had a pale, steel-gray face. Sometimes, when her position called for it, this face would force out a grin that was so steely that it would make kids stutter or wet their beds until age twenty or so. This time, for better or worse, the headmistress wasn't smiling.

"Listen to me," she hissed in a typically didactic tone. "What's your name?"

"Lena…"

"Not Lena, but Olenka! Listen to me, Olenka. You're Ukrainian and you should never forget that. Your grandfathers and great-grandfathers sacrificed their lives so that you could call yourself a Ukrainian."

"My grandfather's alive," Lena managed to squeeze in. "It's just that he drinks a lot. But my great-grandfather's dead, that's true. He was very old."

"You're not hearing what I'm saying, Olenka! I'm not talking about your grandfather and great-grandfather but about other ones. About many other grandfathers and great-grandfathers."

"Ah! Well, you should've said so from the get-go!"

"…who sacrificed their lives for Ukraine. They died and you're living. In a free Ukraine. And you don't have the right to betray this country. You'll live and work for the good of this country, and you'll talk in Ukrainian, which has been preserved thanks only to your grandfathers and great-grandfathers."

Lena flinched again.

"…I meant to say, thanks to the many other grandfathers and great-grandfathers who laid down their lives so that the Ukrainian language could continue to ring freely."

Lena listened a bit longer, in order to appear well-raised and to avoid eliciting needless wrath, and then went right back to her main concern: "So you'll let her talk to us in Russian?"

The headmistress snapped.

"You're unworthy of calling yourself a Ukrainian! To betray your native language like that, when your grandfathers and great-grandfathers are lying in the ground!"

"My grandfather's still alive…"

"Get out of here! Apostate!

Lena bolted out of the office, analyzing along the way in

which category of offensive terms the word "apostate" belonged. But Big Lump had even bigger problems as a result of this conversation. The headmistress convened a special commission, something along the lines of a public trial, which was supposed to decide her fate once and for all.

But her fate decided itself on its own, as fate usually does.

Lena remembered that day very well.

It was May, and everything was blooming and fragrant. Lena had gotten a new dress, which happened rarely at that time because her parents had long been working without pay. The dress, a maroon one with tiny maple leaves, was about two sizes too small.

When the rest of the children had fallen asleep after lunch, Lena came to Big Lump and said that she wasn't going to sleep because she didn't want to take off her new outfit. In reality, Lena simply couldn't take it off: she was scared that she would either rip it or suffocate in the process. Big Lump understood everything and let the girl sit with her in the classroom for a while.

Big Lump was sculpting a light blue swan out of Plasticine. She tended to like light blue. She said to Lena, "Close your eyes and imagine a rainbow."

Lena did as Big Lump said, but no rainbow was coming.

"Do you know what a rainbow is?"

"I do," lied Lena.

She had, of course, seen rainbows before, but had no idea where they came from or where they disappeared to. Lena's grandpa used to say that rainbows were bridges between rivers, but it's very possible that he was lying because he did like to tell a good lie now and then.

"A rainbow is a string of colors that all come together once in a while in order to beautify the world," said Big Lump. "List the colors that you know."

"White, black, red, green, yellow…"

The teacher stopped Lena. "White and black aren't colors."

"How are they not colors? Look, you're wearing a white shirt."

"You think that it's white. In fact, it already has all of the colors in it. It's all the colors combined. It's a miracle."

"Well, I don't see any other colors, just white."

"That's precisely why it's a miracle — because you can't see it. You need to know how to see miracles. You have to learn to see them."

"Will you teach me how?"

"I'll teach you how," Big Lump said sadly, attaching a Plasticine head to her swan.

A real May thunderstorm was brewing outside. It grew as dark as night. Somewhere not far away some homeless dogs let out a howl.

"In thunderstorms like this, a black horseman rides into the city on a black horse," said Big Lump.

"I've never seen him," Lena replied.

"Exactly. No one's ever seen him because everyone sits at home during thunderstorms. But that's when he rides around the city on his horse."

"What does he want?"

"No one knows. Maybe he's just out for a ride, but maybe he's looking for something."

Big Lump would often tell the kids all kinds of unbelievable — at times even terrifying — stories. About supernatural forces, about volcanoes, about aliens and about ghosts in prison castles. The children would listen to her with their mouths gaping. Later, incidentally, they would repeat these stories to their parents, and the outraged parents would go to the headmistress to file complaints against the teacher.

Outside it thundered and lightning flashed. The frightened children, wearing only their underpants, came running into the classroom.

"Go back to your cots," said Big Lump. "I'll be with you in a minute. I'll just shut the window."

The teacher got up from behind her desk and moved in the direction of the window.

And then something flashed in the air.

A fiery orb as big as a soccer ball hovered over the children's heads in the middle of the room spewing short white sparks in all directions. The orb was vibrating but almost seemed frozen in place in some kind of eerie anticipation. All of the children froze too, staring at it spellbound, their eyes overflowing with tears from the brilliant light.

Lena knew what this orb was. She had heard about the phenomenon of ball lightning from the teacher a million times. It was a popular topic in all the science fiction magazines at the time. Everyone talked about ball lightning, but no one had ever seen it. Everyone knew that you shouldn't panic and run away from it, that you shouldn't move. But they didn't know for how long because there wasn't a single witness to this bizarre phenomenon. A single living one, that is.

The teacher also realized what it was. Lena noticed the fear in her eyes and was a little surprised. She thought that, if anyone, Big Lump would be able to get them out of this mess.

It all lasted a matter of seconds. The children, numb with terror and wearing only their underpants, were already on the verge of making a run for it. Big Lump cut them off. She lunged toward the window and hollered with all her might, "Now isn't *this* a miracle, Lena?"

That very second the ball lightning broke loose from its position, and the teacher blazed up in all the colors of a rainbow. The children shrieked while Lena stood and watched.

Big Lump disintegrated into a spectrum of color, dissolved as if she had never been. Only the intolerably vile smell of burnt flesh hinted at the teacher's former existence.

Lena was still standing and watching when the entire preschool came running into the classroom at the kids' squeals. The headmistress interrogated the kids about what had happened, but it was useless because no one could even utter a word. Everyone was crying, and a few kids had fallen to the floor unconscious. The headmistress was asking Lena, "Olenka, what happened? Where's the teacher?"

The blue Plasticine swan stood in splendor on Big Lump's desk. Lena took it for herself as a keepsake.

"Olenka, Olenka!" the headmistress was yelling.

Lena said, "I'm not Olenka. I'm Lena."

And she went home.

For a few months after that, she spoke only in Russian. The doctors said that it was a result of the shock she had experienced and that Lena had made it through relatively unscathed because some of the other children had completely stopped talking.

Lena was transferred to another preschool, while a commemorative plaque was hung in Big Lump's honor at the entrance of her previous one. "To save the children, she offered her own life." Lena never saw this plaque because she was very busy.

She was always waiting for great people to finally come crawling out of her.

Lena got good grades in school and read a lot because she thought that she had been granted no other talent. She had no friends. She was always alone with her books and textbooks in a made-up world, which very little resembled this world that we know.

Only some kind of forlorn creatures who had taken a beating from life were drawn to Lena. She later described them in her memoirs under the heading "The inner beauty of forlorn people": "Miserable and unwanted by anyone but me. Such, for example, was Ivanka, my best friend at the time. I called her Dog and she didn't take offense.

I suspect that she even liked it. Dog had barely learned to read and write by the sixth grade. She was simple and good, agreed to all of my shenanigans, went everywhere with me, and if I had suggested walking to the ends of the earth, she would've followed. There were nineteen other people in her family. That's why Dog spent all of her time on the street or at my house. I fed her, told her my tall tales, brushed her hair, at times I even treated her like a doll."

They sat next to each other in school, and Dog would always copy homework from Lena's notebook, nonetheless being wise enough to make mistakes in the process and get Ds. But grades were unimportant to her, as was school. Dog didn't regret anything because in order to have regrets you need to know how to think, and Dog didn't know how to do that, which is why she was happy and carefree. Lena, having taken upon herself the responsibility for Dog's education, would relate to her friend what she had learned in biology and physics, in both lit classes (Ukrainian and world) and in history. Lena particularly liked this last one because she felt no inhibitions and would concoct things to her heart's content. Lena didn't consider history to be a legitimate branch of knowledge and didn't believe in it. Dog paid dearly for this a few times, blurting something out in class she had heard from Lena. The stern Ukrainian history teacher would get so furious that he would kick her out of the room.

That was the first time that Dog got upset with Lena. She began to doubt Lena's authority. But as she had nowhere else to go, she came back to her before long all the same.

"Lena, you're a rotten liar."

"And you, Dog, are a dimwit."

And so they began chatting and once again became friends.

Another forlorn creature in Lena's world was a florist, the caretaker of the school's greenhouse — an elderly woman, with one leg twelve centimeters shorter than the other. When she walked, she looked like a ship that was being rocked from side to side by waves and carried farther and farther from shore. Lena called her Baba Lida.

There was a true jungle in Baba Lida's greenhouse. It smelled of dampness, heat and the ozone in there. A gigantic three-meter ficus stood resplendent in the entryway. Next you had to tear your way through hostile thickets of lush Monsteras with cropped leaves that looked like octopus tentacles on alert. Beyond that grew rows of agaves and snow-powdered old man cacti, as well as hundreds, no, thousands of the most varied plants, which Lena would never again see anywhere.

Baba Lida would water her forest with a solution of chicken droppings, and that's why, as she would say, everything grew and flourished so well. Like leavened bread. The cacti bloomed year-round, and the Monsteras bore fruit, which for them, as subtropicals, was far from characteristic in a temperate climate. Even ordinary geraniums (botanical term *Pelargonia)* looked like exotic princesses at Baba Lida's.

Lena and Dog would spend their entire recess in the greenhouse. They would sit on tiny stools under the Monsteras and keep an eye on how Baba Lida's forest was growing. Once in a while, the greenhouse would be graced with a visit from the school directress — a fleshy hideous hag with thickly painted frog lips. (For some reason, Lena never managed to meet normal people in this position.) While the directress raised her usual ruckus in the greenhouse, Lena would sit on her stool and imagine that the three-meter ficus, which could also hear all of this, was hammering the directress into the concrete greenhouse floor with its thickest branch so that she would finally shut up, so that she would stop picking on Baba Lida.

The directress would yell, "Lida! What a jungle! Where am I going to put all these plants? I don't need ficuses and

Monsteras! They won't fit in any office! And these cacti? Why are they here? The schoolchildren will poke out their eyes on the spines! This is criminal!"

"I have other plants too," Baba Lida would answer softly. "Look how pretty the hydrangeas are. The calla lilies have bloomed already too…"

But the directress wasn't interested in hydrangeas or calla lilies. She just hated Baba Lida, and that was when Lena realized that there were people in this world who hated just because.

In the winter, Baba Lida would keep hens and their chicks in the greenhouse. She hid them in boxes under the shelving and screened them with flowerpots. It was terribly cold in her teeny wooden house not far from the school, but here in the greenhouse it was warm and cozy. The chickens, by all indications, enjoyed wintering in the jungle. They would bestow their droppings on the plants, and the plants, in return, would give their warmth.

The directress didn't know anything about the chicken coop in the greenhouse and, in fact, shouldn't have found out about it. When she would come for a routine check, Baba Lida would cover the boxes with planks, and the chickens would sit quiet as mice.

One day the directress showed up with no warning, and Baba Lida didn't have time to conceal her crime. The directress, as usual, began to yell in response to a new family of succulent plants until she suddenly heard a cheeping of unknown origin. She pricked up her ears, and Baba Lida turned pale.

"What is that, Lida? What's squealing?"

"I didn't hear anything…"

"No, no, something's squealing, almost like…" the directress listened closely, "almost like mice…. or chickens…"

"There are no mice in the greenhouse, Raisa Volodymyrivna, or else they would've gnawed up the pots. And chickens… how could they have gotten in here?"

The directress dove between the racks of shelving. Baba

Lida, pale as death, was left standing in the entryway. She would no doubt lose her job for the chickens in the greenhouse.

That was when Dog saved her, completely surprising Lena with her quick wits. Dog sprang out from under the racks and squealed with such skill and such volume that a whole flock of chickens wouldn't have been able to mimic it. The directress jumped back in fright and knocked a pail of soaking chicken poop onto herself.

"What is this, Lida? What is this shit here?"

It wasn't clear what she meant by "shit" — the chicken droppings or the squealing Ivanka. Her black polished shoes and magnificent silvery suit were spattered with the digestive products of fowl.

"That's chicken droppings. I water the plants with them. They grow better like that."

"I don't want to see this here anymore! Watering plants with shit! Are you insane?"

"I won't do it anymore," Baba Lida promised, smiling.

That time she kept her job, but not for long. The directress nevertheless managed to find a reason to oust Baba Lida and to take the greenhouse, along with all of its green inhabitants, into her own hands.

Lena would still go there out of habit and saw how irreversibly swiftly the process of extinction was going. The ficus yellowed and lost all of its leaves. Within a year it had been chopped up for firewood. The Monsteras were sold off by the headmistress to shady businessmen for their fashionable offices. They reportedly went for two hundred dollars a pop. The cacti shriveled up. The geraniums hung on the longest: They're very hardy plants in general and die only when there really is no other option.

After the greenhouse, Baba Lida got a job as a cleaning lady at the polyclinic.

Over the course of her life, she worked in all the lowliest possible jobs. The greenhouse really was the single more or less respectable exception. For some reason, Baba Lida had no luck, and she used to admit this to Lena herself.

She would say, "This is all payback. It's my own fault that I live like a beggar. When I correct everything that I've messed up in the past, things will get easier. Not in this lifetime — no, no — but in the next one perhaps. Or in the one after that."

Baba Lida was a fan of esotericism and of many other similar philosophies about hidden knowledge and hidden worlds. She read the Russian occultists Helena Blavatsky and Nicholas Roerich as well as pseudo-academic books about Ukrainians as Aryans, spent whole days holding séances, deciphered messages encoded in the Bible, believed in signs and omens, and made batches of rose petal jam for the winter. Lena would later say that Baba Lida's way of making it through this life was not the craziest of all possible ways. It could've been markedly worse, but Baba Lida hung on and never fell into despair.

She would say, "I was very pretty in my youth. Boys chased after me in droves, but I didn't pay them any heed. I would insult them and make fun of them. I was very proud. And then the war began and a bomb fragment found its way into my stomach. They operated on me on the front line, amid the catacombs and the filth, without anesthetic, then doused the wound with moonshine. The doctor didn't believe that I would survive, so he sewed me up like a pig. Hundreds of other wounded soldiers were waiting for him. But I survived. And after that, Lena, not a single day passed that I didn't regret it. All of my relatives died in the war, all of my friends. At age seventeen I began to roam the world, and nowhere did I find a true home."

After the operation, Baba Lida's leg ended up twelve centimeters shorter, and she became a cripple. In the 1950s, she came to San Francisco and got her first job as a cleaning lady. She cleaned public restrooms. There, in a public restroom, Baba Lida met a young fellow who had by chance stopped by to relieve himself and fell head over heels in love with him. The fellow, by the looks of it, wasn't indifferent either.

Their romance dragged on for years with varying degrees of success. The fellow's parents — they were either respected professors or influential stomatologists or something along those lines — didn't sanction the union of their only son and the stray cripple. They tried to pay her off, threatened Baba Lida, even sent her off to jail a few times for made-up petty thefts. When none of their plans worked, they sent their son off to work in Vladivostok. Baba Lida had just given birth to a daughter by him.

It's not that this fellow was bad, Baba Lida would tell Lena, he was just weak-willed. He loved me, she would say, he wrote me letters and promised to think of something. A few years later the letters stopped coming. Apparently he didn't manage to think of anything. He was a little short on imagination in general.

The fellow's parents would occasionally pass along modest gifts to Baba Lida's daughter on New Year's. Baba Lida would say that they were from Grandpa Frost, and the daughter believed in Grandpa Frost until she turned eighteen.

"Look at me, Lena," Baba Lida would say, "what was there to love about me? A cripple with no family or home, I spent my whole life cleaning up. So much effort, so much redone work, and the world's still not any tidier."

Baba Lida always had one and the same nightmare. That she's flying up against the ceiling, and people in white lab coats are running around the room and are trying to catch her. There's a giant meat grinder in the room. It's running at full throttle. It's grinding. Baba Lida hears the sound of human bones crunching and is very scared. She smells the scent of blood, hears the cries of small children and the moans of proud men. Then she notices an open ventilation window. She flies out through it and says to herself, "Thank God, I escaped. I made it. Now I'm free." But there, on the other side of the ventilation window, is the exact same room, the exact same meat grinder, grinding in exactly the same way.

Lena was so scared of this meat grinder from Baba Lida's dreams that she too began to dream of it. Baba Lida would reassure her: "You have nothing to be scared of. You have a family, you're a good student. Things will go differently for you."

Lena would munch on her rose jam and nod yes, yes.

"I have straight As," she would say. "I'll grow up to be great people."

"Well, mind you, don't forget Baba Lida when you grow up to be a great person."

"I won't forget! I'll come visit!"

With time, Baba Lida came to look like a good old witch. Lena saw her once a year, sometimes once every two years. They always talked about "high and lofty" matters, probably because people who know only "base and mundane" ones at times find it nice to dream a bit.

And then Lena forgot about Baba Lida. They weren't traveling down the same road. One still very much wanted to live; the other had already lived her fill and was awaiting something new.

2 GOD IN HEAVEN AND ON EARTH

Sometime in the seventh grade, Lena began to have serious problems with her faith.

God, to whom Lena politely prayed every morning and every evening, suddenly lost all sway over her because she just couldn't take him seriously anymore. Lena's old grandma had told her about him. She had lent him to Lena for a while, to use until Lena found her own. Grandma taught Lena to pray, which she herself did before sunrise and after sunset without fail every day. Grandma had two Gods: One hung on the wall in the summer kitchen (Lena liked that one more) and the other in the room where she slept with Grandpa. Grandma prayed to the second one in the mornings and to the first one in the evenings, after she had washed her feet. Incidentally, Grandma never brushed her teeth. Lena figured out why only much later. She no longer had any.

In the evenings, Lena's grandma would wash her face and feet, would take off her work clothes, and — thin as a rake, in just a nightgown that reached all the way to her heels — would fold her hands on her bosom and pray in a language unknown to Lena. The beginning was always identical and always came out as one word: "Arrfatherwhoartinheaven." Lena, who didn't wash her feet because she was lazy, would sit on the trestle bed next to her and listen. She liked her grandma's God, which was exactly what she called him, "Grandma's God." He was strict but fair. He was almighty and looked very respectable. He was about sixty years old, and Lena found this to be the best age for a God — not too young because no one would listen to a little punk, and not too old because people would think that he was senile. This sixty-year-old God of Grandma's had a magnificent beard and a gentle face, which could nonetheless change its demeanor depending on how much Lena had sinned over the course of the day.

She would often talk to him. Typically she would propose some kind of shady deals. For instance, you, God, give me this or that, and I'll believe in you forever. As if it mattered to God that people believe in him.

Once in a while Lena would test him. She would say, for example, "There's a candy in my mouth. Prove that you exist and make this candy fall out of my mouth. Then I'll believe."

And sometimes the candy would fall out.

Lena's grandma made different kinds of deals. She would make requests on behalf of Lena and all her other children and grandchildren, without offering anything in return. She would also ask for nice weather and a good harvest. That the cow's calving go smoothly and that the pigs stop demolishing the floor in the hog house. That Colorado beetles not devour the potatoes so brazenly. That the hay last till spring. That Grandpa drink less, and that everything go well for Lena's parents so that they could finally buy the car they'd been dreaming of.

Grandma would always finish with the words, "I have sinned without measure. Forgive me, Lord." Lena didn't understand this part because Grandma never sinned. She was infinitely good and was satisfied with everything that she had, even though she always had little. People like that don't exist anymore, Lena would say in time. These days people want everything, they only do what they want. But Grandma rejoiced in the very fact that she was healthy and still kicking.

Grandma didn't have any teeth, and now and then, when she got an awful hankering to eat a pickle, she would grate one on a fine grater and would gulp it down like porridge. Her desires were very modest, and if they weren't satisfied, then Grandma didn't particularly suffer.

Lena's grandpa, now he was a completely different story. He had, truth be told, only two desires: to drink and to smoke. These desires were strong enough that in his old age, when his God had ceased fulfilling them, Grandpa took vengeance and stopped believing in him. He lay helplessly in his room, without a cigarette or a tumbler of moonshine, and would see demons.

That was when Lena promised herself that she would never desire anything too much because she didn't want to meet these demons herself.

Lena prayed every morning and every evening for many years. If she unexpectedly forgot to do so for some reason, she would torment herself and dread getting punished. She would think to herself, well, that's it, I won't be able to buy a cup of ice cream or a pastry on Sunday, or I'll make some stupid mistake on a test and get a B in Ukrainian grammar for the semester. Or, most likely, I'll just fall into a puddle somewhere in the street and half the town will laugh at me.

Grandma's God saw everything and forgave nothing. He sat inside Lena and watched over everything that she did and thought. And if she did or thought something bad, she always got what she deserved.

Lena lost her favorite mittens because she didn't want to help her mom tidy up the apartment. Lena couldn't figure out how a protractor worked because she had silently called her dad "stupid" the night before and said, "When I grow up, I'll get back at you."

Everything was interconnected like this. The relationship of cause and effect functioned predictably, like an adding machine. Lena would obediently accept her punishment and continue on with her childish sinning.

"This was a type of pastime," Lena would later write.

"My childish God and I would wink at each other. I at him, and he at me. In this way neither of us got lonely."

Till one day, sometime around age thirteen, Lena suddenly realized during a routine evening prayer that she didn't feel anything anymore — neither fear of punishment nor gratitude for her existence. She realized that someone had pulled this borrowed childish God of hers off the wall, and now a big black hole that could in no way be shut gaped in his place. She realized that the game was over and that they were both now on their own. Do what you want, sin as much as you can: There will be no punishment for the bad and no reward for the good.

Lena stopped praying and nothing happened. The ground didn't split open beneath her feet. A few more times, mostly out of force of habit, she involuntarily said to herself, "Forgive me that I no longer pray to you, God," which was supposed to mean, "Forgive me, Lord, that I no longer believe in you."

With time, Lena recognized the complete absurdity of such words and stopped making excuses for herself altogether. From the outside her life hadn't changed. Well, except for the fact that once in a while Lena would try to convince her schoolteachers that God didn't exist because she didn't see him.

The so-called "public" God, if he did in fact exist, was also acting very weird and didn't inspire trust in Lena. People who had for seventy years believed only in a bright socialist future all suddenly rushed in a hubbub to prostrate themselves in newly built churches. These churches differed from one another in nothing on the outside. Even after you stepped inside one, it was hard to figure out precisely what denomination and nationality that particular God was and how much he expected to be paid for salvation. Polytheism was in full bloom. There were Russian, Ukrainian, Orthodox, Greek and Roman Catholic, Protestant, Baptist and Evangelical Gods, even Gods of the Seventh-day Adventists and of the Warriors of the Kingdom.

In the last Soviet-style social housing neighborhood, which is where Lena grew up, five churches appeared, all of different denominations. Some people went here, others there. Old couples got married in churches after having lived together for forty years. Others got baptized in accordance with all the canons and rituals. Still others signed over all of their possessions to the church in blissful ecstasy. And they all stood together in confession lines on the eve of Easter.

Lena's Christian Ethics teacher also led the entire class to confession. This was the one and only time that Lena publicly repented her sins.

The children were standing in a very long line, discussing their transgressions. Lena was very scared because she didn't know what to say. That was when her classmate Ira helped her.

"This is what you have to say: I gave my parents attitude, I was lazy, and I thought ill of others."

Lena repeated everything verbatim to the priest. The priest patted her on the head and ordered her to recite the Our Father twelve times.

"Excuse me," Lena said to him in parting, "but I also don't really believe in God."

The priest didn't even glance at her. He just said, "Then thirteen times."

Lena's uncle — actually, he wasn't exactly related to her, but that's a long story — not only didn't pray himself but also preached against God whenever a convenient opportunity presented itself. And an opportunity would always present itself. He just couldn't let it go. He was always trying to convince others that faith in God contradicted the principles of science.

Lena called him Doubting Thomas.

This sudden universal turn toward religion tormented

her uncle more than his lack of money, the infertility of both his daughters, and the fact that his son had died in Afghanistan for no good reason. Waging war against God was in essence his profession. In the past, the uncle had taught atheism at the local university and, as rumor had it, also had a side gig working for the so-called "organs."

What exactly these "organs" were, Lena didn't know. She thought maybe it was a reference to some kind of underground hospital where they performed abortions on teenage girls or transplanted poor people's kidneys into rich party officials. Whether her uncle wrote scandalous reports about other professors and handed them over to the KGB, or if he personally sat somewhere in some office and determined people's fates with the stroke of a pen, was unclear. But the man's reputation was pretty shady. He also looked intelligent and well-bred, as befits a servant of the devil. (That's what he was called behind his back.) And he knew how to engage in conversations in a professional manner without resorting to shouting and always won in a debate. He had no match at the holiday table in the apartment where Lena grew up.

The uncle and his wife would come visit religiously once a year, on the day after Easter, and while everyone gobbled homemade sausage and eggs stuffed with cheese and horseradish with gusto, her uncle would explain how stupid everyone at the table was because they were rejoicing in the fact that a human cadaver, in defiance of logic and science, had ascended into heaven.

Lena was personally rejoicing in the sausage and eggs, which she only saw once a year, and didn't get involved in the conversations. Lena, by the way, always associated her uncle with sausage. Even his cheeks had that same sausage-reddish tint. He would say, "How do you not understand that religion was contrived for people like you, the poor and unfortunate, so that you sit quietly, dream of the afterlife and not want anything in this life? It's been scientifically proven that Jesus Christ was a historical figure. It's possible that he had certain paranormal abilities, but so does every other person in China! Even around here you can find a psychic on every corner."

Lena's grandpa, the one who only wanted to drink and smoke, loved her uncle but didn't respect him. When Grandpa drank more than he ought to, he would say to the uncle, "Shut up for a bit already. Things are abominable enough with you."

Her uncle would get offended and wouldn't come back till the following Easter. He had a pleasant wife of few words who was always manicured and dressed to the nines (Lena's mom would hide her hands under the table in shame), and two daughters whom Lena never saw. One was studying in Moscow, the other in Kharkiv. Both were on track to become diplomats.

But one Easter the uncle didn't come. Everyone at the holiday table felt a bit awkward. The sausage just wouldn't go down. Someone called to let them know that the uncle had gotten very sick. Cancer, the final stage. There was no hope of recovery.

His pleasant wife of few words, who by default didn't believe in God either, settled on a desperate measure: to bring Doubting Thomas to a certain old woman who could supposedly raise the dead with a single glance. Thomas, strange as it may seem, agreed to the experiment. He obviously didn't want to die because what he believed in promised him nothing good after death. His bones would rot, and that would be the end of that.

(Lena would later say that death is atheism's biggest weak spot.)

The uncle — withered, ashen, barely standing, and a bit shamed — arrived in the village of the healer along with his wife and Lena's dad. The latter's role was to play bodyguard in case of an unforeseen situation.

The old healer was a hundred and twenty. She was sitting in her yard and gazing into the sky. She was receiving her clients one by one. About fifty patients had gathered, but the old woman was spending no more than a few minutes on each of them. First the patients put ten dollars into the cash box. (Ukrainian money wasn't accepted there.) Then the old woman asked them just one question, and it had nothing to do with health. Lena's dad called it the sixty-four-thousand-dollar question. At the end, the old woman would do some kind of hocus-pocus with her hands over the patient's head and order them to drink some stinky herbs for the next month. They were included in the service package and distributed on the way out.

When Doubting Thomas's turn came up, the old woman asked, "Do you believe in God?"

"I don't."

"Then why did you come?"

"Is there no way without God?"

"There's no way."

The old woman lowered her head, and it became evident that she was blind.

"I'll pay," said the uncle.

"You already paid. You can drink the herbs, but they won't do you any good."

The uncle walked off to the side. The old woman sat silently for a bit, then added, "To die by the will of God is a great joy. I've been waiting for a long, long time for him to summon me. But to die like this, like a dog, from rectal cancer…"

The old woman spat with disgust into the grass at her feet.

She had guessed the diagnosis.

Lena's uncle paced around for a while, mulled things over, and a week later went to confession for the first time. To the exact same priest as Lena, but, unlike her, he spent six hours on his knees. After his conversion, he didn't live all that long, it's true — about a year or eighteen months. He died surrounded by his family, quietly and peacefully.

"In his case," Lena would later write, "the important thing wasn't believing in God. It was ridding himself of fear and making peace with the inevitable. Maybe he wasn't really an atheist after all. Maybe he was just pretending. They say it's the most combative ones that become diehard believers. I, for one, have never waged war against God. I didn't seek proof of his nonexistence, quite the opposite. I kept waiting for him to appear. And once in a while he would appear, but I, unfortunately, didn't realize it a single time."

Lena's best friend, the one she called Dog, caught everyone by considerable surprise a second time when they turned fifteen. Out of nowhere, she got married.

Lena had never heard anything about the groom from her. Dog was as silent as a partisan. Maybe she was ashamed, or maybe she didn't say anything because she thought it wouldn't interest Lena. She wasn't one for much thinking in general. And she was too good, which typically also tends to be self-destructive.

She and Dog had seen each other less often in the last few years. Lena was interested in different things and different people, whereas nothing seemed to interest Dog. Maybe she was mad at Lena and got married out of spite, to give herself away to someone else if Lena didn't want her.

Dog's family was thrilled to hear the news because now there would be one less mouth in their house. Aside from Dog, there was still a bunch of kids of various ages, an itty-bitty doughnut-shaped mom and a one-armed cripple of a dad. It's a wonder they managed to make so many kids.

Dog met her future husband in one of the five neighborhood churches. She said, "I was bored." But she offered this explanation with such inexpressible sorrow that it's possible she meant "lonely."

"Dog!" Lena was yelling. "You need to go to school! It's never boring there!"

But school had lost all ontological significance for Dog

long ago. Dog had learned to read and write, and that was enough for her. She didn't foster any great hopes regarding her own future, and no one had told her as a child that you needed to wait until great people came crawling out of you like intestinal worms. Dog took after her mom in stature, had never been pretty, and always plaited her hair into a thin dingy braid.

"So what, you've already... slept with him?" Lena asked cautiously.

"Yes," Dog answered calmly, without a trace of shame, "and not just with him. With lots."

The husband, who was older than Dog by about twenty years, hauled her off to a remote village of ten people. Dog looked content. Now she had her own house, her own bed and her own TV.

But things with the TV didn't turn out to be all that simple. The first thing that Dog's husband did was to forbid her to watch it. Religion didn't allow it. There's no need to clog up your head with raunchy TV shows and fabricated news! Why he kept a TV at home at all was a mystery. Maybe in order to strength-train his willpower and grope at the depths of his faith.

Since Dog's faith and will amounted to zilch, she would watch TV on the sly all the same, and this illicit TV-watching would bring her twice the pleasure. Until the husband caught Dog red-handed one day. He didn't say anything to her then and there and didn't talk to her at all for the next two months. At first Dog thought that this was some kind of joke, that he'd get angry and give up, but the husband had strength-trained his will for years, and it was iron in the literal sense of the word.

After two full months of silence, the husband finally preached his version of The Word to Dog: "TV is evil. You shouldn't watch it anymore. Think about your wretched soul. How it suffers in such a hostile world and such a worthless body. If you turn on the TV one more time, I won't talk to you for six months."

That was when Dog realized that he wasn't joking. After two months of silence, she was ready to talk to her own shadow or the mice in the pantry. She didn't turn on the TV anymore because she was scared. But the TV was just the beginning of her spiritual enhancement.

The next stage was food. You couldn't eat much because digestion impeded knowledge of God.

This was a blow below the belt for Dog. Eating was the thing she loved most in the world. In fact, Dog considered food to be the sole proof of the existence of higher forces. If she had enough to eat on a given day, that meant that God existed and that He was good.

"You can only eat black bread," the husband would tell Dog. "I don't want to see any white bread at home. Forget about meat and sausages. Once in a while you can eat an egg, but not often. Rice can't be eaten because it's from China, and they don't believe in God there. Potatoes, beans, I'll allow. But the best food for a believer is still black bread. And water. You catch my drift?"

Dog would steal pocket change from her husband, buy herself cocktail wieners in the only store in the entire village, and furtively devour them at night as her husband slept the dead sleep of the righteous. She didn't know how long her husband wouldn't talk to her if he caught her with the cocktail wieners but sensed that it would be a long time.

Dog began to fear everything. She dreamed horrible dreams in which she was hanging on a crucifix, like Jesus Christ, and the whole world around her was strewn with cocktail wieners and doused with ketchup.

Dog was also forbidden to wear T-shirts with short sleeves, use sanitary napkins during her period, sing, visit her relatives or even call them. She wasn't allowed to laugh too loud (not that she wanted to), wash her hair more often than once a month, smoke (which Dog had picked up with Lena and now had to quit), contradict her husband (because he was a vicegerent of God on earth) or even look him in the eye (because looking at God wasn't permitted, that was hubris).

Eventually, in order to avoid misunderstandings, a precise system of penalties for all transgressions was compiled and concisely and clearly written on a sheet of paper. This paper was attached to the door of the empty fridge with a magnet.

Silence wasn't the only form of punishment. There was also hungering for a week or two, kneeling, and — this was the husband's personal forte — holding the old front door above your head on outstretched arms all night.

Dog spent most of her time crying. Sometimes her husband would console her. He would say, "Cry. Tears are cleansing. They wash away disobedience to our Lord. You have to wrap your head around the fact that you're evil. You catch my drift?"

Dog would nod her head that yes, she caught it.

One day, when Dog's itty-bitty mom and one-armed dad came to visit her, Dog's husband didn't let them into the house. That was when her parents filed a complaint with the police. The following day a policeman came to assess the situation. He told Dog that she could leave with him if she wanted to. Dog turned down the invitation.

"I've been informed," said the policeman, "that your husband is abusing you. Is that true?"

"It's not true," Dog answered. "He doesn't beat me."

It all came to an end three years later. That was when Lena started college.

Dog's husband said to her, "You're beyond redemption. Now I know this for sure. The greatest evil in the world is to not have children. You're barren. Why don't you have any children?"

"I don't know," replied Dog.

"But I do. You don't have any children because you're evil. You catch my drift?"

That was when Dog began to bleed out of all of the orifices that exist in a person. The blood flowed without stopping for several days, as if it wanted to escape from that canine body. The whole house was bathed in blood, and Dog's husband was in the meantime praying for her sinful and unredeemable soul. The mailwoman, who had come by with the unemployment check (Dog and her husband lived exclusively off it), saw the scene and called an ambulance. She apparently even whacked the husband with a stool, and he went splat on the floor, howling from pain as if he was feeling it for the first time.

The paramedics had never seen blood gushing out of all of a person's orifices like that. The doctors in the regional hospital weren't able to make a diagnosis either. They just kept plugging Dog's ears and nose with cotton tampons.

In three months, Dog recovered.

She and Lena would go for walks on the hospital grounds, and Dog rarely said a word. Even though they had begun their journey together, a bottomless chasm now gaped between them.

"Do you remember," Lena would say, to at least say something, "how you scared the directress with chicken squeals in Baba Lida's greenhouse and she knocked a pail of shit onto herself?"

Dog didn't remember, and Lena couldn't blame her.

She would later say that no one was guilty, regardless of what they'd done. To blame someone else was to make excuses for yourself. And Lena could find no excuses for herself. "I," she would admit, "have a million regrets for nicknaming Ivanka Dog. It's my fault that she lives like a dog. I didn't protect her, though I had the chance. The only thing that I take solace in is that dogs are resilient animals."

"It's good that you guys didn't have any kids," Lena said to Dog in parting for some reason.

"Because in order to have kids," replied Dog, "you need to give a damn about them once in a while. You catch my drift?"

3   HOW SHE PROMISED HERSELF
    NOT TO LOSE HER MIND

It all boils down to money, Lena would say. People without money are frightening because they lose their diversity. Poor people become thieves or philosophers. There is no third option. I, for example, never had any money but was too much of a coward to learn how to steal.

Lena's parents had money once in a while, when they would manage to pilfer something somewhere. Unfortunately, they wouldn't manage to all that often because others weren't sitting around twiddling their thumbs either, and there wasn't enough to go around. A country of thieves, Lena's dad would say, as he pilfered decommissioned aluminum wire from the plant that once produced secret parts for secret nuclear submarines.

"When will you finally have stuffed yourselves already," Lena's mom would mutter, as she smuggled a kilo of May Night bonbons out of the chocolate factory in her bosom.

Her dad at all times smelled like aluminum, her mom like chocolate. Together they exuded this strange, artificial smell of a new era, though there was no old era for Lena. There was just this one. Lena didn't know that other eras had once existed, but most of the people in her life still remembered them. Some mourned for them because everything in those days was clear-cut and ran according to five-year plans. You could buy all of three products in the grocery stores, underwear was cotton, and there were savings books into which you set aside money in order to buy a car in ten years when it was your turn.

But now, in this new era, there were no groceries, no underwear, no cars. Everyone walked around broken and tattered. The new era wasn't promising anything good, just kids that wanted to eat and kids that had nothing to wear.

When butter would arrive in the local store, the line would stretch all the way into the next neighborhood. Lena would skip school that day because there was butter in town. Her mom would go to the chocolate factory and come back at 5 p.m. It was at about that time that Lena would finally be working her way up to the counter. The limit for butter was 150 grams. They would eat it all week, one gram at a time.

Lena hated butter and often said that she couldn't understand why it had been invented. She loved meat and could eat it three times a day.

That was when Lena's dad would say to her, "There are people in North Korea who don't even know the word 'veal.'"

He had read this somewhere in a magazine. Lena wasn't very sure what veal was either, but when you're told that someone somewhere is worse off than you, it makes things easier. Thank God that someone somewhere is worse off because otherwise it would be completely unbearable here.

"Now you have yourselves an independent Ukraine!" Lena heard this often while standing in some line and would get really annoyed.

"What, aren't you glad?" she would say. "Ukraine wasn't free for nearly three centuries. And now it's independent! We should be rejoicing."

"What are you rejoicing about, child? That you spend your days waiting in line?"

"Well," Lena would object, not as confidently anymore, "it's just like that at the outset. But later we're all going to be happy and rich. Because we're our own masters."

The "masters" would reply, short and to the point, "Shut your trap!" Even though secretly they were fostering the same hopes.

Lena would imagine Ukraine as a vast wheat field. Cornflowers are bluing, and field poppies are reddening here and there between the wheat. The sky is a pale, pale blue, and the sun is brilliant and exceptionally Ukrainian. The girls are in embroidered blouses with wreaths of flowers on their heads; old men in traditional Hutzul jackets are playing jaw harps; men are working in the field, either mowing or standing and smoking. And everyone is happy and rich. The second point was particularly important, while the first was just proportionally determined by the second and in reality meant the same thing. Everyone is happy and rich.

In order to somehow make it through the new era, people began to leave for various places. Some to Poland (though it seems there wasn't anything better there), some to Italy (though Ukrainians had long ago become Italians, since they only ate pasta), some to Portugal (Lena didn't know anything about that country).

Her dad also made up his mind to leave.

He and Mom would sit in the kitchen and, after a tasty pasta dinner, would talk.

"Go!" Mom would say. "Go because we'll croak."

"And where would you have me go? Well, where?" Dad would demand.

"Go to Italy. Look, that Myrosia I used to work with went. She sends back an awful lot of money."

"Who do you think I am, Myrosia? She's not making money with her hands over there."

"If not with her hands, then with what? She sent pictures. She lives with an old man and woman in their villa. She looks after them and has everything. She's fed, clothed, and gets a day off once a month. She got herself a new hairdo and now looks like a real human being."

"Then you go!"

Mom was silent.

"I won't go to Italy because that's where the Mafia is," Lena's dad decided at last.

He was always watching the Italian TV series *The Octopus* about an honest police commissioner who singlehandedly takes on the immortal Mafia. The series made it look like the whole country was Mafia. Commissioner Cattani alone was honest, for which he ended up paying with his head. Apparently they even threw him into a pool of sulfuric acid and shot up his family, but he dug in his heels and that was it. He was honest. Later they shot him too, and with that the series ended.

"I'll go to America," said Lena's dad.

"America?" Mom hadn't even dared to consider it.

"America it is!"

America is an entirely separate story, but everyone probably knows it. America is paradise on earth. The roads there are paved with dollars. Just take — grab — as many as you want. True, there are a lot of blacks there, former slaves. Rumor has it that when you look at them you always get the urge to laugh, but you can't laugh because they'll put a bullet in you. In America, everyone and their mother has a gun. Kids, for example, shoot at teachers and babysitters when they do something to piss them off. But everyone tolerates it because it's better to live a short life with dollars than a long one without.

Once every two years, the distant American family of Lena's grandma would send a wooden crate full of kerchiefs and various sweets that would manage to spoil while the crate sailed across the ocean. But Grandma really ly loved the kerchiefs and always called them "American." She would say to Lena, "Child, hand me that American kerchief from the wardrobe."

"Do you know English?" Lena's mom would ask.

"I studied it in college," Dad would reply. "Doo yoo speek Engleesh, yes ay doo! I studied German too, so don't worry, I'll get by! Shprekhen zee deutsch!? Natyurleekh!"

In order to get to America, Lena's dad needed to "win"

a green card. This card was sold on every shady corner, just pay up and bon voyage. But it cost a lot, and Lena's dad didn't have that much. The cheaper option was to buy, there on those same shady corners, a fake invitation from American relatives who never existed in which these relatives implore you to come visit them for a month. They would pay for everything. They would feed you and take care of you like their own child. The important thing was to not mess up the names of these relatives and to have a calm demeanor at the interview at the American consulate. A demeanor that elicits trust. That says to the consulate staff, "Don't you worry. I'm definitely coming back. I'll just visit for a month and will be back in a jiffy, sooner than you can say boo. I need that America of yours, with its former slaves and guns, like a hole in the head. I live just fine right here. This here isn't Ukraine, mind you, it's a downright miracle of economic development."

That's how you needed to come across.

Lena's dad spent an entire month rehearsing in front of a mirror. He was learning to control his facial expressions so that his veins wouldn't pop out every which way from fright. He was learning to control his voice so that it would be confident. But not too much so because overly confident voices also arouse suspicion.

Lena's dad was scared of going to Kyiv alone, so he talked his best friend Tolik into the adventure. To come along for company. Tolik was tall and had black hair. He looked like a music teacher. Even his fingers were long and thin like those of a pianist, though he most likely played the violin, if he in fact played anything at all. He had two children and a young wife.

They headed off to Kyiv. Lena's mom escorted the delegation to the station with tears in her eyes. Lena, in the meantime, was busy telling everyone that she needed to urgently learn English and would miss Ukraine till the end of her happy and rich days.

But something went wrong in Kyiv. Lena's dad's face betrayed him after all. Or something was off with his voice. Or he messed up the names of the "relatives." Or he wore the wrong shirt. Or he just didn't have any luck. In a nutshell, they denied him a visa and forbade him from applying for one again for the next five years.

"Good that they didn't throw him in jail," Lena's mom would later say.

But Tolik, who was in general just coming along for company, got a visa. Evidently the music teacher façade worked. Tolik guiltily gathered up his paraphernalia and left for the land of dollars. In two years, he brought his wife over. In four, his kids. Now Tolik lives in New York and manages a company that constructs plastic American housing. He wrote a letter to Lena's dad: "There are a lot of Ukrainians here. I live as if I had never even gone anywhere." As if that was supposed to make someone feel better.

Lena's little old grandma, the one who walked around in American kerchiefs, remembered not only the old era but even the so-called prehistoric era, which existed until the time when the proletarians of all countries united and showed up at her field to plow. She referred to this era as "in the days of Austria." It's true, she would sometimes get confused and say "in the days of Poland," no doubt meaning one and the same thing. For Lena's grandma, the prehistoric era was the best time in her life. Maybe because she was young and pretty then. And had teeth. And could eat pickles. Although, from what she told Lena, it was hard to figure out whether or not people had money. Lena suspected that they in fact didn't because, as she would say, "There's something improper about being rich in our land. Then people take you for either a thief or an opportunist."

As a child, Grandma had to plow an enormous, boundless field on her own. Her father — whom Grandma called "Djedjo," or Grandpa, which is why Lena always thought that he was Grandma's uncle, or "Djadja" — went off to the First World War and would send photos from there. He kept sending photos from there even when the war had ended and even when ten years had passed since the war and even when a new war had begun.

At first he lived in Czechoslovakia, then in Austria. Then he migrated to America, and it was most likely some kids or grandkids of his that eventually fell into the habit of sending wooden crates of kerchiefs and sweets. Djedjo simply never came back.

Lena's grandma told a lot of such stories but did so, surprisingly, without malice, at times even trying to justify the deserters just a teeny bit. In this house over here, she would say, the husband didn't come back either, and the wife went a little cuckoo in the head from grief and shame. But there were nine kids here. Their mother locked them up and ran off to America with a lover. The kids sat in the house for three days, waiting. No one heard a single peep, and by the time the neighbors got a clue, four of them were already dead.

And Grandma would smack her toothless lips and say, "And so it goes."

Lena's grandma would also say, "At the end of the day, some good always comes out of everything."

Lena would say, "Not everything."

In the meantime, Polish priests arrived in Grandma's village to restore the local Roman Catholic church.

For half a century this church had stood in the middle of the village as an exhibition space for toilet art. The local head of the Communist Party (when it was still in existence) used to pay boys to spray-paint vulgarities all over the church and to do whatever they wanted there in general. They would've done it for free, with pleasure, but for money they went at it tooth and nail. The church stank worse than a public restroom, had no windows or doors, was missing an iconostasis, and crows and snakes had nested under its roof.

The Poles showed up and fixed up everything. This was some sort of noteworthy monument of their (namely the Polish) culture. The grand opening and first mass were supposed to take place on the feast of St. Anthony, which was also some sort of big holy day of theirs. Ten buses of pilgrims and tourists came rolling in from Poland. Many of them once had relatives in the village, and they roamed the old Polish cemetery hoping to find familiar surnames on the graves and weeping like children.

The local residents got decked out too and gathered next to the church, as if at any moment they might all fall to their knees as one and swear allegiance to the Pope in Rome. In reality, they were all waiting for presents.

Someone had started a rumor that the Poles had brought bulging sacks with them and would be giving out expensive Polish clothing and overseas delicacies to the locals during the ceremony. For free, out of the goodness of their hearts.

The locals gathered and waited eagerly. Not far away, the children milled about and prepared to pounce at the first command.

The ceremony dragged. People shifted their weight from foot to foot. The Polish priest, a likeable young fellow, was delivering a moving speech about time and memory in broken Ukrainian. He thanked the locals for their safekeeping of the Polish church, and some of the men in the crowd lowered their eyes in shame.

Finally the long-awaited sacks of goods started getting carried off the buses. The eyes of the locals blazed. They knew this was for them. Not waiting for permission or the last few solemn words, they lunged at the sacks like coyotes at a dead antelope. The Poles carrying the sacks at first tried to defend themselves but quickly realized that they'd get trampled and bolted.

The sacks burst at the seams with a crackle and tons of caramels came pouring out. The locals didn't even have time to get disappointed. Even caramels can be a hit if they're free. Everyone was stuffing their pockets and bosoms with them. Kids snatched the booty from each other, and adults snatched it from the kids.

Lena would later say that she would've done the same thing if her mom hadn't worked at a chocolate factory. Lena had long ago developed an allergy to sweets. Now, if they had been handing out meat or some kind of hot dogs or sausages, Lena wouldn't have been left standing on the sidelines.

Some old man dropped to the ground and was picking caramels from the grass as if they were nuggets of gold.

"Have some shame," old women were hollering at him. "Leave some candy for the kids! Let the kids eat it!"

And right then and there they too fell to their knees to gather up the rest.

When the caramels had run out, the locals quickly dispersed, and the Polish priest celebrated his mass in empty silence.

Later the locals grew embarrassed about how they had acted. "Really, as if we'd never seen caramels before," they were saying. Lena felt sorry for them. She felt sorry for old man Kysylytsia, who had torn his pants on the caramel battlefield. And she felt sorry for Zhenia Prokopovych, who had accidentally stepped on her grandson and broken a finger on his right hand. "Poor people are frightening," she was saying, in tears. "As if I needed those caramels. But everyone started running, and I did too, like I was some kind of herd cow. What if someone had gotten killed?" Zhenia sobbed.

Lena felt for Zhenia Prokopovych. Zhenia was living proof of the fact that what is written in the Bible may actually be The Truth. I'm getting hit, and I offer the other cheek. Zhenia got hit by anyone who could be bothered, but she loved everyone. Zhenia got hit by her son Mykola and by her grandchildren. Lena was sure she would get hit by her great-grandchildren too, but they were too little for now and couldn't reach her face. Zhenia looked like a skeleton, but a deformed one. She was hunched and contorted. Her jaw was too big, her nose too small, her arms too long, her legs too short, and her knees bent to the back instead of the front. The thin cotton dress she wore highlighted her dystrophic figure perfectly.

"You would get the urge to cry when you saw her," Lena would later write in her journals. "You would get the urge to wrap your arms around her and smother her to death in your embrace so that she wouldn't suffer anymore."

Zhenia's son Mykola — a coarse, cruel and somewhat dimwitted ass — would spend entire days lying on his bed slurping vodka straight from the bottle. In the meantime, Zhenia would be spoon-feeding him potato dumplings, which he would then fling back in her face. He also enjoyed dumping freshly cooked borshch onto Zhenia's head or smashing empty vodka bottles against her head, then making her scuttle to the store for a fresh half-liter. In the winter, he would chase her out into the street in a nightgown and sometimes even tethered her to the well so that she wouldn't go complaining to the neighbors. But Zhenia wasn't one to complain.

She always walked around bruised and swollen, and when someone would ask what had happened, she would reply:

"It's no big deal. I fell."

"I slipped."

"I tripped on the doorstep at home."

"A gust of wind swung in the door and it slammed into me."

"I was chopping wood, and a hunk of wood popped out from under the ax right into my face."

"The brakes on my bike gave out."

"I don't know. It swelled up overnight. Maybe a tooth is rotting."

Mykoltsio, as Zhenia fondly called him, spent one year in jail. Zhenia had been screaming a lot during a routine nocturnal booze-and-beat binge, and the neighbors had called the police. They all chipped in for a bribe so that the cops would lock up Mykoltsio for as long as possible. The cops scrupulously delivered. Mykoltsio was gone for a year. But Zhenia didn't get any happier. Her "granddaughter" Olechka came to live with her. How she's technically not related and why she showed up all of a sudden is a long story. But if you, as Lena would say, had also decided to live on top of Zhenia for a while out of nowhere, she wouldn't have refused.

The granddaughter abused Zhenia in a different way. She would take away all her money and not let her eat. For a year Zhenia went hungry and lived off whatever the neighbors gave her now and then, though even that she wouldn't eat completely. She would stash it in a baggie and bring it to the prison for Mykoltsio every week.

After a year, Mykoltsio returned and promptly established some order. He kicked Olechka out of Zhenia's house, and everything went back to its same old routine: drunken debauches, nightly rows and Zhenia's swollen face.

"What's with these kids of yours?" the neighbors wouldn't even ask, they would simply say.

"Kids are kids," Zhenia would answer, smiling. "Kids are the same the world over."

"Mine don't beat me like a mare in a stable."

"Neither do mine."

"So why is your face swollen?"

"A tooth's rotting."

Zhenia's story ended just as it had begun, biblically. Don't dig a grave for another or you'll fall in it yourself. Mykoltsio had decided to kill Zhenia.

He had no intention of going back to prison. So he cooked up an ingenious plan: to poison Zhenia with carbon monoxide. So many people die from carbon monoxide in these parts that Mykoltsio likely figured no one would suspect it was murder. An old stove is the perfect murder weapon. Even in the neighboring village a young couple had recently gotten poisoned on the day after their wedding. In another village, a whole family never woke up.

At that time, as Lena would write, people actually died most often from carbon monoxide and motorcycle crashes.

When Zhenia came back home in the evening, Mykoltsio told her to go to bed while he set about tinkering with the chimney and stove. He knew how to make the carbon monoxide go into the house instead of the chimney because he had been a stove fixer back when he still pretended to have a job. He did everything to a T.

He just didn't factor in that he had drunk too much vodka. And so, there next to the stove, he passed out.

Meanwhile, that very evening Zhenia got the urge to go to the hospital to have a chat with the head doctor because Mykoltsio's health was troubling her. "It's almost as if something's poking him on the right side." The head doctor, an older and compassionate woman, let Zhenia eat the leftovers from the hospital dinner and convinced her to spend the night in an empty patient room. When Zhenia arrived back home in the morning to prepare breakfast for her dear little son, he was already cold. They say that the locals had never heard such wailing at a funeral, so distraught was Zhenia over her Mykoltsio. She was bawling, "It was I that was supposed to die, not you!"

Lena's old grandma was smacking her toothless gums and saying, "And so it goes. Such are folk."

But there were all kinds of other "folk" too.

There were people who ate pig's head all month. Lena met them at the train station. They were sitting on a bench, most likely a husband and wife (at the very least, a man and woman for sure), with boozed-up blue faces, in some kind of dreadful and dirty overalls, and were smoking.

Lena asked them, "What are you eating?"

The woman laughed, traces of a garish lipstick glimmering red on her lips like blood.

"Seriously?" she asked.

"Seriously," Lena replied.

Two unfinished bottles of beer stood beside them on the bench.

"OK, look," said the woman. "When we get our disability check at the beginning of the month — I'm disabled, just so you know — we immediately go to the bazaar and buy a pig's head. At home we divide it up into portions and put it in the fridge. And we have food for the whole month. We cook meat jellies, soups, some kind of chowders. We don't have enough money for anything else."

There were people who would tether their kids to a table leg so that nothing would happen to them while no one was home.

There were also people who didn't tether them, and the kids would do whatever they wanted while no one was home. For instance, they would cut flowers out of the new tablecloth and stack them into neat little piles on the floor. That's what one five-year-old boy from Horodenka did. When the adults got home, they were furious. The frightened boy crawled under the bed, and as he got dragged out from under there by his dad, the dad kept swatting his hands with a belt. He swatted so hard that the boy later had to have his hands amputated at the regional hospital. As they walked out of the hospital, the boy said the following to his dad, and all the doctors and nurses heard it, and later all the local and regional newspapers published it: "Dad, I'll never cut flowers out of the tablecloth again. Just give me back my hands."

There were all kinds of people and all kinds of stories. Lena did her best to file all of them away in her head for statistical purposes in order to some day, down the road, understand where evil came from. At the time, it all seemed to come from poverty. Someone who's constantly thinking about money doesn't have the time to work on himself in order to become better because it's easy to be evil. You don't have to exert yourself to be evil. But being good, on the other hand, requires a little effort. You have to have a clear head, sleep a minimum of eight hours a day, eat healthy, work out, and take walks in the fresh air, preferably in some park. Per Lena's modest statistics, people in her immediate world didn't do any of this. They drank often, slept late, ate pasta and potatoes, and when they weren't working, they were sitting at home in front of the TV. Those kinds of conditions weren't conducive to social goodness. Something had to be done about it.

But even at the very outset, Lena stayed away from the thankless notion of saving the world. "This world hardly needs someone to save it," she would maintain. "I'm not concerned about the North Koreans who don't know what veal is or don't even know the word 'veal' for that matter. I'm not concerned about the starving Africans on the banks of the Nile or the poor Indonesian children whose work is exploited from age three. I'm not concerned about anything that I don't see and don't hear. It's just this pig's head that wasn't getting out of my head. Dog wasn't getting out of my head, Zhenia Prokopovych, the handless boy from Horodenka... I had to do something about all of this so that my own life would be more livable, so as not to lose my mind as others had."

4   SCIOPODS, ARIMASPIANS AND OTHER DOGHEADS OF NATURAL PHILOSOPHY

In 1996, everything definitively went to pieces and San Francisco sank into the black waters of the free market.

Dad's plant, the one that used to produce secret components for secret nuclear submarines, was turned into a night club. Mom's chocolate factory became a bootleg distillery. Both of them, like everyone else in Ukraine, were left to their own devices and no longer had anything to pilfer. That's what always happened with thieves, Lena would say. When all is said and done, they end up even poorer.

But at the end of the day, some good always comes out of everything. A new American word suddenly entered, or rather burst into, Ukrainians' virtuous post-communist souls — *business*. Granted, it had a slightly different meaning here: If you couldn't steal from the state, then you had to steal from one another.

The global economy rests on this postulate, Lena's dad would say. Pull one over on the guy next to you, otherwise someone will show up from some faraway place and pull one over on you both.

Everyone began to do business. In practice, doing business meant having a stall at the bazaar.

Several architectural monuments from the eighteenth century were torn down in the center of San Francisco, and a huge area got fenced off as the bazaar. Now *this* was the center. What's more, it was the center in every sense — economic, academic, cultural and spiritual. Those who had something to sell sold; those who had money bought; and those who didn't just strolled around, inhaling deeply the aroma of Chinese pleather and synthetics. But everyone was there. At a minimum on Sundays. It was where the hope for something better was being revived, where the nationwide depression was being healed. Half of the professors from the local university, doctors, teachers, newspaper editors and journalists, artists and writers, soloists from the regional folk chorus and actors from the local drama theater all came to peddle their wares at the bazaar.

At the bazaar, there were discussions about post-colonialism and globalization, about contemporary European cinema and postmodernism in the arts. There were discussions about Warhol and Marquez, about Kurt Cobain, and about the philosophy of deconstructivism. Often in the evenings, when the customers had all left but no one felt like going home yet, someone would scramble up on the tracksuit racks and recite first their own poems, then those of others. (The tracksuits, incidentally, were the hottest item, as if the entire city, possibly even the entire country, did nothing but play sports.)

The rest stood around and applauded. Or smoked and drank.

That was when Lena noticed that intellectuals, even though they have no money, won't drink cheap alcohol no matter what. They'll scrape up what they can to buy the good stuff. It's a matter of the utmost honor for them.

Some would also sing at the bazaar. Others did magic tricks. Lena liked watching the bazaar concerts. She would often stop by there because her parents were also doing business. Her mom sold "going-out outfits" while her dad got himself a job as a packer and loader. Lena would come by to help each of them in turn.

Lena's dad was a worthless loader, probably because he knew how to build ships. His boss was always complaining about him and threatening to fire him because Dad, instead of simply loading, was perpetually contriving odd ways to make his job easier, dreaming up new loading technologies, or building some kind of mechanisms and iron mini-cranes. In a nutshell, he was enhancing efficiency.

The boss would shout to Lena's dad, "Load with your hands! With your *hands*! There's no need to concoct anything. Just grab a crate and load it. Load it!"

Lena's mom was a good saleswoman, but the "going-out outfits" weren't selling well. People had nowhere to go out to in the outfits. She was constantly saying that she needed to give up on the outfits and switch to undergarments. Underwear is always in demand. No matter how poor you may be, flashing a bare backside is disgraceful.

The "going-out outfits" reeked horribly and sparkled like a New Year's tree in the dark. Their labels didn't offer any tips regarding the temperature at which that miracle of the textile industry should be washed but did have the same warning you see on deodorants: Highly flammable, keep away from fire. At the time, Lena figured that the outfits had been designed specifically for customers on their way to the crematorium so that electricity could be conserved. Strike a match and poof, the cadaver would burn away on its own in a matter of seconds. Not just economical but beautiful to watch too.

Lena had two of these outfits, and her mom had three. But her dad stubbornly kept on wearing his one and only pair of jeans and said that jeans were a symbol of democracy, it was jeans that broke up the Soviet Union. This made Lena's dad very happy, and he would remain loyal to his jeans till his death.

As befitted an employee of a secret plant, he had previously been a member of the Communist Party. But in the late 1980s, when the roast began to smell, he was the first to go turn in his party card. He went in his jeans. The guy sitting behind the table and accepting the party cards glanced at Lena's dad with judgment in his eyes and said, "Ekh, you really have no conscience!"

But everyone was missing a conscience, or so it seemed to Lena. And not having one was turning out to be a lot of fun. The bazaar intellectuals, whom Lena saw every evening, had also long since lost their collective conscience and were busy making fun of everything and everyone.

There was a former professor of Ukrainian literature named Theophilus Bunny, who also worked at the bazaar. Not a single day would pass without someone poking fun at this old man. At first they made fun of his name, because "Theophilus Bunny" was a pseudonym that the professor had adopted at age seventeen. Later they made fun of just about everything else about him.

The professor would go peddle at the bazaar as if going to the university to teach, carrying a black suitcase and wearing an old but neat leather overcoat, glasses and a tie. He was tall and awfully thin as well as a bit hunched, as if he were very ashamed of something or had lived through a horrible tragedy. Theophilus Bunny sold a variety of headgear, from straw bonnets to baseball caps to fur hats with ear flaps. He was a lousy haggler, which was understandable since Theophilus Bunny knew absolutely nothing about what he was selling. When, out of desperation, he would try to actively entice customers, he would spew out something along the following lines: "Buy a hat. Your head will look bigger, and no one will realize it's empty."

Theophilus Bunny was officially recognized as a misanthrope by all, although he hated not just people but anything else you could only imagine as well. He hated communists and nationalists, he hated children and senior citizens, he hated the bazaar and his straw bonnets, and he hated the university that he worked for and the literature that he taught. The vendor in the stall next to Bunny's, a jolly bearded fellow nicknamed The Artist, would say, "Tell me, who in the world gave you such an idiotic name?

You really should get rid of it sooner rather than later. Theophilus Bunny, hmph!"

"It's none of your fucking business," Theophilus Bunny would reply.

The professor always expressed himself very crassly, but he never used Russian curse words because he believed that the starving proletariat had discredited this vocabulary. And Bunny hated the proletariat above all else. He called Lena, for example, a "goddamned child of the proletariat." But Lena wouldn't get overly upset because it wasn't fully clear to her what this phrase meant.

"You'll never comprehend the essence of things," Theophilus Bunny would say to Lena, even with a touch of sympathy. "This was denied you by the mere fact of your birth. Your brain just doesn't have the necessary wrinkles. You'll spend your entire life agonizing over it, poor thing, and you still won't figure anything out."

"And what have *you* figured out, Mr. Bunny?" Lena would ask.

"What I've figured out will always remain beyond your reach, you proletarian misbirth. You don't even have the necessary vocabulary to begin to wrap your head around it."

That was when the other academic and artistic types would come to Lena's defense: Mila, an "actress of the burnt-down theater," who had once starred in two movies but now sold glassware "a la Bohemian crystal," as well as her lover Shtick, who had been writing a novel for some years now about a miraculous land of gophers (but Lena only ever heard him recite Pushkin poetry).

Mila had an irrefutable trump card in her fight against Theophilus Bunny: She had once been his student. On top of that, she had a whole network of informants and could find out absolutely everything one could possibly want to know about a person in a matter of seconds. In the evenings, when the professor was packing his unsold headgear back into crates, Mila would say, "So is it true, Mr. Bunny, that you picked out your name all by yourself?"

"None of your fucking business." Bunny's reply would be curt and clear.

"And what did you have against the last name Donkeytail?"

Theophilus Bunny would hunch over even more, and his naturally swarthy face would take on a deep purple tint.

"It's not the name that makes a person beautiful," he would mutter in response. "But you wouldn't understand that. Otherwise you wouldn't shake your naked titties in front of movie cameras."

Mila had starred in two films and both had involved sex scenes. Unlike one might think, she took pride in this.

"Why, if it weren't for my boobs," she would say, "we would still be living under the Soviets! I revolutionized the movie industry! All the execs did was lecture me about my conscience and my duty to the Party! But who am I talking to? You, Mr. Theophilus, have never even made out!"

One day she brought her old notebook from Theophilus Bunny's lectures to the bazaar and staged him a public execution. The professor nearly had a heart attack. Mila climbed up on her rack of "crystal" and began to read excerpts from Bunny's old lectures out loud: "On April 23, 1616," she read, "the English author William Shakespeare died. On that very same April 23, 1616, the Spanish author Miguel de Cervantes Saavedra also died. And – this will knock your socks off – on that very same day of that very same year, April 23, 1616, the Peruvian author Garcilaso de la Vega died too! On the basis of these facts, I conclude that all three men were in fact one and the same person."

The bazaar erupted with laughter. Mila paused expressively, then asked Bunny, "Esteemed Professor, kindly reveal, if you would, to the no less esteemed audience, on the basis of *which facts* did you make this brilliant conclusion?"

"I can explain." The professor was jabbering, but no one was listening to him.

"With your permission, I'll proceed," Mila said. "There

are so many interesting things here in this notebook! I just can't take it! I particularly like the passage about monsters."

The crowd of bored vendors swarmed around Mila as if she were handing out free sausage.

"In your lecture number five," she continued, "you, Mr. Theophilus Bunny, claim that monsters are — and I quote — 'mistakes of nature. Nature blunders and appropriates either too much or too little matter to some creature. When too much, a foal, for example, is born with two heads. When too little, an infant, for example, is born with no arms or legs. In such a case, the parents of the bizarre creature are normal.' Have I gotten it all correct, Professor?"

The professor pulled a bottle of booze out of his pleather briefcase and began slurping. Mila decided to take this as an affirmative response.

"Then we'll go on. I prefer the next part. 'But there are monsters in the world about whose parents nothing is known. Or whose parents and all their ancestors are monsters. These include dragons, asps, basi... basilisks and other wild animals of Africa and Libya. They also include pygmies, who measure twenty to thirty centimeters in height, and giants, whom the Bible calls enormous towers of flesh.' Is everything correct, Professor? I haven't mixed anything up, have I?"

"Everything's correct! Read on!" the riled up audience answered on behalf of Bunny.

"Next, Mr. Theophilus, you enumerate the following monsters. Lord, help me pronounce this! Sci-o-pods!"

"Sciopods," Bunny was repeating with doom.

"These are monsters that consist of nothing but lower legs. The only thing known about Long-Eared Creatures is that their ears reach all the way down to their feet and they can lie down on one ear and cover themselves with the other."

Mila was reading louder and louder: "'A-ri-mas-pi-ans... Arimaspians.' Don't interrupt me, Professor, I know how to read! 'Arimaspians have only one eye, on their forehead or on their shoulders, and have no nape. Dogheads have a canine head and are able to simultaneously bark and talk!'"

The audience was rolling with laughter. Lena was too. The bearded Artist addressed Theophilus Bunny with a straight face: "Dear Professor, what do you think this is, *biology?* You supposedly teach literature. *Li-te-ra-ture!*"

"This is the natural philosophy of Teofan Prokopovych," Theophilus Bunny was saying almost in tears, and, as usual, no one was listening to him.

But Mila wasn't done yet. She hollered from her podium, "Professor, do you remember how you told us about the hairy tortoises?"

Bunny perked up.

"I remember. Green-winged tortoises. They live in the Chinese province of Henan. Athanasius Kircher wrote about them in his *Illustrated Encyclopedia of the Chinese Empire.*"

"No, no! Don't get ahead of yourself, dear Professor! You say here that these hairy tortoises can supposedly fly too! That's going a little far. I took the time to double-check this. And I discovered that these tortoises are normal tortoises! There's no hair growing on their shells! Because that's im-pos-si-ble! And you, dear Professor, know that perfectly well. There's no hair growing out of their shells."

"There is," Bunny objected, drinking down the last of his bottle, "in certain cases, as, for instance, in the case of the green-winged tortoises from Henan Province."

"That's where you're wrong, Mr. Bunny! I checked. It's not hair on those tortoises' shells but algae and moss! Algae and moss! You hear me? They're just very old and live in swamps, so they get overgrown with algae that looks like hair. But it's not hair, Professor, it's algae. Algae, algae, algae!"

In despair, Theophilus Bunny abandoned his hats as they were, not packed, and fled the bazaar.

The bazaar intellectuals still teased him about the monsters and tortoises for a very long time. Sometimes they would call him Doghead, other times Sciopod.

The term Sciopod in general got firmly entrenched in the jargon of the late 1990s and signified anything you could have a good laugh at.

Mila tossed the notebook with the unfortunate lectures in the trash, from where Lena dug it out and took to reading it in her spare time. She liked the beginning in particular:

Dear students, I ask you to trust me unconditionally with respect to everything. Even if it sounds like I'm lying. I ask you to believe in everything that you will hear from me because anything is possible in this world. Absolutely anything. That you can or can't only imagine. There is no truth versus untruth. There is only that which is said. And if it is said, it's already in existence. Before his death, Blaise Pascal told his priest that he believed in everything and believed wholeheartedly. I ask you to believe like this as well. That same Pascal said that the entire world deceived people, that it deceived us deliberately so that we wouldn't reach the truth. But the search for the truth is already the second step. Only when you believe in everything will you be ready to find the truth in the false world.

And remember that it is better to know more about this world than less. You need to be open to everything that the world tells you. Because after you leave it, you won't find your way into another. It's not worth comforting your indolence with tall tales about other worlds, where you will be able to make up for what was lost in this one. There are no other worlds. If they did exist, God would not conceal their existence from us. God has no reason to conceal his grandeur.

Lena had her first kiss at the bazaar and would later recall it with great shame. She would say that the pig heads were to blame for everything.

A Biography of a Chance Miracle

The little alcoholic couple from the train station left her no peace. Lena decided to find the relevant pig-head vendor and have a chat with him. As it turned out, he wasn't that difficult to find because pig heads were sold in only one place.

Not only could you buy just a head there, you could also buy ears by themselves. You could get meatless backbones, skinless tails, or just the skin itself. Teeth could be bought separately if you wished, and cow udders and bulls' balls were also for sale. Whoever sold this stuff had to be a downright pervert, Lena had no doubt.

A young guy by the name of Misha was in charge of this assortment of porcine and bovine anatomical specimens. Both his cheeks and the whites of his eyes had a bluish tint, which didn't at all surprise Lena. It was precisely like this — with those bluish eyes, rather short, with a buzz cut and a little paunch, in shorts and rubber flip-flops for swimming — that she had imagined a true maniac would look.

Misha always wore the exact same T-shirt, which advertised: "Vegetarians Are Also Meat." The T-shirt was spattered in blood, whose origin you couldn't be one hundred percent confident in.

"Listen, so where do you get the pig heads?" began Lena the first time they spoke.

Misha smirked at her and didn't respond.

"Some people I know come here every month. They buy a pig's head. And eat it."

"So what?"

"You remember them? A husband and wife, they look a little… poor."

"I have a lot of customers. I'm not supposed to remember all of them. And none of them are swimming in gold, that's for sure."

"Well, these two are hard to forget. They're a little… they have very memorable faces."

As they talked, Misha was poking out the eyes of the next pig in line. He was born to do this work.

"What do you want?" he asked Lena nervously.

"I want you to stop selling them pig heads."

"To what do I owe this pleasure? You think I'm standing here for shits and giggles, or what?"

"I'll pay you."

Misha was clearly surprised. Lena went on. She had a clear-cut plan.

"You see, I really don't like that they eat pig heads. I dislike picturing it and even just knowing about it. I'm going to pay you, and you sell them normal meat. Just enough to get them through the month. Not too much because I don't eat meat every day either, but just, well, you know, just enough for a month. There's no need to tell them about this."

Lena laid out her modest savings, which she had spent a long while sneaking out of her dad's pockets one kopiyka at a time, on the table in front of Misha. Lena's dad was always very careless with money. When he had any at all, he had it all over the place. And he never noticed if he was running low because he never knew how much he should have left. This was Lena's saving grace, especially when she began to smoke regularly and was on a perpetual hunt for funding for her next pack of cigarettes.

"OK, fine" said Misha, raking up Lena's hryvnias. "There's only one little problem. These aren't the only two that buy pig heads from me. There are a lot of other customers too."

Lena was prepared for this little problem. She had a clear-cut plan.

She said, "Other people don't concern me. Let them eat what they want. The only thing that matters to me is that these two stop."

Later Lena would come to monitor the situation.

"They were here today, the little dears," Misha would say to her. "I sold them meat."

"And what? They weren't surprised? They didn't ask anything?"

"They asked nothing, just grabbed the meat and bolted. They were probably afraid that I had made a mistake and would take it back in a second."

Lena was happy. She would picture the little couple from the train station getting home and the woman with the traces of lipstick on her lips frying little cutlets for her husband. Or some potatoes with gravy. Or whatever it is that she was able to come up with. Lena realized that they likely kept on drinking but also knew that booze affected the body differently on a full belly. When you have a good meal, the urge to drink subsides. Instead, you get the urge to sleep. Lena had studied this phenomenon on her old grandpa. When he ate, he would always go to bed. But when he drank, he never ate.

"How old are you?" the butcher Misha would ask Lena.

"Sixteen. I'll be seventeen soon. I'm starting college this year."

"Seventeen, and so…" and Misha wouldn't go on.

"What? Stupid? Nah, I'm not stupid. I just have a clear-cut plan."

"So what's the plan?"

Lena wouldn't say, and Misha wouldn't pry.

At their tenth or so encounter, she let herself get kissed. It was her first kiss, and Lena told him as much too. Misha responded, "So now, in your world, we're supposed to get married?"

"Only after I finish college."

Misha began to laugh and laughed for a long time, while Lena didn't sleep that whole night. She was restless and developed a fever. Her old childhood ghosts surrounded her bed and shook their heads in sadness as if to say, "Look, our little girl is all grown up. She's wanting love, oh my, my."

Later Lena would say that there had been no money, no conscience and no love around her. No one loved anyone; they just all tolerated everyone. They tolerated each other for lack of a way out. Because they had no other option. Or

at least they thought they didn't. For convenie
this was called "no-other-option-but-to-love" l
parents "loved" each other, and all of her neig
friends "loved" each other. But if you took a closer look,
it was easy to detect the contempt that they were barely
able to restrain in talking to or accidentally touching the
shoulder of their most cherished better halves. That's how
wild animals that are locked in the same cage hate each
other — without cause, simply because there isn't enough
air for two.

Everything's going to be different for me, Lena would
say. I'm not going to hate anyone just because I can't
breathe.

The following day she was already at the bazaar early in
the morning. Misha was ignoring her and pretending to be
very busy, even though pig heads aren't at the height of demand in the morning. The people who subsist on them are
typically off solving other, considerably more important
problems of the day, namely where to find a shot or two for
a morning pick-me-up.

"Why is it you won't even look at me, Misha?" asked
Lena.

"Listen, I don't have time to talk right now."

"What are you so busy with?"

"I need to get everything ready."

"What is there to get ready? Just chop it off and plop it
on the counter."

"Leave me alone! Isn't it time for you to go to school?"

"There's no school today."

"Since when is there no school on Mondays?"

"Misha," Lena said seriously, "don't you love me?"

Misha was laying out fresh bulls' balls on the counter
before her. He said, "What does love have to do with it?"

"What do you mean, what does it have to do with it?"

"We made out once and I'm supposed to love you already?"

"Shouldn't you?"

"Nah."

"Then why were you so eager to kiss me?"

"I wanted to sleep with you too."

A terrible suspicion gripped Lena.

"Did you sell meat to the two of them or no?"

"Lena, you really could use some psych treatment."

"Why? Because I wanted to help them?"

"Come on, they spit on your help!"

"That was *my* business! *My* plan! I gave you money!"

"Take your money and get out of here."

Misha gave Lena back her money. Lena counted it over, then went to the train station.

Only the woman was sitting at the train station. As usu-al, she was smoking and drinking beer. She was dressed in shorts, and her bare legs were covered in wounds and bruises. The road home the previous night had probably been rough.

"Where's your husband?" asked Lena.

"Give me a smoke," said the woman.

"You're smoking already."

The woman tossed her cigarette under the bench and grinned at Lena with a handful of sparse teeth.

"I'm not smoking anymore."

"Where is your husband?" Lena stubbornly tried again.

"What husband? Ivan? I don't know, asleep somewhere, the dick. Or do you mean Petro?"

"So you have two of them?"

"Hah! I have a whole slew of them!"

Lena sat down on the bench next to the woman and asked, "Why are you drinking?"

The drunk had apparently answered this question a million times. And she was very convincing. She hollered across the entire station, "What else is there for me to do?"

Lena said, "I don't know, anything. Get some kind of job. Have a kid. You know, just live differently…"

"Let me tell you something!" The woman sprang up, but was too drunk to reach over and smack Lena in the face.

"You have no conscience! Just look at you! People have gotten so brazen these days! There are simply no words to describe it!"

Lena was completely unable to decide what she wanted to do when she grew up and what she should major in in college — whether she should study foreign languages and be a translator, or become a lawyer and defend thugs, or study philosophy and be a philosopher. The last profession enticed her the most, although Lena didn't understand what it was exactly that philosophers did.

One day at the bazaar she met an elderly lady who had taught philosophy for forty years and had even written a doctoral dissertation entitled *The Meaning of Life*. Lena asked her what the dissertation was about and what the meaning of life was. The lady was unable to answer. She said "Well…" and nothing more. Apparently "Well…" was the only thing that could be said about the meaning of life, concluded Lena.

Lena's dad also said "Well…" when he got fired from his lucrative loading position. But he didn't fall into despair. He wasn't one of those people who were easily defeated. "Loading," Lena's dad would say, "is a profession with no prospects, and I still have a lot of living to do. I'm going to take up farming! I'm going to grow beets. Or potatoes. I need to carefully think through what's going to sell better. I'm going to be a big farmer. A big landowner. Sow the land and ye shall reap. The land isn't stingy. It'll keep giving and giving."

There really was a lot of land lying around. You just had to go and stake your claim. No one was rushing at it too eagerly because there was nothing to work it with. You could make it through a small field with a hoe in hand if need be, but you couldn't pull that off with acres. The collective farms and equipment garages stood looted and overgrown with elderberry bushes. Plots of the former collective land had been distributed to lucky peasants who didn't even know which acre was whose. The fields were abloom with wild flowers and rosehip bushes.

"Not to worry, not to worry," Lena's dad would say dreamily. "I'll read a few books and set up a farming business. I'll be a trailblazer. The important thing here is not to miss the moment. Everyone will get fed up with the bazaar. They'll come flocking to the land, and there I'll be!"

His great-grandfather, Lena's great-great-grandfather, had had acres of farmland and supposedly even some kind of sugar factory or dairy. "If he could do it," Lena's dad would say, "why can't I? History unravels in a spiral; now is the time to once again return to our roots. Ukraine was always an agrarian country. The Commies wanted to make it into an industrial one, but that turned out to be a big flop. All the factories have ground to a halt. It's dreadful to look at. And our dear land is all that we have left. But it's not just any old land! It's *chornozem* — black soil! It's not for nothing that the Germans exported Ukrainian soil by the trainload. They weren't stupid. Whatever gets tossed into Ukrainian soil grows. In 1947, during the famine, people didn't have anything to plant and would throw potato peelings into the soil. And what do you think? The potatoes that came up were bigger than the world had ever seen. As big as watermelons!"

Lena's dad would say all of this while sitting on the balcony and nursing a beer. Meanwhile, Lena's mom would be nursing a cup of valerian tea in the kitchen. At the time, valerian tea was dirt cheap, and still is actually.

"So, what do you think?" Lena's dad would ask her.

"I think that something needs to be done," Lena would reply seriously.

"Exactly! Brilliant minds think alike!"

Her dad had always wanted to have a son, but he had had no luck and Lena alone was born. He tried to make a

real man out of her, and his efforts were partially successful.

"You couldn't even last as a loader!" Lena's mom would
be yelling from the kitchen.

"What is there to last at? I had no intention of spending
my whole life stacking Moldovan tomatoes!"

"Mr. Big Shot!"

"You just wait. I'm not a big shot yet, but I will be someday soon!"

"We can barely make ends meet, and he's going to be
a big shot someday soon! You have a kid starting college,
and there's no money!"

"No one held my hand when I was her age, and no one's
going to hold hers. She has a head on her shoulders. She'll
figure things out."

All of Lena's classmates had long since picked out their
future professions. One was heading to Kharkiv to the police academy to rob people, another to medical school to
kill people. One went off to music school, but she truly
had a talent for music. Many wanted to be econ majors
to count the money that didn't exist. One guy decided to
major in politics. It's true, he was stupid, but he was likeable, and in politics being likeable and a man is all that
really matters. Two or three girls from her class got hitched
right out of school and announced that they were done
with knowledge. Two others joined a convent, which was
fashionable at the time. Lena alone was flopping around
all over the place, trying to decide what her greatest talent
was.

She couldn't seem to pinpoint any particularly great
ones, but small ones — well, she had a whole mess of
those. Lena knew just enough about everything to get by.
She could be a physicist, or a biologist, or a mathematician
(this one required a little effort), or a psychologist. (This
one wouldn't require much effort, Lena would say, since
she could crack people like nuts at first glance.) Or she
could major in environmental science. Lena loved nature

and would later often complain that this had been her first major mistake, not going in for environmental science.

And so she submitted applications to all the more or less respectable departments and settled in to wait for the entrance exams. Lena wasn't scared of these exams because she was opinionated. And being opinionated, she would say, is very important. Then you can get yourself out of any mess with dignity.

Lena's dad, in the meantime, had leased a few acres of land from some villagers and was mulling over what to plant to make his fields sprout gold. He had a friend in the village named Havrylko. They joined forces and set up a co-op.

"Let's plant potatoes," Lena's dad would say to Havrylko.

"But first you need to have potatoes in order to plant them. Then you sweat over them, poisoning Colorado beetles and digging them up, and in the end you get pocket change for them at the bazaar. We won't even make back what we spend on gas."

"Alright," Lena's dad would agree, "let's plant sugar beets."

"And what are you going to do with them later? Suck on them like sugar cubes? You need to bring them to a factory to get processed, and only then will you have sugar. For a hundred kilos, you only get twenty or so kilos in return. Nah, I'm not signing up for that sort of thing."

"OK, fine, then wheat."

"The rain will beat it down, and you'll be left with squat."

"How about barley?"

"Diddly-squat. Besides, I've hated barley since I was a kid. If it gets in your pants, you spend all day scratching yourself, as if you had picked up some gonorrhea or something."

"And peas?"

"The neighbors will steal them all."

"Cabbage?"

"You're completely joking, aren't you?"

"Corn?"

"It could work, but everyone plants corn. We need something different, unique…"

Lena's dad would run through any other produce he could think of in his head. He would muse out loud: "Watermelons don't grow in these parts. That's too bad. Watermelons would've been a good business. Cucumbers I have no interest in. That's all I eat all summer, and I always end up feeling like a rabbit."

"Rabbits eat cucumbers?"

"They eat everything. Just show them a finger and they'll bite it off! Oh! Tobacco! A friend of mine once planted his whole garden full of tobacco. It was so pretty when it bloomed!"

"There was nothing to smoke back then, so people planted their own. But these days you can buy an unfiltered pack in every corner shop. What are you going to do with all that tobacco?"

"Listen, how about poppies? Let's grow poppies! They're also very pretty when they bloom."

"You'll have addicts from the whole province knocking at your door."

"I've got it!" Dad shouted. "We need to go back to our roots. Back to tradition! What did Ukrainians always grow?"

Havrylko didn't know. And, to be honest, Lena didn't guess it on her first try either, even though she was supposedly well-versed in Tradition. Her dad was very happy.

"Buckwheat! We're going to grow buckwheat, just like our ancestors."

Havrylko wasn't a fan of this idea, but he couldn't come up with a single strong argument against it.

"Buckwheat will make a good business!" Lena's dad set about persuading everyone. "We'll break our way into Europe with buckwheat. We'll develop such a fantastic European import market that we won't have enough room to stack the dollars. We need to do everything just right. We'll launch an ad campaign. I can see it now: Return to your roots, eat buckwheat! We'll name the company Agro-Firm Buckwheat Farmer. Doesn't that sound awesome?"

Even Lena's mom got pulled in by the men's excitement and handed over everything she had earned on her "out-fits" to buy seeds. Havrylko was in charge of the agro-technical aspects of the business. He rented an old tractor and somehow managed to plow up the field.

Sowing the buckwheat was a family affair.

"Stomp it down! Stomp it down!" Lena's dad was com-manding his squad. "So that it goes all the way into the ground, otherwise it won't sprout."

"So, who exactly eats buckwheat?" Havrylko would grumble with displeasure. "That's the one thing I don't understand. It would've been better to plant beans. You can at least eat them in lieu of meat, so they say. Lots of protein. But buckwheat? What's buckwheat? Some kind of culinary torture."

"A lot you know," Dad-the-Businessman would fire back. "Buckwheat was around even before potatoes. Ev-eryone ate it and lived to be a hundred. But now, chips are all kids think about. Pure chemicals."

"And what are you going to do? Take away the chips and stuff buckwheat down kids' throats?"

"I have a few ideas. Don't you worry."

To everyone's surprise, the buckwheat actually sprouted, and what's more, it even blossomed. The field stretched white past the horizon and up to heaven. Lena's dad glowed with pride, and her mom strutted around among the buckwheat flowers like a peacock. Havrylko told ev-eryone in the village that going back to the roots had been his idea and, out of sheer joy, even gave up drinking in preparation for his newly rich future.

The villagers also came to have a look at the field.

"Congratulations," they would say to Lena's dad. "Con-gratulations. Finally there's some youthful vigor in our village. The village will come back to life. We'll live like people now, not peasants. Now this here is a real farmer! Just look at that buckwheat! That's not buckwheat, it's a marvel!"

"You just wait until we really get rolling!" Lena's dad would reply. "Once we set up a process here, then you'll really be impressed. This year, all of the money from the harvest will go toward expansion and for the purchase of equipment. Next year, we'll buy an office, so that there's some place for management, namely me, to sit. I'll hire myself some agronomists. After that, you just watch, I'll open a sausage shop. We're going to make the buckwheat into blood sausage. So that no one can say that buckwheat isn't sausage. You'll have your sausage too."

On sunny days, Lena's dad would sit on the balcony, nursing his beer, and say, "Shine down, shine down, dear sun, on my little buckwheat."

When it rained, he would say, "Pour down, pour down, dear rain, on my little buckwheat."

He regressed into childhood.

In August they were supposed to mow the buckwheat. Lena's dad barely found a mower because there were only two in the entire province and both had been standing rusty and idle for many years. He was getting ready to mow it by hand, but someone told him that you couldn't do that with buckwheat: This isn't just some old hay, all of the seeds will fall off. They ended up having to get one of the mowers repaired. So dad borrowed some money from Lena's old grandpa and grandma. The two of them were saving up for their funerals.

Lena was busy with entrance exams all of July and didn't take much interest in how the family business was blooming. She just kept telling her dad, "Look, the important thing is to mow the buckwheat in time because the seeds fall quickly and then the entire harvest will be in the ground back where it started."

"You just study," her dad would reply, "and don't let my swaying buckwheat lull you into daydreams." And while he was at it, he would add, "I still think you should major in economics. You can help me with the business. Later, when the money comes rolling in, you'll be able to set up everything properly for us. You know, so that we can evade taxes and pay our employees under the table, but so that the books all add up."

"You'll hire someone," Lena would say. "I'm going to be a philosopher. That's my big plan."

But things with philosophy started heading in the wrong direction from the very start. You needed to know history to get through the entrance exam for the philosophy department, and Lena had had issues with history back in school. She had a tendency to get creative and to twist things around. And to get opinionated. As it turned out, the professors were only looking for the exact names and dates of the Hetmans, and they wanted them in chronological order to boot. But, as Lena would later complain, there was a whole butt-load of these Hetmans. Sometimes there were even two ruling simultaneously. It was simply impossible to keep all of them straight!

She said as much to the professor administering the oral exam: "What's the point in knowing all these Hetmans if they fucked everything up anyway?"

The professor said to Lena, "Child, you're applying to the wrong department."

"What do you mean the wrong department?" Lena was yelling. "I'm applying to philosophy, not history! What does a philosopher need to know the Hetmans for! This whole history thing is just intellectual babble anyway!"

Lena got so worked up that the professor sent for the nurse from the university clinic, who injected her with a sedative. That's when Lena realized that a career as a philosopher wasn't in the stars for her. On the following day, she went to take the physics exam.

Everything should have gone smoothly with physics because there, unlike in philosophy, everything was considerably more clear-cut. It was based on formulas and free of intellectual babble. But the devil got Lena to trip up on her own. Her exam question was: "The speed of light and the theory of probability." Lena knew and liked this topic. She spoke quickly and clearly while the physics professor just twisted his mustache in silence and nodded his head with satisfaction. At the very end Lena got the urge to explain a little more, to demonstrate that she could not only regurgitate textbooks but think with her head too.

She said, "You know, Professor, I think that the speed of light isn't the most fundamental constant. It isn't the greatest possible velocity."

The professor perked up from his apathy and craned his neck. "Indeed?"

"Yes, I think that Eynstein, or whatever his name is, Einstein, was a little off in his calculations. He bit off a little more than he could chew. Three hundred thousand or so kilometers per second — just think about it. Is there really no higher velocity?"

"Is there?"

"Why, of course! Eynstein was thinking objectively and was trying to find the greatest velocity in the world around him. He got that part right, of course. In the objective world, the speed of light is the fastest. It exists outside human consciousness. But Eynstein didn't take man into consideration. There is something within man which moves faster."

The professor bounced up in his chair. "And what do you think that is?"

"Thought! Human thought moves faster!"

The professor laughed. He had heard similar theories from his students many times before.

Lena forged on. "What's so funny? Thought is infinitely

fast. Take a look. Poof, and now I'm in Kharkiv! Seriously! Poof, and now I'm on the moon! Poof, and now I'm in the constellation of Andromeda! And that's a whopping two million light years from here!"

"So you think you're in the constellation of Andromeda right now?"

"That's right! I think! Therefore I'm there!"

"Child," the professor said to Lena, wiping the tears from his eyes with an old-fashioned monogrammed hand-kerchief, "you're applying to the wrong department. You should apply to philosophy…"

At the sound of this word, Lena had a nervous break-down once again.

"But they didn't accept me in philosophy! They said that I was applying to the wrong department! Why are all of you people messing with me?"

The same nurse from the university clinic once more in-jected Lena with a sedative. This nurse was a pretty nice girl, and she and Lena would cross paths a few more times after that. At other exams. The nurse copied Lena's exam schedule and would be waiting in the hallway with all her gear until she got called.

Lena bombed everything and didn't get accepted into any department.

And in the meantime, her dad was mowing his buck-wheat.

He had picked just the right kind of day: not too hot so that the buckwheat stalks wouldn't get too dry and the seeds wouldn't fall to the ground during mowing. Behind the wheel of the mower sat its owner, an old man who had volunteered to work for free just to watch first-hand as agriculture was revived in Ukraine. Well, and out of gratitude for the refurbished machine too. This old man mowed while Lena's dad walked proudly behind him, weighing the pros and cons of running for head of the local village council that year. So it went for about half an hour, up until the old man on the mower leapt down from the cab onto the field. He peered closely at the buckwheat and cried out, "What is there to mow here, Mr. Business-man?"

Lena's dad was at a loss for a moment. "Mow the buck-wheat. What do you mean?"

"But where's the buckwheat?"

"Right here. There's a whole field of it in front of you."

"There's a field alright, but where's the buckwheat?"

"Do I look like a moron to you?"

"No, but you apparently think that I look like a moron! There are stalks here, but there are no seeds. Take a look. It's all empty!"

Dad plucked a few stalks. The stalk were stalks, nothing special.

"Take a closer look. There isn't a single seed," the old man was shouting at him. "If there was at least one, fine, but there are none!"

"But it bloomed," Lena's dad was muttering.

"Listen, Mr. Businessman, did you bring bees over to the field?"

"What kind of bees?"

"Normal bees! Did you bring over beehives with bees? To pollinate the buckwheat."

"Should I have?"

"My, my, aren't you a businessman! How's it supposed to work without bees? The buckwheat pollinates itself on its own?"

"I didn't know that you needed bees for buckwheat too…"

"If the neighbors had had some hives around here some-where, OK, it wouldn't be the end of the world. But no one has beehives anymore. Take a walk around the village. No one has any. These days everyone cooks honey from Polish powders. My, are you a businessman! The whole field is one big barren flower. You could've at least asked someone, if you were that clueless yourself."

"Who would've thought that buckwheat's that crafty. You need to bring bees... Who knew?"

The old man gave a dismissive wave of the hand and took off with his mower to wherever he had come from. And Lena's dad sank into an indefinite post-capitalist depression.

"Whoever set this up was really crafty," he kept repeating while sipping some sort of apple cider concoction on the balcony. "You need bees for buckwheat! What a craftily complex world it is!"

In order to somehow pay back their "funeral funds" to her grandparents, Lena also began peddling at the bazaar. She now had lots of free time. A whole life's worth.

She sold "accessories," specifically, anything and everything pleather you could possibly need or want — mostly gloves, caps, change purses, handbags and belts. Lena wasn't trusted with pleather jackets yet because that involved serious money. On top of it, when buyers would walk up and ask if the jackets were leather, you had to reply without a blink of an eye, "Yes, yes, they're leather!" But Lena wasn't good at that.

Her fellow vendor, the former lit professor Theophilus Bunny, would say, "So, child of the proletariat, did you end up going to college?"

"You know," Lena would reply, "those college people don't really like it when someone's opinionated."

"And what kind of opinions could you possibly have? You're a numbskull by the mere fact of your birth!"

"Why do you say that, Mr. Bunny? You just get a kick out of offending people for no good reason."

"For no good reason! There *is* a reason, and a very serious one at that. You haven't even figured out that you should be bringing your money to the university, and not your opinions!"

"What money? Education is free of charge in Ukraine."

"Well sure, now you can sit at the bazaar free of charge!"

Lena spent a few days mulling over Theophilus Bunny's words, then sought him out herself.

"Mr. Bunny, what did you mean when you said that I should've brought my money to the university?"

"I meant just that. A bribe for the head of the admissions committee. Or for one of the professors. But you need to have connections. You need to know who to give it to."

"Do you have connections?"

"Do you have money?"

"I'll find some."

"Well, when you find some, then come back to me. But don't go dallying because as of September no one will accept you anywhere anymore."

Lena set off to her grandparents' to ask for money. In addition to their "funeral funds," they also had so-called "rainy day funds." That was the money she was counting on. Grandma gave away the savings without any hesitation. She said, "Education is sacred. Study, child. That which you learn a fire won't burn and water won't wash away." Lena teared up. She thanked her grandma and wished her and Grandpa a long life. After all, they now had no other choice but to live long. They had to save up for their funerals again.

"It's not enough." Theophilus Bunny smacked his lips when Lena gave him what she had wheedled.

"I don't have more."

"I'll see what I can do with these kopiykas, but I can't promise anything."

"Mind you, don't get it mixed up. I want philosophy. Remember that."

"Philosophy! Hah! You, a proletarian misbirth! It would take a whole eternity of teaching to get you educated. I have a philosopher on my hands!"

"Philosophy! Don't forget!"

Within two days Theophilus Bunny had arranged everything; he hadn't lied. He told Lena, "Go, get ready! Buy some notebooks and highlighters. You're starting classes on the first of September. You'll be a college student. I arranged everything. You'll be thanking me till the end of your vacant and meaningless life."

Lena promised that she would. She was unbelievably proud of herself, even though she had gotten into college by not entirely honest means.

"Honesty is a relative thing," she would later write in her journals. "You need to choose your priorities and sacrifice small truths for the sake of greater ones. How would Ukraine have benefited from me remaining uneducated? And in this specific instance, I didn't even cheat anyone. On the contrary, I got cheated and was forced to pay for free education. And my healthy young body got poisoned by strong sedatives to boot."

In her excitement, Lena forgot to ask Theophilus Bunny the most important thing: Into which department had she been "admitted"? Bunny got a little flustered and began to stammer. He always stammered when he was nervous.

"Don't sweat it so much, Mr. Bunny," Lena was saying. "The exact department isn't all that important to me. I wanted philosophy, but if that didn't pan out, it's not the end of the world. Others aren't that bad either. At least I'll have a college degree."

"For phi... phi... philosophy," Bunny was stammering, "there wasn't enough money."

"No worries! I've been a philosopher for some time now. When you have no money, there's not much else left but to philosophize."

"And for phy... phy... physics too," Bunny continued.

"Oh, I've had enough of that physics for a hundred years! It's obnoxiously boring. They only know how to look at the world through formulas. But I'm not like that, I want to look with eyes wide open!"

"In short... I got you set up in phy... phy... phys ed."
"What? Phys ed!"

That, of course, was one Lena hadn't been expecting.

"Is there even a phys ed department in the university?" she asked through tears.

"Where would it have gone? It's always been there."

"Are you joking? Mr. Bunny! But I can't even do two pushups in a row!"

"You're a young, healthy girl. You'll learn! You'll tone up your abs and develop a nice little figure. You'll become a real woman," Bunny said and gave her an encouraging slap on the back.

5   HOW SHE LEARNED THE BASICS
    OF VALEOLOGY

The phys ed department, Lena would later say, wasn't that bad a place to study, truth be told, if you happened to be a burly guy with a small, barely existent brain. After graduation, or even during the course of your studies for that matter, you could get a gig working as a bodyguard for gangsters. The pay wasn't bad, and the risk of getting killed was as good as nil because the gangsters of San Francisco got along well and didn't venture onto each other's turfs.

Should you nonetheless insist on exhibiting an inkling of intelligence — nothing too egregious, just a bare trace — you could even help the gangsters in their "gangsta business" and gangsta a little yourself.

Among the student athletes, specializing in boxing or kickboxing held the most prestige. (Boxing, Lena would explain, was when two monkeys pummeled each other whereas kickboxing was when two baby monkeys bopped around.) Weightlifting also got a whoop-whoop. (That was when the King Kongs entered the ring.) Everyone else, losers that they were, was left with either running ten kilometers a day like demented squirrels, which was called "light athletics," or contorting their bodies into such obscene poses in the gym that even the Kama Sutra's authors would've marveled at such perversion. This too was called "light athletics."

On September first, when the students were picking their concentrations, Lena walked up to the department chair and announced that she was going to specialize in chess.

"That's a sport too, isn't it?"

The chair looked at her with pity. He was an intelligent man and understood immediately that Lena had only had enough money for phys ed.

"So you're completely useless when it comes to sports?"

"I'm useless," Lena replied honestly.

"How about skiing? We have very few skiers right now."

"The only thing I'm mobile on is a bike. There's no dancing, huh? I know how to do the lambada…"

"You can do the lambada at a disco. This is a university here."

Lena began to cry.

"Stop bawling," said the chair. "You can also do research here, if you like."

"Research — that's for me! I'm smart, I swear! I actually wanted to major in philosophy!"

"OK, fine, then you'll do research. You have two options: contemporary valeology or physical therapy."

The word "valeology" struck Lena's fancy. What it meant only a valeologist could know. The word kind of lolled on her tongue, so Lena thought it must be the study of how to properly loll around in bed and do nothing. That's why she chose contemporary valeology and happily went off to do her first laps, which she was unfortunately still obliged to do.

"Right now, to be honest, I hate physical activity in all its manifestations, without exception," Lena wrote in a journal entry under the heading "Other stuff that I hate." "I hate running, I hate squatting, and I hate playing games where you have to run or move at all for that matter. I also hate looking at other people who are running. Watching them makes my head spin. I get the urge to shout at the runners, 'Stop for a minute already! Where are you rushing to?'"

Running, in Lena's opinion, was actually hazardous for the heart. She had read this in the journal *Science and Religion*. The heart only beats a certain number of times over a lifetime. Accordingly, the slower it beats, the longer a person will live. But if you abuse it foolishly by running, then you might not even make it to thirty. You need to conserve your heart. Even without your abuse, the poor thing has to endure a great deal.

Lena's, for example, had endured a lot.

Her parents had invited her to the café Sweet Treat for a serious conversation. Her dad ordered a beer, her mom wanted nothing, and Lena got a beer too. And so they sat in the café at a large wooden table, while whipped-cream pastries sprinkled with last year's blueberries rotted in the display case beside them.

"We have to have a serious talk with you," said Lena's mom.

"I'm listening."

"We're getting a divorce."

"What?"

It turned out that Lena's parents had both had lovers for many years and were living together only for the sake of their daughter.

"You're all grown up now," said Lena's mom. "You're in college. You'll understand us. We gave you everything that we could, and now we want to live a little for ourselves."

"Then, please," cried Lena, "go live! As if I've ever stood in your way!"

"We're going to sell the apartment and buy two one-room ones instead," her mom continued, all businesslike, "one for your dad, and one for me."

"And me?"

"I guess you can live with me for a while." Her mom hesitated a bit. "And with Uncle Stepan."

"With Uncle Stepan?"

A Biography of a Chance Miracle

"You know him. He worked with me at the Bon Bon."
(That's what Lena's mom called the chocolate factory.)

"Or you can live with me for a while," her dad broke in,
"with me and Tamara."

"With Tamara? You guys are kidding!"

Lena packed up her modest belongings and set herself
up in the college dormitory. To do research. At that time,
she was constantly reminding herself that it was too soon
to get disillusioned, that things were just beginning. How
things were beginning didn't matter. The important thing
was that they were beginning and that where they would
go from there depended on her.

Lena's new roommate — a discus thrower named Vasylyna, who looked like a clothes wardrobe, two meters wide
from every angle — was a big fan of the Russian singer
Zemfira. She was constantly playing Zemfira's songs at
full blast and bursting into bitter tears, all while chowing
down on a pot of pasta. One of the songs included the line
"If we can't fly, we'll just go for a swim." Lena would sniffle
along to the beat too.

"You could also crawl," she would say, "or leap, plod,
swing, eat, devour, gobble, or sleep. But I would still much
rather fly around a bit."

"In order to fly," Vasylyna would insist, "you need a rib
cage that's six cubic meters in volume."

"Where'd you get that?"

"Well, I am a discus thrower, after all."

Lena didn't see the logical connection between the question and the answer, but Vasylyna was like that, illogical.
And she was a discus thrower. That part was true.

But back to valeology. This is the study of health. Of
how to make an ordinary person into a healthy one without the use of force. So that a person begins to want to
be healthy of their own volition. "There's not much to it,"
Lena would later say. "It's a superficial science at best, be-

cause what is health anyway? Some kind of fiction, nothing more." Lena's old grandma described health as the state when a different body part aches every day. There is no better definition. It's the God's honest truth. Besides, there's something intrinsically impossible about people being healthy when they're not quite right in the head.

Valeology has an ingenious classification system. People are divided into the healthy, the sick and those who are "in a third state." This "third state" interested Lena the most.

"You, Vasylyna," she would tell her roommate, "are a prime example of the third state."

"No, I'm a specimen of the fifth generation," Vasylyna would object. "But anyway, what's the third state?"

"The third state is when you're neither healthy nor sick."

"Is that really possible?"

"It turns out it is. So anyway, what's the fifth generation?"

"It's the final generation of people, who are starting to appear on earth right now. They're super-humans and have special powers. They can even walk on water, like Jesus Christ. Actually, Jesus was the first specimen of the fifth generation."

"So what sort of special powers do you have, Vasylyna?"

"I'm in the process of finding them. But I'm definitely from the fifth generation. There's a mark on my forehead."

Vasylyna was a very hefty girl. A giant, in fact. Her face alone, which was round as a muffin top, measured one meter in diameter. When she ran — and Vasylyna ran only when revving up to throw a discus, even then she didn't really run, just took a running start — she could knock over and kill an innocent bystander with her flapping cheeks. Vasylyna barely had any hair, and whenever some would sprout, she would crop it with nail scissors. Her dorm bed collapsed beneath her the first time Vasylyna sat down on it. She had to buy another one, an iron one with reinforced springs.

Vasylyna came to college not from high school but from prison. Apparently she flew into a rage and hurled some man a distance of twenty meters because he had called her a gorilla. The man broke all of his bones, and Vasylyna served a year for inflicting grievous bodily harm.

"People," Lena would say, "are very reckless in their use of language. They have no compunction about what they say. That's their big problem."

Vasylyna was a big help to Lena right from the start. The owner of the pleather accessories that Lena sold at the bazaar had accused her of skimming profits. But Lena hadn't skimmed anything. The bazaar bigwigs often resorted to those kinds of ploys. They would say, "You skimmed. Pay up or we'll file a police report for theft." They, of course, had buddies on the police force who would write everything up as though you were really a thief.

And so this little guy showed up at Lena's dorm to scare her. Lena said to him, "I didn't take anything from you. And besides, I barely sold anything in the whole time that I worked at the bazaar. I'm a lousy salesgirl. Research is what I'm good at."

"Let the cops figure out what you're good at."

Vasylyna reacted to the word "cops" quickly and unequivocally. And, no doubt, with good reason. She said to the little guy, "What did you say, dude?"

But she said it in such a way that the "dude" nearly wet his pants.

"I'm not talking to you."

"I don't give a hoot. I'm talking to you!" Vasylyna growled and made a menacing move toward him.

The little guy barely reached her bellybutton. Lena even got a little scared because if Vasylyna decided to hurl him, the end result would involve much more than broken bones. Fortunately, the little guy realized this too and scurried away. Lena never saw him again.

"Vasylyna, I owe you one," she said.

The discus thrower scornfully sized Lena up from head

to toe and replied, "You need to work out. Anyone with an ounce of oomph can kick a wimp like you and you'll fall over. You need to learn to defend yourself."

Vasylyna had even taken part in the Summer Olympics but ended up unable to compete due to a severe upset stomach.

"I spent the whole day sitting in the bathroom," she would recount later on. "But it doesn't matter. I don't give a hoot. So it wasn't meant to be."

Lena respected Vasylyna for her optimism and for the fact that she accepted all failures with her trademark "I don't give a hoot." I-don't-give-a-hoot Vasylyna didn't know what depression was, or even a bad mood for that matter. She was a true sportsman. When she sensed that the blues were encroaching, she would turn on Zemfira at full blast and have herself a good cry. Or she would go to the stadium to throw discuses. Vasylyna had no family. She grew up in a group home, and often at night, when they couldn't fall asleep, she would tell Lena stories about what had gone on there. These stories were typically horrid: Girls got raped from age twelve, and those who weren't getting raped, raped one another.

"For some reason, everyone was very nasty there," Vasylyna would say. "They loathed each other and could've even killed if they hadn't been scared of getting punished."

"This is all a result of them never having known love," Lena would philosophize.

"What love? What love are you talking about? There's no such thing. There's only survival. Man is a beast."

"Vasylyna, have you ever loved anyone?"

Vasylyna was silent. After a moment, she said, "Let's suppose that I have. And that I still do. So what?"

"Who?"

"It's none of your business."

She kept silent like a partisan. She never went anywhere and never met up with anyone. Her day was planned out

down to the minute, so Lena always knew what Vasylyna was doing at any given moment. Her world comprised
only the stadium and the dorm room. Well, and the tape
recorder with Zemfira too.

Vasylyna's mysterious love sat inside her quiet as a mouse,
and Vasylyna never said another word about it again.

When Lena fell in love with a certain gymnast and
spent a few weeks lying in bed all miserable, Vasylyna kept
feeding her and repeating, "Now, now, Lena, take it easy.
This too shall pass. You'll laugh about it later. It's just hor-
mones. You know that. We just crave some intimacy every
now and then. We get an urge to be with someone so that
things don't seem so terrible. It's a weakness. Are you a
weakling or what?"

"I can't live without him!" Lena would wail.

"You've lived without him this long, and you'll go on
living. Guys are scum anyway."

"Not all of them. This one's wonderful!"

"He's got a different girl every night. What's so wonderful about that?"

"He just doesn't realize that he loves me."

"Why, he realizes everything perfectly well! He goes on
and on to anyone who'll listen about how you trot around
after him like a puppy."

"That's not true!"

"Look at me," Vasylyna would say. "Do you think I
could make up something like that?"

Lena would concede that she couldn't. Vasylyna had no
imagination. The part of her brain that was responsible for
imagination had atrophied while she was still in the womb
of the mother she never knew.

"So, tell me, Vasylyna," Lena would say, in order to distract herself from the pain, "have you ever seen a rainbow?"

"You mean in the sky? Yeah, I've seen one."

"And did you know that there are night rainbows?"

"I don't give a hoot."

"There are."

"Don't lie."

"Honestly. Every now and then, very rarely, all the colors come together in order to beautify the world."

"You can beautify it or not beautify it. Shit will still worm its way in all the same."

"And there are also hairy tortoises. Hair grows out of their shells. Just imagine."

"Lena, you really do lie a lot."

"Athanasius Kircher wrote about the hairy tortoises in his *Illustrated Encyclopedia of China*. They live in Henan Province. Look it up. I'm not lying. Maybe you'll find the book in the university library. There's so much in this world that's miraculous, yet we're somehow so callous and so cruel."

(As it later turned out, no one in the University of San Francisco library had ever heard of the above-referenced encyclopedia.)

Whenever someone would start getting sentimental, Vasylyna would get anxious and dismiss it as "centimeteral" talk, namely, talk resulting from your worldview narrowing to one centimeter.

"Well, if you want, I can beat him up!" she would offer.

"There's no need to beat him up. I'll lie in bed for a while and then I'll get up."

Later on there were also a kayaker, a skier and two volleyball players. It was always the same story. Lena would lie in bed, and Vasylyna would feed her pasta. All she knew how to cook was pasta. She would toss it into boiling water and fish it out fifteen minutes later. "Simple and nutritious," she would repeat as she cooked.

But one day Vasylyna came back from the stadium unusually excited.

"Get up, Lena, we're going to Kyiv on the night train. I bought the tickets already, third class, OK?"

"And why is it we're heading to Kyiv?"

"Zemfira's performing. We're going to the concert."

That was when it began to dawn on Lena, but she said nothing.

They packed up one backpack for the two of them and set out on the night train for the chestnut-filled capital of Ukraine.

Lena had never seen Kyiv before, or a live concert for that matter. The skier (or was it already the volleyball player then?) had gotten hung up on some girlie from the linguistics department, and Lena was now open to new experiences once again.

The train pulled out of San Francisco in the evening and arrived in Kyiv in the early morning. Vasylyna was sitting on her third-class bed (she could only fit sitting) and gazing out the window. The train chugged along slowly and with a rumble, as if it had gotten sick to death of transporting these fate-shortchanged passengers in their stinky socks, with their parcels of smoked sausage, bread and quartered onions.

Lena said, "I'm your best friend. Tell me. Are you in love with Zemfira?"

Vasylyna curled up and said nothing.

"How is it possible to fall in love with a singer?"

Silence.

"You've never even seen her, after all."

Silence.

"OK, fine. She's a good singer. I like her. She's very… It's evident that she lives like she sings. She's fierce but genuine. But to fall in love?"

"I'm not in love," Vasylyna finally squeezed out of her gigantic body. "It's just that people call it that."

"So you're in love. Let's get real!"

"She's so, you need to understand, she's… brilliant."

"And so what that she's brilliant? You know so many brilliant people. Are you telling me I'm supposed to love all of them?"

"Brilliant people are few and far between," said Vasyly-na. "They're like your night rainbows. They pass through very rarely, only to beautify the world a little with their presence."

Lena hollered, "Centimeteral talk!"

"I don't give a hoot," Vasylyna grumbled and didn't say a word more.

"She was illogical, this Vasylyna," Lena would later write in her journals. "Yet another forlorn creature, which I ended up having to live with for four years. Forlorn creatures were drawn to me, probably because I was always making myself out to be a hero. Incidentally, it's very easy to be a hero. You don't need to do more than have faith in your own strength and tell everyone, 'See, I'm a hero.' And everyone will believe it. At least most of them will. And there's really no need to talk to the ones that don't. Avoid them and that's all. And that's how you can be a hero in your own little heroic world."

They arrived in Kyiv at six in the morning. They roamed around downtown for a few hours, froze a bit on Independence Square, ate some cat shawarma, and drank some tea out of a dispenser in a street underpass. After that they barely made it to some park and took turns sleeping on a bench so that no one would steal their stuff.

Lena said, "So where are all the chestnut trees here in this Kyiv? Have you seen even one?"

"All trees are chestnut trees to me," Vasylyna replied. "I don't know the ins and outs of biology."

But she wasn't listening to Lena. She was dreaming. And at the concert she also sat very quietly. She just watched as Zemfira sang and didn't breathe. At the time, Lena was pretty sure that her manly discus thrower, who was one minute shy of being an Olympic champion, had died like that, with eyes wide open. And it's possible that Vasylyna in fact wanted just that. It's possible that she wanted what she was seeing at that moment to imprint itself on her eyes forever. Because the concert would end and Vasylyna would return to her dormitory rat hole, to live there as she had lived before, with a tape recorder and a pot of pasta. But now she'd have something to remember, and that memory, which would inexorably fade with time, would become her hell. She would replay it again and again, anew and anew, but the day would come when all that remained of the memory was words. Like the skeleton of a dead person.

Even when the concert had ended and the audience began to exit, Vasylyna went on sitting and gazing motionlessly at the empty stage.

"She's brilliant," she was whispering.

"Maybe you could come up with something else to say?"

Lena was trying to pull Vasylyna out of her seat, but it was like trying to move a sleeping elephant from its spot.

"Let's go, Vasylyna! Or is your ass glued to the seat? Did we come to Kyiv for nothing? Come on, let's go talk to her."

"To who?"

"What do you mean who? To your love."

"To Zemfira? Talk? Can we really do that?"

"We can do anything! She's just human, same as us. Let's go!"

Vasylyna trudged off after Lena as if heading to her execution, barely lugging her feet along.

"What will I say to her, Lena? I don't have anything to say to her."

"You'll come up with something."

"I ca-a-an't."

Lena's target was the stage door. She had often seen on TV how fans lay in wait for their idols there. But, apparently, Lena wasn't the only one who watched TV because a massive crowd of people had already gathered at the stage door, and they didn't stand a chance of elbowing through it.

The fans were shouting, "Zemfira, you're our God! Zemfira, we love you!"

Standing on the edge of the crowd, Vasylyna looked comical, even pitiful.

"Well, go on," Lena urged, "squeeze in! You can knock all of them down with a single swat if need be."

"I can't," Vasylyna was muttering in response. "I don't have anything to say to her."

"You'll tell her that you love her! Isn't that what you wanted?"

"A million other people are already yelling that at her. Can't you hear?"

"Well, not many people manage to be original when it comes to love."

Vasylyna stood there, and down those same cheeks with which she could've killed someone, gathering momentum, flowed tears, gigantic just like Vasylyna.

"Let her live her own life, and I'll live mine," she was whispering. "Let her sing, and I'll listen."

The crowd let out a roar. This was supposed to signal that Zemfira had come out of the building and was trying to make her way to her car. Vasylyna's eyes sparked for a second but instantly faded. She turned away, wanting to run. But the mob, which had by now engulfed her, instead lunged in attack at the object of its infatuation. The few guards were of little use. They got trampled into the asphalt in a matter of seconds.

"Zemfira, you're our God! We love you!"

That was when Lena concluded that such love was worse than hatred. There was something lethal in it.

"What are you doing?" someone was yelling. "You'll suffocate her!"

But that's exactly what the fan mob wanted. To divvy

up Zemfira into little pieces among themselves and take her home as a souvenir. To stick her between the pages of a thick book and preserve her like a dried flower. In order to have something to boast about to their grandchildren and great-grandchildren when they're old.

Suddenly someone behind Lena roared with such ferocity that Lena's blood changed course in her veins and began flowing in the opposite direction.

"Back off, bitches!!!"

With a raging howl, Vasylyna plunged into the crowd, and people began flying every which way like hunks of meat. She stomped and clambered over torsos and heads. Oh, woe to those who ended up in Vasylyna's path!

She snatched Zemfira up into her arms and just like that, on outstretched arms, carried her out of the field of battle as if she were a plastic mannequin. Next to the car, Vasylyna gently lowered her precious cargo onto the ground.

Zemfira shook herself off, glanced at Vasylyna, smiled and, as she climbed into the car, said in Russian: "*Spasiba.*"

Vasylyna replied in Ukrainian: "*Bud laska.*"

She smiled too.

Zemfira's car pulled away and quickly disappeared into the darkness. Vasylyna stood rooted to the ground, still smiling. She murmured rapturously to Lena, "I talked to her. She thanked me."

"You see, and you were scared. I told you that you'd come up with something."

A few years ago Zemfira released a new album that, co-incidentally or not, was entitled *Spasiba*. Vasylyna thinks that it is dedicated to her.

6 How She Turned Down Being a Master

Lena never had much of anything, but she did have a sober mind. Sober and lucid. A little cynical perhaps, but cynicism can serve as a self-protective mechanism in state-of-emergency conditions. Lena's mind was her last bastion of hope.

But with time, it's true, she began to notice to her great regret that even this sober and lucid mind of hers was slowly proving less reliable. For one, it wasn't always sober in the literal sense of the word, but alcohol was never the cause, only a consequence. Second, problems also began to arise with its lucidity. I stopped understanding what was happening around me, Lena would say. And this haziness tormented me. I didn't want to end up not understanding anything.

Having lost her faith, Lena threw herself into other, more earthly pursuits in search of meaning. In order to grasp the spiritual essence of what's happening around you, it's sometimes necessary to first make sense of the real world. Intellectuals like to ignore reality, and though she was no intellectual, Lena had this same proclivity. Ignoring reality was a big mistake, so decided Lena. You could spin it however you liked, but the only concrete thing we humans had been given was reality. So our first job was to learn to cope with it somehow.

There was this guy at the university that everyone called

Darwin because he was living proof that Darwin was right, that people had descended from apes. OK, so this Darwin was studying swimming and not how to swing from tree to tree. But everyone called him Darwin anyway. He wasn't that bad-looking. He had plump red lips, a well-developed muscular body, white-blond hair and blue eyes — in short, a textbook Aryan. But, unfortunately, he wasn't all that bright.

What irritated Lena about Darwin was that he never had doubts. About anything. However he called it, so it was.

"Physical activity is the most important thing in life," Darwin would say, for instance, and it was impossible to convince him that man couldn't survive on physical activity alone. It was the most important thing, period.

And so it was with everything else.

"People need to eat beets," Darwin would say.
Period. Beets and under no circumstances cabbage.

"A person should work for the good of the society in which he lives."
Period.

"Arguing with parents isn't allowed because they've lived life."
Period.

"The goal of Russian propaganda is the destruction of Ukrainian independence."
Period.

Sometimes Darwin would contradict himself and preach two completely incompatible ideas. For example, he would claim that sacrificing your life for the sake of the motherland was a great honor. But on another occasion he argued that you could choose a motherland, and he had chosen Ukraine. Lena came to the conclusion that you should choose a motherland in such a way that you didn't end up having to sacrifice your life for it.

But, unfortunately, a motherland is precisely a motherland because it isn't chosen. "If I had had the option," Lena would later say, "then Ukraine would certainly not have been at the top of my list. I would've probably chosen Greece because the sea there is this beautiful true-blue. Not black, like the Ukrainian one. Or Great Britain because then I would've known English from birth and wouldn't have had to spend years studying it in school. Because this English has really worn me down. I'm forever studying it and studying it but still can't string two words together when the need arises."

One day Darwin walked up to Lena during her lunch break. She was sitting in the university courtyard munching on an apple. He said, "Listen, Lena, you don't strike me as being all that stupid."

"Thank you," replied Lena.

"Then why haven't you joined our organization yet?"

"What organization?"

"Our organization of young nationalists."

"I didn't know there was such a thing."

"There is. It's called the Resistance Movement. I'm the deputy."

"But what is it you're resisting?"

"Well, it's a nationalist organization. We bring nationally conscious young people together. You're conscious, aren't you?"

"That I am," said Lena.

"Then join us. We meet up three times a week at 7 p.m. We discuss the news and are developing a plan of action. We swap ideas about how best to help Ukraine. You're in agreement that something must be done, aren't you?"

Lena was in agreement with this.

"To live and do nothing is decadence," Darwin went on. "Action is necessary. You agree, don't you?"

"I agree."

A Biography of a Chance Miracle

The Resistance Movement rented a room in an old building in the center of town. The room was almost empty, save for a few chairs, a table and a large portrait of the WWII pro-Ukrainian activist Stepan Bandera on a white wall. Lena liked this type of ascetic atmosphere. She found it conducive to the generation of ideas that would change the world before long. Lena felt like a member of a secret revolutionary movement and attended meetings for a number of weeks with considerable enthusiasm.

They spent the meetings studying and discussing the biographies of great Ukrainians: political and military activists of the inter-war period such as Dmytro Dontsov, Yevhen Konovalets, Symon Petliura and Stepan Bandera too, of course. Him first. A short but very chatty student from the history department presided over the sessions. When he spoke, he would flail his arms and gaze intently into the eyes of all the movement members. After every one of his observations or assertions, no matter what it concerned, he would cry out, "Isn't that right?" And the members would readily nod their heads, "Ye-e-es." Not because they actually supported this particular opinion or idea but because they felt like he was asking their permission, like he was reckoning with them.

Something about this chairman reminded Lena of Lenin from the old Soviet films in which Lenin would wave his arms around before the working class while hiding behind a podium. So that they couldn't see what a shrimp he was.

At the tenth or so meeting, after a detailed exploration of all the foundational biographies and fundamental postulates of Ukrainian integral nationalism, Lena asked, "So what are we going to do? How are we going to change the world? I'm ready for concrete actions."

The room responded with vocal support.

"There's plenty to do," said the chairman. "Isn't that right?"

"Ye-e-es!"

"Someone has just submitted a proposal that we initiate the renaming of Builders Street to Stepan Bandera Street."

"But what have the builders done wrong?" asked Lena. "Aren't they people too? Building is a fine profession. They build houses, and that's not all that easy, let me tell you."

The shrimp grew a bit nervous but was too intelligent to get tripped up on such a triviality.

"Building is certainly a fine profession, but why should they have a street named after them? Naming streets in honor of the working classes is a Communist tradition. Builders, firefighters, miners…"

"So are divers on that list?" Lena asked because she was genuinely curious.

"Maybe, somewhere," grunted the chairman. "But that's not the point, isn't that right?"

And once again, they all said in chorus, "Ye-e-es."

"A nationally conscious society," the spiritual leader would say, "names streets in honor of its heroes and doesn't borrow names from a totalitarian regime, which is what the Soviet Union was."

"OK, fine," Lena agreed. "Then let's do away with these builders if they're such an eyesore. Although I would personally rather give our city back its old name of San Francisco, instead of whatever they're calling it these days. What do we need to do?"

"We'll submit a request to the local authorities," said the chairman. "But that's not enough. They take a very long time renaming streets. We may not live to see it happen. We need to proceed more radically."

Lena was ready for radical action and was typically the first to run into battle. Under different circumstances, in a different period of history, she would've made a very good partisan or revolutionary. Courage and romanticism, that's what drives revolutions, and Lena was both courageous and romantic.

A Biography of a Chance Miracle

This is the plan they came up with: to show up on this street of the working class at night, paint all the "Builders Street" signs there white, and then write "Stepan Bandera Street" in black paint on them. Simple and straightforward.

Lena took I-don't-give-a-hoot Vasylyna along just to play it safe should problems with the local drug addicts crop up. But problems of a different nature cropped up. The partisans didn't find a single sign to paint. Everyone in town knew that this was Builders Street, but there were no signs to confirm this fact. The old ones had either worn away or fallen down, and the local housing office apparently didn't have money for new ones.

The young nationalists paced around for a while and, disappointed, were ready to give up and head home. That was when Lena said, "Who needs these old signs anyway? We'll just write the new street name right on the buildings and, voila, the job's done! It's even better that the signs are gone. It means less work. Isn't that right?"

The "Isn't that right?" tactic worked like magic. Everyone nodded in agreement, even Vasylyna, who technically didn't belong to the movement. The chairman, incidentally, was absent from the operation, having excused himself for health reasons.

Everyone set about meticulously painting the new street name in black paint. On every building. It was hard work. Lena, for example, couldn't feel or lift her arms for the next few days she had so worn herself out. They wrapped up the operation at sunrise and trotted off to sleep satisfied. They didn't encounter any drug addicts either.

The local residents, however, weren't overly impressed by the young artists' masterpieces for some reason. None of the "artists" actually knew how to paint, and the signs turned out crooked, if not quite ghastly. Many of the painters even made spelling mistakes, likely from fatigue.

Over the course of the week, the locals painted over the scrawls. They weren't cheap about it either and even paid for the paint themselves.

At first the young nationalists were thinking of executing the operation again because, let's be honest, it's a shame to let fine work go to waste. They figured, let them paint over it, and we'll just show up again! They'll paint over, and we'll show up again! And on and on, until the locals finally get sick of buying paint. Reviving the national consciousness of the ex-proletariat isn't that simple. It requires exerting some serious effort. But then another national matter arose, which was considerably more serious than that of urban toponymy.

At an extraordinary meeting, Darwin announced, "Colleagues, I want to bring something to your attention. Do you remember the bookstore in the center of town?"

Everyone remembered it, of course, because it was, after all, the only bookstore in town.

Darwin went on. "I stopped by there recently, and do you know what I saw? All Russian books, without exception. Only two or three Ukrainian ones, tops. Well, maybe five. This is a disgrace, not a bookstore! Unabashed propaganda of the Russkis! How can we talk about a national consciousness when children are reading their first books in Russian?"

The word "children" worked like dynamite. The colleagues began to rumble.

"If you want to convince someone that you're right," Lena would later write, "say the word 'children,' and in the name of the children the bookstore will get wiped not off the face of the city, but off the face of the earth. Not a stone will be left unturned."

Darwin was on a roll. "That's not all! I wanted to buy a book that touched on some national issue and, naturally, I didn't find any. But I did find this vile opus by some Kyiv scholar in which the great Ukrainian poet Taras Shevchen-ko is slandered as an alcoholic. We can't allow such things. Our national icons are being mocked!"

"Yippee!" Lena perked up. "We're going to Kyiv to have a chitchat with the scholar! I'll bring Vasylyna. One good little chitchat with her and the scholar won't know what hit him."

"Why do we need to mess with the scholar?" objected Darwin. "Let him write what he wants. We need to burn down the bookstore that sells such abominations!"

The bookstore it was then.

Lena was a little uncomfortable. Burning books seemed a little immoral, regardless of the language they were writ-ten in. But things were rolling, and it was too late to back down. Sometimes it's necessary to sacrifice a smaller con-viction for the sake of a greater one.

Someone got hold of a Molotov cocktail. It needed to be tossed in the front window of the bookstore, and from there things would take care of themselves. The store would burn down and not a trace would be left. Lena proposed organizing a reading of Shevchenko's poetry the evening before the raid to get themselves psyched for battle, but no one supported the idea. People were still recovering from all the Shevchenko they had read back in grade school.

The honor of hurling the explosive concoction through the front window of the bookstore fell upon Lena. Because she was courageous and romantic.

Vasylyna said to her, "You're wasting your time on non-sense, Lena."

"Now maybe on nonsense, but this is just the begin-ning. Next, we're going to seriously change the world. I've always aspired to this. It's my mission. I want the whole world to be happy."

Vasylyna shrugged her shoulders, as if to say, then go, burn your bookstore if you must. I don't give a hoot.

So Lena went.

Four a.m. is the best time for criminal activity. The streets are completely empty and everyone's asleep, even those who will moan in the morning that they didn't get a wink of sleep all night.

The spiritual leader was absent once again, this time on the grounds that he was cramming for an important exam.

The partisans crept up to the bookstore. The store window was well lit. It showcased books, lots of books, all very brand new and with vibrant covers. *Castles of the Lviv Region* in Ukrainian, *Egypt's Gold* in Russian, *The Great Illustrated Encyclopedia of Dinosaurs* also in Russian. A rather light assortment, Lena would later write, but books should be entertaining too, isn't that right?

"Listen, Darwin," she whispered to her world-improvement comrade-in-arms. "So what sort of books do you typically like to read?"

"For me, sports are the most important thing in life," replied Darwin.

"You don't read books?"

"Well, I've read a few."

"Which ones exactly?"

"I don't really remember. Why are you pestering me?"

This answer alarmed Lena.

"Darwin, what if it wasn't Russian books for sale in this store, but athletic equipment, some kind of, I don't know, Russian sneakers, for example?"

"These days all sneakers are Russian."

Lena yelled, "Oh no, my dears, it's not going to go down like this! So we burn Russian books but wear Russian sneakers? What a double standard! How are books any different from sneakers? Why aren't we burning down stores that sell sneakers? I would very happily do that. I don't like sports at all."

"Sneakers, unlike books, don't influence a person's worldview."

"And what kind of influence on a person's worldview does a history of dinosaurs have?"

"Give me back the bottle," ordered Darwin.

"I won't let you burn down the bookstore!"

"We'll kick you out of the organization! With a dishonorable discharge!"

"So kick me out, for the love of God!"

Lena took off as fast as she could from the bookstore. She hid the Molotov cocktail under her mattress in her dorm room. It might still come in handy someday, she thought to herself. Maybe, someday, there'd be something else she needed to blow up.

The following day the partisan-revolutionaries burned down the bookstore nonetheless, without Lena. They scrawled OUN/UPA on its façade in embers, hoping to place blame on the WWII Organization of Ukrainian Nationalists and its Ukrainian Insurgent Army, and the local branch of the OUN/UPA was forced to prove its non-involvement in the incident to the cops. The bookstore was closed down for lengthy repairs.

Later the local Orthodox church of the Moscow Patriarchate was burned down in the same manner, and the priest, who happened to be spending the night there because he had drunk too much after the evening service, barely made it out of the fire alive.

Lena no longer showed up at the group's meetings and made a blanket decision that collective action wasn't for her, that she was by nature an individualist and had to work independently.

It was about then that Lena by chance met a certain Jamaican who had come from that Jamaica of his to Ukraine to study Ukrainian at the university. For the first time ever, the foot of a black man had trodden the hallowed ground of the Ukrainian San Francisco. People craned their necks to catch a glimpse of the Jamaican when he went to the store for bread. Children, feeling no shame, pointed at and ogled him, while the really little ones cried out in fear and yelled, "Bogeyman!"

The Jamaican was truly black. Almost bluish-black. He had long black fingers and pastel-pink palms. His wide nose stretched across half his face, and his hair was coiled into thin little snakes, which he called dreads.

The Jamaican spoke something that closely approximated Ukrainian, while Lena spoke something that closely approximated English.

Lena would say, "You're really so black that it's almost terrifying. Is it so that you can prowl around undetected at night?"

The Jamaican (his name was Ishion or something along those lines) would smile.

"So why did you come here at all, huh?"

"To study the *ukrainska* language and *ukrainska literatura*."

"Well that's obvious, but *chomu? Why?*"

"It's interesting."

Ishion talked a lot about Jamaica. Lena understood half of it; the other half she filled in with her imagination.

"I was born in Jamaica," Ishion would say. "My parents, grandparents and great-grandparents were fishermen. But actually we're from Africa."

"That's all very interesting, but there's only one question that's bothering me. Tell me honestly, why in the world did you schlep all the way to Ukraine?"

Ishion didn't know the word "schlep." There was, in fact, a lot that he didn't understand, and Lena was happy to learn that there were people who understood even less than she did.

"In Jamaica," Ishion would say, "all the men are Casanovas. But they don't just take advantage of women. They serve them too. Women worship Jamaican men, and even when the men ditch them, the women go on being happy. Jamaican men make Jamaican women happy. On top of that, all the men have guns and shoot at each other every now and then. They all dream of going to America, and once in a while they succeed in getting there. Everyone also sings Bob Marley songs, and Bob Marley's children — there are fifteen of them by various women – are considered the unofficial princes of the island."

Out of gratitude for the lessons on Jamaica, Lena told Ishion the history of Ukraine, as best she was able, and showed him the noteworthy local sights, in particular, the palace of the Polish prince, which now housed the barracks for new army recruits, and The Goldfish bar, which served the cheapest beer in town.

They hung out often at The Goldfish. Lena would drink beer while Ishion would flamboyantly order cocktails. (He didn't know the word "flamboyantly" either, of course.) The waitresses couldn't stand Ishion and would explain to him every single time: "We don't have cocktails! We only serve beer and booze!"

"Mix some booze into some beer and you'll have a cocktail," Ishion would reply in Ukrainian.

But the waitress of the night, now on the verge of tears, would beg Lena anyway, "Explain to him, will you, that we don't do such things here!"

"Bring him a Bloody Mary," Lena would suggest.

"That's tomato juice with vodka?" the waitress would ask with a bounce of joy. "Coming right up! I'll bring it in a jiffy!"

Lena would protect Ishion from the Ukrainians and the Ukrainians from Ishion. And everyone was content. The owners of The Goldfish secretly took pride in the fact that they had a foreign regular and would turn a blind eye to his skin color. Over time, in fact, this bar became shrouded in legends, the last of which was that Bob Marley himself had been there. Now, in his honor, the bar is known as Bob's and serves the most expensive cocktails in town. The walls are decorated with a Bob Marley "autograph" and "Feel the heat of high-proof spirits" signs, though it's highly doubtful that Bob Marley ever wrote or sang that.

But then unforeseen problems arose for Ishion with Lena's former comrades from the underground. They became apparent one day when Darwin walked into The Goldfish with his musclemen and grunted, "What are you doing hanging out here?"

"Is it bothering you?" Lena snapped back.

"Not really, I guess," Darwin replied and moseyed off to the bar.

He hung out at the bar for a few hours, sipping mineral water and keeping an eye on both of them.

"Don't worry," Ishion said in an effort to comfort Lena. "I'm used to racism. It doesn't bother me. I beat my own drum."

"All that matters is that you don't beat your own noggin."

"What's a noggin?"

"In some cases, the same thing as a drum."

It was then that the Resistance Movement issued an operational directive prohibiting any relations whatsoever between foreigners and Ukrainian girls. In reality, the directive pertained only to Ishion and Lena because Ishion was the only foreigner in town and Lena was the only one who talked to him at all.

Ishion got hunted through dark alleys on a few occasions, but he managed to get away unscathed each time. Ishion was actually a fast runner and said that everyone in Jamaica was a fast runner because there was no public transportation there.

And then Lena received an "official" invitation to attend a meeting of the Resistance Movement because the discussion that was scheduled to take place "directly concerned her unacceptably heathenish behavior."

Here's what Lena subsequently wrote in her journal:

> It was interesting to listen to the idiots. I told them as much at the outset.
> "You people are all idiots!"
> The shrimp, flailing his arms around as usual, gave a short speech and ordered that I sit down on a chair in the middle of the room.
> "You've staged an entire trial here!" I laughed.
> "Is it really possible that you couldn't find a single Ukrainian guy in the entire city to be friends with?" the chairman asked sternly.
> "Obviously, I couldn't. Take a look at yourselves. As if someone could be friends with you. You're young communists and fascists wrapped up in one package!"
> Darwin sprang out of his chair, as if stung by a scorpion.
> "Calm down," ordered the spiritual leader. "We've gathered here in order to have an informative discussion."
> "And if you don't succeed in convincing me with words, are you going to beat me?"
> "Just think about what color your monkey-babies are going to be!" Darwin cried.
> "Tell me, Darwin," I said, "why do you think people call you Darwin? Monkeys can be light-skinned too, you know."
> "I see that the informative discussion has been unsuccessful," the shrimp summed up.
> The organization members — there were about twenty of them — all stood up as if on cue and began to pull the belts out of their pants.

At this point, I must admit that I never really went to any meeting. I just wanted to more vividly envision how such a conversation might have gone.

I don't like to beat people up and don't enjoy getting beaten up by someone else either. But one of these two things would've definitely happened had I accepted the invitation and gone to this meeting. No, I didn't go anywhere, of course. The only way to fight guerrillas is to beat them at their own game, with guerrilla warfare.

The building in which the Resistance Movement rented a room, despite its hundred-year history (rumor had it even the famous Ivan Franko had given a reading of his poetry here), had long since been discredited in Lena's eyes. Its other rooms were rented by organizations that were in no way better, including Liberty or Death, Red and Black Flag, and Young Nation.

Everything went flawlessly. In the middle of the night, Lena smashed the window of the Resistance Movement's meeting room, tossed in the Molotov cocktail that she had set aside for better days, and the room instantly burst into flames. The chairs burst into flames, and the table, and the portrait of Stepan Bandera too. Lena felt bad for him. Stepan Bandera just happened to be hanging there, with no bearing on anything, but sometimes you had to sacrifice a lesser conviction for the sake of a greater one.

(The cops, fed up with the fires in the city and not finding any other culprits, arrested the victims. That's how it always goes,) but in this instance Lena wasn't too concerned with global injustice. The spiritual leader of the Resistance Movement spent fifteen days in a holding cell and in the end handed over every last one of his like-minded colleagues. He also filed a complaint against Lena, but the cops were apparently too lazy to go digging that deep and made do with just him and his deputy Darwin. They were both given a year of probation and got kicked out of the university.

A few times after that, Darwin stood outside Lena's dorm window, crying like a child, punching the air with his fists and yelling, "It was you. You set all of this up!"

"I don't know what you're talking about," Lena would joke.

"I got kicked out of college because of you and your darkie!"

"What makes you think, Darwin, that you can dictate what others should do? You think you're some sort of great master?"

"Yes, I *am* a master! I'm the master of my own land!"

This pronouncement threw Lena for quite a loop. It seemed generally reasonable and valid yet illogical at the same time. "Because how can land have a master," Lena kept asking herself. "As if you could hide land in your pocket and say, 'This is mine, not yours!'? You can't. No more than you can air, or a tree, or a river, or a mountain. Then why waste so much energy conquering something that can't be conquered, trying to own something that can't be owned, if you don't even own your own life and will have to give it back when the time comes?"

Later Lena would write, "When someone says, 'I'm the master of my own land,' I don't know how to respond. I'm at a loss. But at the time I yelled back at Darwin, 'The master is the one who's craftier. And in our case, that's me!'"

Soon after, the Jamaican announced that he had grown bored in Ukraine and was itching for something more exotic. So he went to Belarus. Lena wished him safe travels.

7 HOW SHE SOUGHT AND DIDN'T FIND

And that was when her nightmares began. No sooner would Lena close her eyes than they would immediately appear. Lena called them her "friends of the dark," probably because she didn't have any friends of the light. Lonely people are full of darkness and very easily spooked.

Lena's nightmares always began the same way: There's a third person in the dorm room, aside from her and Vasylyna. And he's hiding. But Lena knows that he is there, this mysterious third someone. What makes him dangerous is that he can take on whatever shape he wants. For example, Vasylyna.

Lena thinks to herself, "It's Vasylyna. Calm down. Don't be scared. It's just Vasylyna standing next to the window with a pot of pasta." And then, just as she has almost convinced herself of this, she suddenly remembers that Vasylyna just went to the bathroom and therefore can't be standing at the window right now.

The real Vasylyna walks back into the room, happy and carefree, and tells Lena, for instance, that they can sleep till eight tomorrow because the movement theory instructor is in the hospital. Lena turns her head toward Vasylyna, her feet rooted to the linoleum in horror, but a second later there's no one next to the window.

Lena looks down at her hands and watches as her fingers fall off one by one, like autumn leaves from a tree, while the real Vasylyna — although who knows whether or not she is real — whispers, "Lena, you need to smoke less. Smoking causes fingers to fall off. You know that."

These nightmares had Lena scared to death, not because they themselves were so scary but because they could be a symptom of some horrible mental disease. And Lena worried about her mental state the most because her mind was the only thing that she had. She was afraid of going mad. Very afraid. And she was afraid of what they say about madness: that it creeps in undetected. It supplants reality little by little, one millimeter at a time, and the afflicted person is incapable of affecting this process. There exists no clear-cut boundary between madness and a sound mind, just as rain has no clear-cut boundary. There is no spot on which you can stand and say, "To the right it's raining, but to the left it's dry. To the right is sanity, but to the left is madness."

That's why Lena trudged off with her nightmares to a doctor she knew. This doctor, Olha Ivanivna, actually specialized in intestines, in children's intestines in fact. But doctors are doctors. They're always willing to prescribe some kind of pills. Olha Ivanivna was friends with Lena's mom and worked in a children's polyclinic. She always looked a little slutty in her miniskirts, her glittery black lace stockings and her boots with three-inch heels, which, since Olha Ivanivna was tall to begin with, always forced her to duck through doorways.

But she liked being that tall.

"From that altitude," Olha Ivanivna would say, "it's less noticeable how the ground beneath your feet stinks."

Lena would visit Olha Ivanivna in her office and head straight for the toddler bed alongside the desk. Olha Ivanivna examined her little patients on it.

"Well, what is it now, Lena?" In the polyclinic, Olha Ivanivna wore a white lab coat, which was two centimeters shorter than her short skirt. Maybe she was still hoping to find herself a good husband. "I don't have time for you,"

Olha Ivanivna would say. "Did you see how many kids there are with diarrhea waiting in the hallway?"

"Olha Ivanivna, I'm going mad. Help me! Come on, you're a doctor!"

"Nightmares are a normal reaction of the psyche to stress. You're not going mad."

"But what if they're a symptom?"

"You have a very controlled psyche. You're afraid of losing this control. That's why you're having nightmares, because it's only during sleep that your brain can finally break free and relax."

"You're not making any sense, Olha Ivanivna. Give me some kind of pills!"

"I can only prescribe ones for diarrhea."

"I don't have diarrhea."

"My point exactly. And diarrhea, I'll have you know, is a considerably more common symptom of schizophrenia than troubled sleep."

"My roommate spends a lot of time in the bathroom. She throws discuses. She's an athlete."

"She has a bad diet."

"But maybe she's a schizophrenic and I caught it from her. Schizophrenia is contagious, isn't it?"

"Lena! I have kids shitting themselves in the hallway!"

Lena shared her reflections about the kind of people that existed in the world with Olha Ivanivna. She liked to come up with classification systems so that the world around her would appear more organized.

"There are good people and evil ones, stupid ones and intelligent ones, the fortunate and the wretched, the lonely and the happy, subjective idealists and objective rationalists, nationalists and communists..."

Olha Ivanivna listed to this for about five minutes then said, "Lena, I'm going to burst your bubble. There are only two groups of people in this world: those who go to the bathroom normally every day and those who will die of colon cancer."

A Biography of a Chance Miracle

In Olha Ivanivna's world, Lena would later say, everything was related to excretion, and in some respects she was no doubt right. But, nonetheless, man lives not only in order to eat and, I beg your pardon, shit. There must be something higher. And my goal was to find this higher something. And to do it before the darkness swallowed me up, together with all my rectal, large and duodenal intestines.

During her senior year, Lena started to suspect that great people would never come crawling out of her unless someone did a crash C-section on her soon. She didn't want fame and success. She simply wanted to be someone, someone specific — not very great, but not small either — and she wanted to do something. As of now, it looked like Lena would spend the rest of her life working as a phys ed teacher in a high school. But she didn't want that. For one, she wasn't too fond of children, and second, she hated running. Combined, these two things could easily kill Lena. You know how it goes — a despicable job, a lonely life, cigarettes and alcohol, and before you know it, there you are at the very bottom. In five years you get a stomach ulcer, in ten you have breast cancer. And that's it, there's no more person. But Lena wasn't ready to pass into other forms of existence yet.

The example of Olha Ivanivna inspired her. This woman didn't wait for heavenly manna to fall on her head. She orchestrated her own manna.

Her job at the polyclinic was only a front so that she could legally call herself a doctor and build a network of potential clients. In reality, Olha Ivanivna was a computer diagnostician.

She rented a teeny little office in downtown San Francisco which housed a large computer. With its help, Olha Ivanivna divested people of ridiculous sums of money.

People had stopped trusting doctors long before because they had discredited themselves with purchased diplomas.

But computers, on the other hand, they trusted whole-heartedly. People didn't entirely understand how that unique machine of zeros and ones worked. And that's why many were convinced that the computer was almighty, that it had its own intellect and that it could talk and think and see right through you, in fact. A computer knew wherein lay your problem. Only it would save you.

Olha Ivanivna would pass the computer mouse over the patient's body. The computer would let out a long piercing be-e-e-e-p, and Olha Ivanivna would cry out, "Well, here you go! Everything is clear now!"

"What's clear?" the alarmed patients would whisper. "Doctor, what do I have? What's it saying?"

"You have worms!"

"Worms?"

"Well, yes. You have worms in your liver."

"In my liver? Is that possible?"

"You're lucky that they're not in your heart."

"You can have worms in your heart too?"

"You can even have them in your brain."

"Good Lord!"

Theoretically, Olha Ivanivna wasn't entirely deceiving her patients because there are actually worms in the body at all times. Every parasitologist will confirm that. Most people simply have no idea of their silent anaerobic existence inside their bodies. Therefore, Olha Ivanivna was actually doing something good. Patients would undergo "worm treatments" and think that now they were healthy. And they actually would become healthy. It was all a matter of mindset. The entirety of Chinese medicine is based on a similar principle. You have to treat the person, not the disease. Convince a legless man that he has legs, and he'll break into a run.

There were always long lines outside Olha Ivanivna's office. People would wait and talk among themselves:

"Did they find worms in you too?"

"In my kidneys. And you?"

"In my lungs. Can you imagine? And I was just thinking that there was this sound when I inhale deeply, as if something was squealing in there. Turns out it's worms! The shit that'll latch on to you!"

Thanks to Olha Ivanivna, a true parasitic hysteria broke out in the city. People were attacking the one and only state laboratory that performed parasitic analyses in droves, and the lab techs who worked there were collapsing from exhaustion. They would holler at the women who were bringing in matchboxes of stool samples by the kilo, "You don't have any worms, for God's sake! What's gotten into you people?"

"That's what you say, but the computer says I do! The computer sees everything. Do the stool analysis! That's what the state pays you for!"

The tests would show that there were no worms, and the women would be outraged. "They're shameless! They can't even perform a stool analysis honestly! They write that there are no worms just to get rid of us!"

The pharmacists, on the contrary, responded to consumer demand with lightning speed, and new super-effective "German" drugs, which killed every living thing inside you with one pill, showed up in every pharmacy display case.

Hundreds of other computer diagnostics offices began to open up in the city since success always breeds copycats. Some streets even had more than one, and San Francisco now had more computer diagnosticians than dentists. But Olha Ivanivna unexpectedly switched to a different medical specialty. She was, without a doubt, an extraordinary woman. She knew how to sense things like when to scoop up your winnings and run from a casino.

Over a single night, the cops banned "computer diagnostics" and even arrested a number of "doctors" for fraud. But not Olha Ivanivna. Like an elusive avenger, she continues to tread the thorny paths of Ukrainian medicine till this day.

I need something like that, said Lena. Harmless, but profitable. Something that everyone is waiting for and that they're ready to pay money for. And people are willing to pay money for happiness and for money itself. So it was, is and shall be.

"What's wrong with being a phys ed teacher?" Vasylyna would ask. She didn't approve of Lena's ambitions of becoming a great person in a little world. "Being a phys ed teacher is a worthy profession. You'll make kids sweat, turn the young generation on to sports, and cultivate a healthy nation."

"You don't get it. I can't do that for a living. This was altogether a mistake — majoring in phys ed. I should've at least majored in ecology. Come on, what kind of athlete would I make? I always wanted to help people."

"You don't want to help them! You want to swindle them!"

"You're right — swindle them in order to help them. That's my goal!"

Lena mulled it over and decided that her first task was to let people know about herself somehow, to attract the public's attention. She, of course, didn't have the money for a large-scale promotional campaign, so she took the route that was free of charge. She placed an ad in the local newspaper.

It sounded a bit improbable perhaps but intriguing nonetheless. You need to intrigue a potential client, Lena would later argue. All great people started out small, but I'm going to go big right off the bat:

A Biography of a Chance Miracle

Miracles to order. Competitively priced.
Payment upon delivery. No requests that harm
other people. Tel: 806-7661-6921 — Lena.

"Do you at least believe in miracles yourself?" Vasylyna would laugh at Lena's ad.

"Of course I do!" she would lie. "Anything that happens but we don't understand how or why it happened is a miracle!"

"My life's been one flop after another, and I don't understand how or why they've happened. So does that mean they were all miracles?"

"You could say that. But you need to look at the problem more broadly, Vasylyna. Everything that's taking place in our country right now, it's all a miracle because no one understands anything that's going on."

"You should be on the radio with that imagination and that mouth."

"I tried, but they didn't hire me. They said my voice was squeaky."

How exactly the business would operate, Lena didn't know yet, but she was optimistic that she would figure it out along the way. The important thing was to attract a client, to intrigue him, because once he was intrigued, getting him to pay would be easy.

"I didn't need much," Lena would write in her journal under the heading "How to conduct business honestly." "I decided to charge ten hryvnias per miracle. Just so you know, ten hryvnias would buy me just enough food to make it through the day. So, one miracle a day and I would have enough to eat. My plan was simple, and anything that's simple always works. What mattered was that the first client bite. Things would go smooth as butter from there."

But no client was biting.

A week later Lena once more placed an ad in the newspaper, and again in two weeks, and again in three. For some reason, no one was interested in Lena's miracles. Ukrainians have completely lost their faith in everything, she would complain.

The two-hundred-kilo voice of Lena's conscience, Vasylyna, wouldn't give it a rest. "I just don't understand why you can't earn a living the same way as everyone else, by getting a job."

"As if performing miracles can't be a job! You can't imagine what hard work it is!"

"Miracles are performed by saints, angels, archangels. That's not exactly your crowd."

It was easy for Vasylyna to talk. She had a talent. She was being retained by the university as a discus coach. There was even a signed contract in her drawer.

Lena would say, "There must be room in the world for my kind too, Vasylynka. I may not be a saint, or an angel, but I'm still capable of performing my modest miracles, have no doubt. It's just that for some reason no one is ordering them yet, and I'm sure as hell not stupid enough to perform them for free!"

Just then the telephone finally rang. At first, Lena didn't even realize that the ringing was coming from her new cell phone, bought for the purpose of taking miracle orders.

The phone rang and rang. Lena kept transferring it from hand to hand like a hot potato.

"Well, why are you dicking around? Pick it up!"

"What if it's the cops?"

"If it is, it's because they have nothing to do! Look at how many maniacs are crawling around the city these days!"

"What if it's a maniac?"

"He won't butcher you over the phone."

Lena put the cell phone to her ear and mumbled a barely audible "Hello."

On the other end of the line, there was silence. Then a snuffle. And then a male voice began to speak. "Good afternoon, I'm calling about the ad."

"Yes, I'm here," Lena said a little more cheerily, although she had expected the first call to be from a woman. You would think that women would be more likely to fall for such ads.

The male voice continued, "So what is it you do exactly?"

"Everything's spelled out in the ad. Miracles."

"Is this some kind of religious sect?"

"This isn't any sect! I'm on my own."

"Ah."

The man was silent. Lena began to chirp, as if selling milk at the bazaar. "I don't charge much. You won't find a better deal anywhere. Ten hryvnias per miracle."

"And what exactly can you do?"

"Everything."

"Can you fly?"

"Fly?" Lena hesitated. "In order to fly, you need a rib cage that's six cubic meters in volume."

"You know, I saw one recently."

"What did you see?"

"A miracle."

"What kind?"

The man blurted out: "I want a hundred hryvnias."

"What?"

"A hundred hryvnias and I'll tell you everything."

"Is this a joke?" Lena jolted at his gall. "I'm the one that's selling miracles, not you!"

"As you wish," the man said and hung up.

After this, Lena spent three days coming back to her senses. She kept saying, "The gall of him. I launched a business, and someone else is already trying to make money off me! And not just a few kopiykas but a whole hundred hryvnias! I get by on that all month long!"

On the third day, she caved and called back the anonymous caller. He instantly picked up.

Lena said to him, "OK, I agree. But I only have eighty."

"So be it. Come see me in the hospital and I'll tell you everything."

"Wait, why are you in the hospital?"

"It's nothing serious. My liver's crap. But I can go out into the park. There's a park here next to the hospital. Let's meet there tomorrow at noon. 12 Builders Street."

Lena knew this street well from the days of her partisan past. And she also knew which building number 12 was. It was the regional drug rehab clinic.

"I'm not going anywhere! Pathetic junkie!"

The man reassured Lena. "I'm no junkie. I just drank a little too much. But I saw what I saw. I'll take the money after we talk. I have no reason to lie."

The regional drug rehab clinic was where men broken by the hard preceding decade healed their spiritual wounds. It was always quiet and calm there. The drug clinic had a large old park surrounded by a brick enclosure. The building itself originally belonged to a family of wealthy local Jews. For alcoholics and enthusiasts of homemade dope, life was good there.

Lena's dad would often say, "Don't judge and you won't be judged." Sometimes he would also say, "All of us will end up there sooner or later." He was alluding not to the cemetery, as one might think, but to this very drug clinic. Many of his acquaintances had passed through those whitewashed walls. The alcohol addiction treatment ended in success only rarely, but to relax a bit there and have a rest, everybody wanted that. Everyone was itching to go there. That's why only those with serious connections got in for inpatient treatment.

It was a sunny summer morning. At the entry gate, Lena was stopped by a well-fed guard. "Where are you going?"

"I have a relative here. He's resting."

"This isn't a resort!"

"Forgive me," said Lena. "I understand. He's undergoing treatment."

"Go on. Just look here, no alcohol! If I see any..."

Patients were shuffling around in the park, all on their own paths. They were staring at the ground with black, despondent faces. On a broken bench sat Lena's longtime acquaintance, the former literature professor Theophilus Bunny.

"Mr. Bunny?" Lena exclaimed in surprise. "What are you doing here?"

The professor looked up at her blankly.

"That's what I thought. Only you could come up with such a moronic ad. Did you bring the money?"

"So you were the one that called!" Lena planted herself next to him on the bench, and the bench nearly tipped over.

"Why are you always breaking things, you victim of the Communist terror! Can't you sit down normally?"

"Who would've thought!" Lena couldn't calm down. "What a coincidence!"

Theophilus Bunny hid his trembling hands in the pockets of his predictable black overcoat. He was even thinner than before and now completely looked like a ghost.

"So how did you end up here, Mr. Bunny?"

"None of your fucking business. Did you bring something to drink?"

"That's not allowed here!"

Bunny spit a glob of black saliva into the green grass and lit a cigarette.

"So, what happened, Mr. Bunny?"

"I won't say anything without the money."

"Here's the money." Lena showed him the tattered bills in a tattered wallet. "I'll give it to you when we're done."

"Like you can be trusted? You have no conscience and don't even know what a conscience is. Little hustler. She performs miracles, my ass!"

They sat in silence for a bit, and finally Lena handed over her eighty hryvnias to the professor. He took them without a hint of shame. Then he nodded toward the other patients. "Not a single intellectual, just one big herd of rednecks. There's no one here to even shoot the shit with for a few minutes."

"So what did you see?" Lena spurred him on.

Bunny said importantly, "I saw a miracle.

"I heard that part already."

"Don't interrupt me! Sit still and listen. Two days ago I returned home in the evening, after work — I now sell books at the bazaar — and holed myself up in my room to get away from my domestic brutes."

Theophilus Bunny always expressed himself very crassly and called his (most likely miserable) wife and his two sons brutes.

That evening, he stealthily made his way to his room, which, by the way, had a dead bolt. Bunny's wife was watching TV in the living room and munching on her favorite dinner supplement: half a baguette with a hunk of boiled sausage and a spoonful of mayo on top. Bunny sat down behind his former desk, now buried in books and papers. He pulled a bottle of vodka, which had been stashed for a rainy day, out of the bottom drawer. He took a swig. But the vodka turned out to be watered-down rubbing alcohol and, without the help of a snack, it kept burning his throat. That's why Bunny, creeping just as stealthily, made his way to the kitchen to get some pickles. Out of the fridge he pulled a three-liter jug of pickles that his wife's parents had sent from the village. Bunny shoved his hand inside and had already found the first pickle, when suddenly his wife came swooping into the kitchen like a witch. The professor gave her a terrified look, his arm still in the pickle jar up to the elbow.

"What are you doing?" the wife asked in a menacing voice.

"I want to eat something, can't you see?"

"You won't get full on pickles."

"I will."

"Leave the pickles!"

"What, am I not good enough for the pickles?"

Not wasting any time, the wife threw herself at Bunny to snatch the jug out of his trembling hands.

"Get off, woman! What are you doing?"

"Alcoholic!" the wife was yelling. "Alcoholic! Leave the pickles!"

Bunny plopped down on a stool exhausted. Drops of pickle brine dribbled from his hand. His wife stood facing him, clutching the rescued jug in her arms.

"Take a look at yourself, you drunk! Every day you hide in your room and drink! You think I don't know? Look at what you've turned into! Take a look at yourself!"

"You take a look at yourself too," Bunny replied calmly.

"At myself? What are you trying to say?"

"I've already said what I had to say."

The wife placed the pickle jar on the table without a word. Her eyes were quickly flooding with tears. Bunny had watched this guileless process a million times, and it had long since stopped evoking his pity.

"What are you trying to say? Huh? That I'm fat?"

"Are you going to tell me that you're not? You spend the whole day sitting on the couch and devouring sausage with mayo."

"Why the whole day?" The wife was crying, but Bunny was calm.

"I do everything possible to take care of you. I clean up after you. I support you. I bore you two children."

"The children are brutes just like you. They're lazy and brainless."

"How can you say that?"

"I'm telling it like it is."

The wife was muttering, "I hate you, I hate you." Bunny snatched up his black overcoat and on his way out of the house said, "You know what I think? That this world is only an illusion. Somewhere out there the real world exists. It might even be in this world, but we don't see it. The real world only appears to us once in a while. When it wants and if it wants."

"And have you managed to see this real world? You drunk!"

"I'll manage to yet."

He ran out into the street. It was well past midnight. He headed for the train station. For one, the train station had a café that was open around the clock where crowds of the thirsty gathered for the night. You could have both a drink and a chat. Second, Bunny had made up his mind to put an end to himself.

"Do you know the story of the cat Salamakha?" he asked Lena.

Lena didn't know it.

"The cat Salamakha sat on a seventh floor balcony for seven years and gazed down. For seven years, he waited and thought. And in the eighth year, he finally mustered up the courage and jumped. This happened in the building across the street from me. He was my neighbor. A real hero. At the time, everyone said that Salamakha had killed himself. Apparently cats can commit suicide too. For seven years he prepared himself for death, and when he sensed that the time had come, he jumped. He fell on the asphalt with a splat. The yard cleaners later scraped him up with a shovel. And nothing happened. The world didn't change without Salamakha. Right now, there's a new cat that sits on that balcony. And thinks. And so I sat on a bench at the train station and thought. To be honest, I'm afraid of death. When I imagine my own death, I feel paralyzed and my eyes get flooded with darkness. It's terrifying. But it's interesting on the other hand too. Because what if it turns out there's some kind of surprise on the other side? Here you're not expecting anything, and all of a sudden utter bliss befalls you just because, by the grace of God. And God says to me, 'Well, Theophilus, this time I forgive you. You grew up to be a worthless man, but God is with you. Here you go!' That could happen too, no? When I drink, I'm less afraid. And then, on Sunday, my fear vanished somewhere altogether. I decided that the time had come. I'd throw myself under a train. I'd had enough."

Then Bunny finished drinking the quarter-liter bottle he had bought at the café, so as not to let a good thing go to waste, and walked out onto the train tracks. According to the schedule, the train was supposed to pass through in ten minutes.

"I felt like that cat Salamakha. I was wondering, should I pray or not? But for that matter, if there is a God, then he'll take me like this, without a prayer. I don't even know how to pray properly, and I didn't want to bring shame upon myself before death.

"I see the train chugging. It was very close, and the light from the headlamp was blinding me. I closed my eyes. Well, I'm thinking, hang on, Theophilus. In a second it'll shatter your bones and squash your skull. Don't be scared. It's just this once, and it'll be quick, like a shot. And, mind you, I've always been scared of shots."

Then all of a sudden something rustled in the air right next to him. Theophilus Bunny opened his eyes and saw a woman in a kerchief.

"She was suspended above me, simply hanging there and not moving, about two meters above the ground. She was gazing at me reproachfully. It all happened in a flash. She was looking at me, and I at her. And in that brief moment I became ashamed of myself. I thought to myself, 'Why is it that you, Theophilus, are wasting time on such nonsense. You can't even live out your worthless life with dignity.' I wanted to jump back, but I realized that there wasn't enough time. It was too late. The train had already almost reached me. Then this granny in a kerchief — she wasn't old, but she looked like a granny — swooped down and snatched me up with ease, as if I were a bag of feathers. She held me over the ground while the train rode through. Then she carried me over to a bench, planted me like a doll, and sat down alongside me. I said, 'Thank you.' She said, 'There's no need to thank me.' I was afraid to even glance at her. I was shaking all over. 'Who are you?' I asked. She didn't answer. But not out of pride, or at least that's what I sensed, but because she herself didn't know. This kerchief of hers was old-fashioned. My mom used to wear one like that, yellow with burgundy flowers. But I didn't ask too many questions. I just didn't have the strength somehow. She also told me that I should stop drinking and that I should go on living. 'Don't worry, everything will be fine,' she said, then ascended and flew away. All I heard was a slight rustling in the air."

Bunny let out a deep, heavy sigh, as if wanting to exhale his soul out of his body.

"I don't believe it," Lena said to him. "People can't fly. Their rib cages are too small. Maybe this woman had wings?"

"She didn't have any wings. She just flew."

"I don't believe it. Mr. Bunny. You're having hallucinations due to severe alcohol poisoning. Such things happen, I know. My grandfather even saw demons on his deathbed."

"It doesn't matter whether or not you believe me," Bunny snapped. "But there's something else."

Out of his breast pocket he pulled the local newspaper,

the same one in which Lena had been placing her ad, and pushed it toward her.

"Here, read it."

"What do I need this newspaper for? I know my ad by heart."

"Take a look at the second page and have a read, if you haven't forgotten the alphabet yet. The crime news section."

Lena turned the page. There was the headline "Virgin Mary Rescues Woman From Grandson." And below, the following article:

> A resident of Solotvyn Village in Koropetsky District, Z. Prokopovych, age 65, claims that she has seen the Virgin Mary. Z. reports that the Mother of God appeared just as her grandson, 25-year-old H., attempted to butcher her with an ax while in a state of extreme inebriation. According to the victim, the Mother of God appeared out of nowhere, wearing a yellow kerchief with red flowers on her head. She intercepted H.'s ax and cried at him so loudly that he lost his hearing. H. is now undergoing treatment in a psychiatric hospital and was consequently not available for comment. The local police department has filed domestic violence charges against him but has refused to comment on the reportedly miraculous salvation of Z. Research reveals that for several years H. has been listed in the Domestic Violence Registry, where he is identified as a particularly violent offender. Statistics provided by family psychologists show that every sixth woman in the province suffers from domestic violence in some form or another. At present, neither law enforcement agencies nor social institutions are in a position to alleviate this situation. As a result of these events, believers have begun to flock to the village of Solotvyn.

"So, did you read it?"

Lena read it. Her upper lip began to twitch with excitement, because she knew this village. It was where her grandparents had lived. And she knew this woman, Zhenia Prokopovych, who was whacked by anyone who had the oomph and who had almost been poisoned with carbon monoxide by her own son. Apparently, the grandson had taken up the cause. No big surprise.

"What a coincidence. Who would've thought that was possible?"

A large ruddy squirrel sprang out of the bushes. Theophilus Bunny tossed it a nut. The squirrel snatched the nut and bolted back into the thicket.

"I feed them often," said Bunny and, without so much as a goodbye, trudged off to his cell to finish restoring his lost inner peace.

Lena took the local train to her grandparents' village. She wanted to have a word herself with the miracle eyewitness.

She later wrote in her journals that she had been burning with curiosity, that she had been thinking the following: Perhaps this flying being, this old woman in a kerchief, was indeed the Mother of God. Even though Lena didn't believe in anything sacred, she nevertheless had to acknowledge the small likelihood of its existence. Moreover, flying should come easily to the Mother of God. Unlike humans, she wouldn't need a rib cage six cubic meters in volume to fly. But there was also another possibility — that this was in fact a person, and that this person could fly. If that were the case, Lena had to see her with her own eyes. That would change a lot of things, she would say.

Lena hadn't been in her grandparents' village since their death. They had died one right after the other, both at the age of eighty-three. The house had been locked up, the chickens slaughtered, and the pigs sold off.

The Roman Catholic church, the one the Polish priests once intended to revitalize, had reverted to an exhibition space for toilet art. It stood abandoned and plundered, as it had earlier, and the arms of the stone St. Anthony before it were extended oh-so-plaintively toward the heavens, as if he still believed that someone was up there.

Lena remembered where Zhenia Prokopovych lived and was certain that Zhenia wouldn't recognize her. She didn't. She was sitting in her shabby, nettle-overgrown yard peeling potatoes.

Lena entered the yard and greeted her. A yappy little dog — the kind that you don't expect will bite but which always does out of fright — lunged at Lena's feet. Zhenia Prokopovych put aside the potatoes.

"Come here, Big Shot!" she cried to her pitiable protector, and the doggie meekly obeyed. Well, naturally, Big Shot, thought Lena. What else could *that* be called?

"Hello," Lena repeated, walking closer. "Forgive me for showing up unannounced. I'm from town. I wanted to ask you a few questions."

Zhenia Prokopovych sized Lena up distrustfully. Zhenia was exactly like her Big Shot, only taller. She had a withered, dystrophic, almost transparent body and crooked arms and legs, as if she had just returned from a concentration camp.

"Are you a reporter?" asked Zhenia.

Lena readily confirmed the assumption. "Yes, I'm a reporter. I heard that you had a certain encounter not long ago, a rather unpleasant one."

Zhenia suddenly burst into tears, and this lasted for exactly one minute. A minute later the tears vanished without a trace, and Zhenia asked in a businesslike manner, "So where's your camera?"

"My camera? Oh yeah, my camera! Actually, I'm a newspaper reporter. I write from memory."

"Well, in that case, sit down. I'll bring you a stool from inside the house."

They settled in facing one another, while Big Shot hid behind his mistress's legs and let out a menacing yap from time to time, as if to let Lena know that he was still keeping watch and was ready to attack at a moment's notice.

"I want to apologize again for showing up like this, without calling first."

"That's fine. I don't have a phone."

"Tell me, if you would, how it all began," Lena asked, trying to slip into the role of journalist. She even found herself enjoying it.

"What should I tell you? There isn't much to tell. I've suffered a great tragedy. My dear grandson is in the hospital. They say he's lost his hearing."

"And how did he lose it?"

"Well…" Zhenia spent a long time choosing her words, apparently fearful of saying something superfluous. "My dear little grandson is somewhat aimless. He drinks a lot. I'm constantly telling him not to drink, that booze has yet to help anyone. He doesn't listen. These young people these days, they don't listen to their elders. They always think that they know best. But otherwise Hryshka's a good boy. A sweetie."

"They say he was running around after you with an ax."

Zhenia flinched. "Who's saying such things? And then we're supposed to believe these reporters! They twist everything around just to tell a lie. He wasn't running, he was just, you know… walking fast. He wouldn't have done anything to me. As if I don't know my own Hryshka? His head was just a little muddled, from the booze. I told you that he drinks a lot. He'd been eyeing that ax for a long time. I saw that it was making his fingers itch, so I stashed it away, to keep him from sin. Because it's not about me. I'm old already. I'll die soon anyway, but he'll destroy his young life."

That's how she always was, that Zhenia, Lena would later say. It was horrible to listen to her because after hearing her out you would get the urge to stick a bomb in the earth's core and press the red button.

"That evening he came home drunk. He has this friend, a bad egg, who's always pouring him another shot, even though Hryshka probably doesn't even want it. Hryshka's soft-hearted. He doesn't know how to say no. He came home drunk, pulled the ax out from under the bed and stared at it. His eyes were gleaming. There was just something completely off about him. He scowled, his eyebrows knitting together and his brow furrowing. I kept my mouth shut, like a fish. I didn't want to provoke him, lest he sin. But he asked me, 'Why are you so quiet?' and whacked me over the back with the ax. It wasn't that deep, you know. Just a scratch really. But the blood went running down my legs. That I felt. So I ran out into the yard to keep from annoying him. He came out after me. I couldn't run far, so I fell to the ground and was lying in the grass. I was thinking to myself, maybe he'll come to his senses or won't see me. But then he bent down over me and laughed in this creepy way that normal people just can't laugh. I'm telling you, his head was muddled. The devil just took him over. That wasn't my Hryshka."

"Had he beaten you before?"

"Why never! Please!"

Lena couldn't help herself and burst out laughing. Zhenia was offended.

"I'm telling you, *never!*"

"OK, I believe you, I believe you. Please forgive me. I just have a tickle in my throat. I must've caught a cold."

"Well, anyway," Zhenia went on, "he bent over me and said something about how he was going to butcher me, like a pig. So I replied, 'Go ahead, butcher me. I've lived too long as it is.' I was completely calm, honestly. Hrysha raised the ax to swing when all of a sudden she came swooping in…"

"The Virgin Mary?"

"Why, what Virgin Mary, girl? The reporters wrote all kinds of nonsense, and you believe it all! As if I wouldn't have recognized the Virgin Mary!"

"Would you have?"

"Why, of course. But this woman was kind of… she was in a kerchief, a yellow one with red flowers, the old-fashioned kind. I don't have that kind anymore. My kerchiefs are all green. The flowers are finer, not as coarse. Where this woman came from I have no idea. I didn't examine her that closely. She flew up to my Hrysha and snatched the ax away from him. Hrysha fell to his knees in shock, and then she started screaming at him like no one's business! God Almighty! She was calling him such nasty names, the likes of which I'd never heard in my entire life! I just don't buy that the Virgin Mary would curse like that. Never! She was calling Hrysha a monster and a bastard, though he's no bastard — he had both a mom and a dad, both useless, but still. Hrysha fainted, and then she helped me stand up and told me to call an ambulance because I was bleeding."

"What was her name?"

"I didn't ask. I just told her that it wasn't nice for a woman to curse like that. She agreed with me and apologized. Then she flew off."

"She just up and flew off?"

"She up and flew off."

"And that didn't surprise you?"

Zhenia thought it over for a moment.

"I was a little surprised, but there are all sorts of people nowadays. Some can swim well, and others, apparently, have learned how to fly. It seems anything's possible."

"That's true too," said Lena.

Zhenia rose from her stool.

"Excuse me. I have to finish peeling the potatoes. My dear Irochka will be back from the store any minute, and I promised to get lunch ready."

"Who's your dear Irochka?" Lena asked, mostly for shits and giggles.

"My niece's daughter, a nice girl. She's staying with me for a while until she finds a job. Hrysha's in the hospital, and the doctors said he'll be there a long time. His head's muddled. He lost his hearing, the poor child."

Zhenia once more burst into tears for exactly one minute. As Lena was leaving the yard, Zhenia added, "Well, you look here. Don't write anything bad about my Hrysha. He's actually a good boy. And this old woman in the kerchief, I just don't know." Zhenia shook her head. "It's unseemly for a woman to curse like that."

When she got back to San Francisco, Lena worked her way through the last few years' worth of back copies of all the local newspapers in the regional studies library, particularly the crime news section. But they just tortured, butchered and murdered in the newspapers. There was no mention of any miraculous rescues. No one had seen the Mother of God either. That is, she was seen, in Pochaiv and Zarvanytsia, for example, but that was back in the thirteenth century, and Lena needed somewhat more recent cases.

In some Transcarpathian village the contours of a woman appeared on the trunk of some tree and thousands pilgrimaged there to pray. A small chapel was even erected next to the tree. But Lena wasn't inspired by that kind of miracle. In another village, in the Chernivtsi region, a certain blind woman suddenly regained her eyesight, ostensibly in response to the sound of a voice from the heavens. This didn't fit either. Yet another curious case occurred in the Lviv region, on the Polish border. Some young guy was trying to rob a migrant worker who was returning back home to Ukraine. The woman was holding out a crucifix in self-defense, as if he was some evil spirit, and the young guy took one look at the crucifix and dropped dead. The doctors pronounced a heart attack as the cause of death, and one of them even wrote a scientific article on heart attacks as a "youthful phenomenon" in contemporary Ukraine.

Lena gave up on the newspaper back copies, bemoaning the lack of professionalism among Ukrainian journalists.

Her next stop was a priest. Any available information about miracles should theoretically converge with the local clergy, figured Lena, and went off to the same priest to whom she had made her first and last confession. She barely recognized him. The priest had plumped up, had upgraded his cassock, and now walked around head to toe in gold. Lena waited till the morning service was over, and then waited her turn in the line of old biddies who were trying to impress the priest by one-upping each other with their list of woes. They talked mostly about money, lamenting the fact that their pensions were insufficient to buy bread. The priest advised them to pray.

"Mr. Priest," Lena said when it was finally her turn, "you probably don't remember me. You once heard my confession."

"I remember you," replied the priest.

"No, you don't," Lena insisted.

"Child, you told me then that you didn't really believe in God."

Lena was surprised but didn't let on.

"OK, fine," she said. "But I'm actually here for a different reason now."

"Have you started believing already?"

"That's beside the point. Listen. Have you ever seen any miracles?"

The priest wasn't at all taken aback by Lena's question. "I see them daily."

"Really? And what is it exactly that you see?"

"I see human souls in search of salvation."

"Ok, no. I'm being serious. I mean real miracles. When something unfathomable happens. Something that just can't be."

"You've lost your way in the darkness, my child."

"I have not lost my way! I came to you because you're a priest, and you're making a diagnosis off the bat. Is that really godlike?"

The priest replied, "Miracles happen perpetually. That's God's business. Sometimes God reveals His greatness to us, His creations. Give the Bible a read. There are a lot of miracles described there. Read the lives of the saints."

"You know, I just don't have the time. Maybe you could give me a few quick examples, if you will. I don't need that many."

"He turned water into wine, brought a dead man back to life, fed thousands of people with three loaves of bread, walked on water as on land…"

"Mr. Priest, that's not what I'm looking for."

"What is it you want from me then?"

"Right now, recently, has anything miraculous happened?" Lena was choosing her words very carefully so as not to arouse suspicion. "Perhaps you heard something, you know, or someone told you something?"

The priest gave Lena an indulgent smile. "I see, my child, that you want to tell me something yourself. Go on, I'm listening."

"Me? No, no. I have nothing to tell. What could I possibly tell? I'm just curious. You tell me, Mr. Priest, have you maybe heard that somewhere some woman ascended into heaven?"

"I did. The Virgin Mary."

"You're completely misunderstanding me! Not the Virgin Mary, just an ordinary woman. A normal, living, flesh-and-blood woman. Well… and she can fly too. You haven't heard anything?"

"They used to burn people at the stake for that kind of stuff," the priest countered sternly.

"Not a witch, for Pete's sake, a good woman! Not on a broom but just like that — through mental power, for example."

"Have you seen a woman like that?"

"I haven't," Lena admitted honestly. "But I would like to."

"Pray, my child, pray a lot."

"I will, I promise, but first tell me what you know!"

The priest lost his patience. "I don't know about such things. And such things don't exist. Go with God, child. You're wandering in darkness. You're looking for proof when you just need to believe. God has no need to convince people like you that He exists."

"And what's wrong with me?" Lena roared across the entire church, and the little old ladies that were praying next to her for a pension increase crossed themselves frantically. "What have I done that's so bad, that I don't even deserve convincing?"

"You're willing to believe in a flying woman," said the priest, "but don't believe in the God who created everything."

He made the sign of the cross over Lena and left her to struggle with her doubts in solitude.

But Lena didn't give up. She had one last stop on her agenda.

The yogi.

Lena had heard about him from the other phys ed students. This man had studied to become a yogi in Kyiv — or was it China. In any case, Lena suspected that he had never actually gone anywhere but had mastered his art through self-teaching guides.

Aged about forty or so, he could do handstands and head-stands. Maybe he could fly too. Who knew? Lena had read somewhere that for a true yogi flying is child's play. In addition to flying, true yogis could reportedly dissolve into thin air, swallow fire, chew glass, talk to animals and plants, and remain motionless in the lotus position for years on end.

The yogi held his classes in the gymnasium of an old school in San Francisco. Lena waited through the whole class in the hallway, and when his followers of Eastern teachings finally began to pack up, she walked in and asked the yogi point blank, "So tell me, can you fly?"

The yogi replied serenely, "I can."

"Great, then you're the man I've been looking for! Tell me, how do you do it?"

"Are you having some issue with walking?"

Lena plopped down beside him on the floor. She had so much to tell him.

"I walk just fine. No issues in the past and none in the foreseeable future. I'm in the phys ed department. I'm studying valeology. But that's just an aside. My point is that I think I know a person, a woman, who can fly. Like, really fly."

"And what is it you want from me?"

"I want to know if it's possible — to fly, I mean. Or if maybe I'm a little off in the head. I worry a lot about my head."

The yogi sprawled out on the floor in the dead man's pose. That's when you just lie down, slow your breathing and imagine yourself dead. It's supposed to make you feel very nice and make all your worldly problems lose their teeny worldly significance.

"Are you listening to me?" Lena was asking the "corpse." "This is very important to me."

"I haven't heard of any other yogis in town. I would know about them."

"But I didn't say that she was a yogi. Well, that is, I don't know if she's a yogi. I haven't seen her. Maybe she's self-taught or something, learned it by accident. What do you think? Is that possible?"

"No. You have to practice a long time."

"How long?"

"A dozen lives or so."

"So what do you have to do? How do you learn it?"

"Do yoga."

"And there's no way to take off without yoga?"

"There's no way."

The yogi stood up. He was two heads taller than she was

and stocky. Not all that handsome, he looked more like a wolf. He was grim and gloomy, with an uninviting gaze, but something about his unapproachability enticed Lena.

"I thought to myself, what if he's my destiny?" Lena would later admit. "I even hopped up, straightened out my denim skirt and ran my fingers through my hair, which was going on week two of not being washed, in hopes of fluffing it into a casually tousled look."

"What's your name?" the yogi asked.
"Lena," she uttered with a broad grin.

"I on the whole smiled very rarely," she would later say. "My smile never became me. My teeth are too big and don't always all fit in my mouth. That's why, every chance I get, I scrunch my face into a pensive look, as if at that precise moment I'm deciding which path to take, the path of the righteous martyr or the path of the proud and un-subdued Prometheus."

In any case, Lena couldn't help it this time and showed the yogi her full set of chaotically aligned teeth.
"My name is Lena. And your name?"
"Paul."
"Nice to meet you."

Yogi Paul pulled on his sweater. His faithful disciples had long since dispersed, and, by all appearances, he too wanted to be on his way.
"Wait! Why are you in such a rush?"
"I'm never in a rush."
"I always am, to be honest. And I'm always showing up late."
"That's a big mistake."
Lena suggested going to The Goldfish. "We'll grab a drink. My treat."
"What's The Goldfish?"

Everyone in town knew The Goldfish, but the yogi didn't. This made Lena wary, even sad. She was suspicious of people who didn't drink alcohol on principle. First off, such people are horribly boring, she would say, and, second, they're a little shady. You can't depend on them.

"They have the cheapest beer in town. Come on! You must know it! It's called The Goldfish."

"I don't know it. I don't drink alcohol."

Lena sighed in disappointment. "Then I'll show it to you."

To her surprise, Yogi Paul didn't resist. At The Goldfish, he ordered an apple juice. Lena ordered a beer and, as the waitress was fetching it, slung one leg over the other. This was pretty much the only seduction trick she knew, but the yogi didn't react to it at all.

"So you really know how to fly?" asked Lena.

"I don't."

"Then why did you say that you did?"

"I thought you meant meditation."

"I always say exactly what I mean. If I were interested in meditation, I would've said so. But flying and meditating are completely different things, no?"

"No."

Lena sighed once more with resignation. Yogi Paul was beginning to irritate her.

"So you think that flying is physically impossible?"

"Why not? It's possible. But what for?"

"What do you mean, what for? In order to fly!"

"Humans are capable of much greater things than that. Flying is just, you know, for kicks."

"But what could be greater than that?"

The yogi shrugged his shoulders in silence. "When someone is eloquently silent," Lena would later write, "that doesn't mean that they're very smart. It simply means that they don't know the answer. And no one can convince me that isn't so."

"There's this woman, Mr. Yogi," said Lena. "I'm pretty sure she can fly. And she helps people who have found themselves in a crisis. She flies in out of nowhere and saves them. Like in the movies. Honest to God."

"And?"

"And nothing. I was hoping that you knew something about it."

"No. I don't know anything."

"And you have no idea where she could've picked this up?"

"None. I have no interest in such things. That's amateur dabbling."

Lena flipped out. "And you're such a professional expert! What have you accomplished? This woman helps people. What do you do?"

"Who said that people need help?"

"Some do!"

Lena began sobbing out of frustration, although she would later say that she was crying because the beer had made her gag. It was easy to understand where she was coming from. Her quest for the miraculous was turning into a big flop.

Yogi Paul waved over the waitress and paid for his juice.

"Well then, see you soon!" Lena said in a tear-choked voice.

"Not likely," the yogi replied and dissolved into the tobacco-filled twilight of samsara.

The following morning the waitress from The Goldfish was telling a girlfriend, "I've never seen a girl get that wasted alone. Her date ditched her. I saw him. He was nothing special. But she completely lost it. She smashed seven beer steins, knocked over two tables and called our bartender impotent, even though that's not true. And all the while she kept wailing, 'Come on. Show yourself to me! Show yourself at least one ti-i-ime!' I can't begin to imagine who she was talking to or who it is she wanted to see."

8　HOW SHE PROTECTED THE SMALL SO THE BIG WOULDN'T GET ATTACKED

Times change, Lena would say, but never in the way we want them to. That's why it's important to change yourself, to spit on time and change, so that time does not butt in of its own volition and make monsters of us.

San Francisco changed. It became wealthier and more beautiful. Several large supermarkets specializing in bulk secondhand goods sold by the kilo opened their doors, and everyone rushed there. The bazaars suddenly emptied. People preferred wearing used clothes from Europe to new ones from China. This was a good sign, Lena noted with delight. The city had become European overnight. At every step hung signs advertising "European Clothing," "Cheap European Clothing," and "Stylish European Clothing." Europe was poking its head into San Francisco unnoticeably, but confidently. People dressed unlike the rest were popping up more and more often in the city's streets. A lot of multicolored and bright scarves, in particular, appeared on people's necks. Lena's closet was also bursting with scarves. You could acquire an entire collection for a single hryvnia, so Lena bought them for these hryvnias wherever and whenever she could. Sometimes she would manage to buy two scarves and steal two more. Lena would even wind them in twos around her neck, saying that she felt safer like that.

It's true, these "European" clothes reeked to high heaven of the chemicals used to disinfect the imported used goods, which meant that all the people reeked of chemicals, and all the apartments, and the whole city in fact. "That's OK," Lena would say, "a little disinfection won't hurt us."

The old downtown was fixed up a bit, and the bazaar, at which the local intellectuals had once peddled their collective conscience, was transformed into a souvenir market. The intellectuals returned to where they belonged, namely the deep underground. Tourists began to arrive in San Francisco, many from its American sister city. During the day, they would scour the souvenir market, and in the evening, while slurping Ukrainian borshch and nibbling Siberian pelmeni in San Francisco's most expensive restaurant, they would say, "There actually is a certain resemblance."

Lena barely showed up at the university anymore, and as a result was expelled with a right of readmission should she suddenly come back to her senses. But Lena wasn't planning on coming back to her senses.

"I'm leaving here," she would declare confidently to her roommate Vasylyna. "I'm going to travel the world. I'll take a look at Europe, and then I'll go to Latin America. I find that part of the world very interesting. I recently had a dream about Paraguay and two hippos."

"And what are you going to do there?"

"Whatever comes up. I don't need much."

"Ukrainian women prostitute themselves abroad," Vasylyna would fire back.

"What's so bad about that?" Lena would reply, solely to piss her off. "Are we not prostitutes here?"

"We're not prostitutes." Vasylyna would disagree vehemently, and, with respect to herself, she was absolutely right.

In order to travel the world, Lena first needed to apply

for an international passport. She couldn't get that done quickly because she didn't have a domestic passport either, and you needed the latter to get the former. She kept insisting that she had lost hers, but the clerks at the passport desk later swore that Lena had never even applied for one.

After each unsuccessful attempt, Lena had to wait half a year and had nothing to do with her time. She would ponder. But she didn't have a chance to ponder long because a cause found her on its own.

Lena came across an announcement stapled to a telephone pole advertising that an unnamed someone was accepting stray dogs for a hryvnia a head. That's how it all began. Lena immediately came to the conclusion that someone must be taking in dogs with the noble goal of rescuing them and placing them in the shelter that had been under discussion for a long time but that had yet to materialize due to lack of funds and volunteers. Lena concluded that those responsible for the shelter had settled on this awkward approach.

There truly were a lot of stray animals in San Francisco, somewhere between ten and thirty thousand depending on the time of year — dogs and cats of the most diverse breeds but mostly just plain old mutts. Some of them were kind and gentle, others wild and aggressive, still others even mad, but all of them for some reason were very big. People were scared of them and complained about them. The good-hearted but often half-witted street cleaners would feed them scraps and shelter them in their apartments on the eve of a scheduled government raid. The scheduled raids were conducted three times a year. They usually took place in the dead of night so that the city's residents, who were sleeping peacefully in their warm beds, wouldn't hear the heart-wrenching howling and the horrific barking. The dogs, now dead, would be driven out to the city dump and thrown into a trench dug especially for them.

"From the standpoint of zoology and population science," Lena would write some time later in a feature article for the local newspaper, "the capture of stray dogs and cats makes no sense and is a useless waste of the city budget. The captured animals are immediately replaced by new ones, strong and healthy ones, that are in their reproductive prime. Murder is not a solution. Cats and dogs are ineradicable. Therefore, whoever murders them is in my opinion doing so for the sheer fun of it."

After the appearance of the strange announcement, there was a widespread outbreak of hunting fever in the city. Homeless bums, of which there were between five hundred and a thousand in San Francisco, instantly figured out that it was more profitable to collect animals than empty beer bottles and dove into chasing their homeless friends through all the city's parks and vacant lots. They packed up the dogs into makeshift cages, and when the cages were full, they brought their loot to the customer. Only living animals were accepted, which gave Lena much hope.

Lena caught two little bitches that had been living around the dorm for a long time and called the number on the announcement. She very much wanted to get involved in a good cause. A polite voice ordered her to bring the dogs to a certain address between 8 p.m. and 10 a.m.

"You're open all night?" Lena asked with surprise, but they hung up right away.

Lena spent a long time hunting down the address. It was an abandoned industrial zone technically beyond the city limits of San Francisco. A humongous line of like-minded colleagues, all eager to earn some extra cash, had formed leading up to the steel doors of the half-collapsed warehouse. The bums stank horribly and were bickering among themselves while the dogs barked their lungs out in their cages and filthy sacks. "It's like some kind of apocalypse," Lena thought to herself and even jotted this down in her journal.

People were being admitted one at a time. The steel doors would open, and a customer would enter with his merchandise. A few minutes later, the next one would go in.

"Why are yours so quiet?" Lena's neighbor was asking her. "They don't take dead ones, you know. Only living ones. And preferably plump."

"Plump? Where do you get a plump stray dog? They're hungry and miserable."

"I fattened mine up for a few days! Rumor has it they'll toss you a little extra if the dog has some padding. You need to haggle."

"This is an animal shelter, right?" Lena asked with her last ray of hope, and the crowd just burst out laughing in response. To her surprise, Lena's neighbor consoled her sympathetically. "Don't panic, you kind soul. Some live and others die. That's how the world works. You'll die, and I'll die too, like a dog, somewhere under a fence probably. So if you think about it, these little guys are even lucky. They'll find their end in elite Chinese restaurants."

"Good Lord!" Lena shrieked and ran from there as fast as she could with her two little bitches and her shattered faith in the human race in tow.

Early the next morning, she was already sitting in the police station. The policeman heard her out attentively, made a few calls, stepped out somewhere a few times, and finally asked for Lena's passport.

"I don't have a passport," Lena told him. "I'm waiting for one right now. I lost my old one. But I'm begging you, Mr. Policeman, go there right away because they'll all run off. There are hundreds of dogs there. They can still be saved."

"Miss Olena..." the policeman began.

"Lena."

"Lena. Are you aware, Lena, that I can detain you for three days until your identity is established?"

"Me? Detain? For what?"

"You show up here raising a ruckus about dogs and Chinese restaurants, but you don't have a passport on you. How do I know you didn't escape from a loony bin? Maybe you butcher people and are just trying to distract me with dogs."

"I don't butcher people!" Lena grew indignant. "Why are you saying that? I just lost my passport. My name is Lena."

"We'll determine what your name is. In the meantime, you'll wait here in the holding cell."

"But the dogs…"

"You worry about yourself. That's my advice to you. And the dogs… they can wait." The policeman gave her a gloating grin.

Lena wasn't at the station all that long, to be honest. They let her go in the evening, without actually fully determining who she was. That's why, in theory, Lena could've both escaped from a loony bin and butchered people. The cops weren't focused on her past. They were concerned with their own reputations because they knew perfectly well about the local dog trade and made some nice pocket change from ignoring it. The bums, whom Lena diligently interrogated the entire following week, told her about this. She recorded the conversations on a borrowed Dictaphone and later mailed the cassette tapes with their detailed descriptions of the racket to the city council. The recordings described a group of local businessmen who had established relationships with all of the large Chinese restaurants in Ukraine (mostly in Kyiv, one in Lviv, three in Kharkiv) and supplied them with fresh dog meat. That's why the dogs were supposed to be alive. To ensure freshness, they were killed right before being cooked.

Lena never received any response from the city council, so she went there in person. She decided that she wasn't risking much of anything because no one on the city council had the authority to arrest her.

"I'm here to see whoever's in charge of animal welfare," Lena announced importantly to the secretary, who was sending visitors wanting to meet with the authorities into the appropriate offices.

The secretary rummaged through the papers on her desk for a long while.

"We don't have anyone like that here, miss, you've come to the wrong place."

"So who protects animals?"

"Why do they need protection?"

"Listen, homeless dogs are getting sold to Chinese restaurants."

"Then you should go to the Business Development Administration," the secretary exclaimed cheerily, as if happy that she had solved the riddle.

"This isn't a business! It's a crime! Don't you understand that dogs are being sold to Chinese restaurants as meat?"

After prolonged arguments and misunderstandings, Lena landed an appointment with the head of the Office of Social Policy. These people were at least in the business of protecting something: retirees, invalids, children and grandchildren of war and labor, Afghan war vets, people without families and those unable to work, orphans, low-income people and even homeless people. Animals weren't on the list, but the important thing was that the word "homeless" was. These people know genuine compassion, thought Lena.

A woman in a suit, presumably the head of the department, greeted Lena with a friendly, somewhat pasted-on smile.

"Good morning," Lena began, still in the doorway, "I recently sent you recordings of conversations with homeless people which expose the terrible plight of trafficked strays."

It was evident that the woman hadn't understood a single word, but she had a quick answer ready: "Unfortunately, the Ukrainian postal system is very unreliable. We haven't received anything."

"Well, then let me tell you about it." And Lena settled herself comfortably in a chair.

She laid out her story in detail, beginning with the announcement and the little bitches from her dorm and ending with her encounter with law enforcement. The civil servant listened without interrupting. Now and then she would jot something down in a notepad.

"We need to act urgently," Lena said in closing. "The cops are covering for the criminals."

"Why criminals right away? And not so loud please," the civil servant (the name plate on her desk identified her as Bohdana Ivanivna) said cautiously.

"You don't think they're criminals?"

"Only the courts can decide whether or not they're criminals."

Bohdana Ivanivna was a person of liberal calm and democratic poise. Incidentally, she religiously went jogging in the city park three times a week before breakfast between 6 and 7 a.m. Jogging was very popular at that time among the civil servants of the city council.

"But you do understand that this is a crime, don't you?" Lena persisted.

"I wouldn't be that categorical about that point either."

"So you consider selling stray dogs as meat to be normal?"

"No, it's not normal." Bohdana Ivanivna abruptly stood up from her chair and made a face as if she was thinking intently, although it's possible that that's actually what she was doing.

"If someone pretends to be thinking," Lena would later write in her journals, "then you never know for sure whether or not they're thinking at that instant."

"You must understand. We live in a cruel world," said Bohdana Ivanivna.

"But it's the duty of each person to fight the cruelty."

"Yes. And we will take what measures we can. Without a doubt. But you must understand."

"What must I understand?"

In order to be more persuasive, Bohdana Ivanivna was trying to look Lena in the eye. But Lena looked away. She wasn't a fan of these kinds of mind-game tactics.

"Just because something looks like cruelty," said the civil servant, "doesn't mean it actually is. You know that the situation with strays in the city has reached catastrophic proportions."

"I do."

"The city is powerless over this situation. We have no funds to remedy it, and we won't in the near future. We receive complaints daily from residents. Dogs attack children and even adults. Over the last year, there have been…" Bohdana Ivanivna pulled a scrap of paper out of her drawer, "…there have been, here, I found it, over a thousand instances of strays attacking people. Eighty of these victims were forced to seek medical treatment. Simply put, they had to get shots. In the stomach. That is very unpleasant. I know firsthand."

"What are you getting at?"

"I'm getting at the fact that in the last two weeks the number of strays in the city has noticeably decreased."

Lena blew up. "But eating dogs — that's not normal!"

"For us, it's not normal. I agree. But in China, on the contrary, it's quite common."

"So let them eat their own dogs! And let them leave Ukrainian ones in peace!"

"Calm down, miss. You must understand that in this… somewhat strange way, the city has won. You and I," the civil servant added for greater clarity, "have won."

"I don't want to win like that! I'd rather lose!"

"But you've lost anyway. Democracy is the opinion of the majority. And you're in the minority. So make your peace with it. Go home and relax."

"Bastard!" Lena cried out, though she had never uttered this word before.

"You know, I would be more careful with my words if I were you. There are courts in Ukraine."

"I'm not scared of your courts!" Lena shrieked as she walked out of the office, which, incidentally, was decorated with cheap landscape paintings such as *Autumn in the Grove*. She really wasn't scared of courts, mostly because she had never set foot in one.

It's unknown whether Bohdana Ivanivna suddenly grew ashamed or if, conversely, she wanted to shame Lena. But when the latter was nearly out the door, the civil servant said, "So you're OK with hunting dogs and tossing their corpses in the city dump, as long as the Housing and Community Services Board is doing it in an official capacity?"

"Hunting?" Lena was at a loss. "Corpses? The city dump?"

"There's no need to pretend to be a saint!"

"I didn't know."

"Well, of course you didn't know, because then you wouldn't sleep like a baby every night. What the eyes don't see, the heart doesn't grieve over!"

The secretary in the corridor gave Lena a sympathetic "Goodbye." As it eventually turned out, she herself was fattening up three stray dogs. The secretary was taking care of them not for ideological reasons but out of that same pity that someone once summed up as: "We're sentimental and yet savage." When her three little strays vanished without a trace one day, the secretary simply shrugged her shoulders and went on living her life.

But Lena couldn't do that.

Late that evening in The Goldfish, where, thankfully, no one recognized her, she sat down at a wooden table with a tall beer and wrote the most famous animal advocate text of her career. It was entitled "A Manifesto to Dogs from a Dog." It even got printed in the creative writing section of the local literary and art magazine *Thursday*.

The "Manifesto" began as follows: "Dogs of the world, unite! We won't let ourselves get eaten!"

That was when Lena made up her mind to act on her own and till the very end. She had a straightforward three-part plan: transparency, subversion, propaganda. These three tactics, she would say, were the most effective in a clandestine war against the system. Lena said, "I couldn't back off because no one had abolished justice. Yes, the world is cruel. They swindle, bully and kill here. I can't change it, and doing so isn't even my intention. My intention is to change myself. But I won't be able to change myself until I get rid of this horrid aftertaste of dog meat in my mouth."

Lena plunged headfirst into the subject of canine homelessness. She discovered that the number of strays in the streets was inversely proportional to human responsibility. The city residents bred puppies, which they later threw out into the street for whatever personal reasons. Either they didn't like how the dog barked, or it ate too much, or someone lied to them about the breed, or they were just too lazy to walk it every morning. "People should get slapped with hefty fines for this kind of behavior," Lena would say. "Only punishment can habituate irresponsible people to order. The city belongs to everyone not to you personally. By tossing a dog out into the street, you harm others. You violate the rights of others not to mention the rights of the dog itself, which presumably have an inalienable right to a master."

But there was no mention at all of Ukrainian dogs in Ukrainian legislation. The country's legal code equated them with "small-sized property," such as, for instance, a chest of drawers or a piece of luggage. They weren't even on par with bicycles because a bicycle was considered a means of transport.

"Human rights," Lena would later maintain, "are pred-

icated on an absolute lack of rights for all other living be-
ings."⟩

And one more thing. The truly dangerous dogs were the
second- and third-generation street dogs. They no longer
remembered that their place in life was to serve a master.
They were their own masters. What's more, they hated
man because man had betrayed them. Their purpose in
life was to survive and to have their revenge at any cost. Violence, Lena would say, is not a solution, to be sure, but we
must remember that it wasn't they who started this war.
Animals are never the first to start a war.

Over the course of a single night, Lena plastered the
entire city with posters admonishing: "Don't Give Dogs
to Chinese Restaurants. Dogs Don't Taste Good."
The posters also included a brief history of the Chi-
nese-Ukrainian business, the address at which the dogs
were being accepted, and photos of some particularly as-
siduous hunters.

The subject was immediately taken up by the mass media, not so much out of compassion for the dogs as for the
tragicomedy of the story itself. Journalists from the capital
arrived in San Francisco. They filmed the lines outside the
abandoned warehouse, recorded the howling of the im-
prisoned animals, and even managed to catch an employee
of the Chinese business from behind. The news spread like
wildfire. San Francisco and its strays made it onto all the
national TV channels. The city's police chief swore up and
down that he had never heard of the Chinese business and
promised to pursue radical measures. The national police
chief vowed to conduct a thorough inspection of all the
country's Chinese restaurants, although the decisive factor
there was likely not the fate of the poor animals but rather
Ukrainians' collective subconscious disdain for Asians and
Asian culture.

Within two weeks, the Chinese business was shut down,
as were two Chinese restaurants in Kyiv.

"That's right," Lena wrote down in her journal. "We should be eating chicken."

Lena was giving interviews all over the place. It was at this time, actually, that she enjoyed the most fame she would ever have in her life. She wouldn't comment on her dealings with the police and the city council because she felt it was no longer that noteworthy. Government authorities were equally dishonest the world over. It was the task of the public, Lena would insist, to teach the authorities to hide their dishonesty. And to be afraid. (For only a frightened government works for its people.)

Lena even got invited to Kyiv to appear on live TV, on the then-popular morning talk show *Get Up, Ukraine*. The host of the show called Lena the Ukrainian Joan of Arc. Lena laughed. She said that she didn't want to be Joan of Arc. She just wanted to be a normal person. In response to the pathetic question "What does it mean to be a normal person?" Lena replied, "It means the same thing as being a normal dog. You do understand what a normal dog is, don't you?"

The talk show host nodded.

"So, you see," said Lena. "Then why don't you understand what a normal person is?"

This host recently published a book of memoirs in which he devoted an entire chapter to the talk show *Get Up, Ukraine*. In it, he mentioned the episode featuring Lena. And he admitted, "Actually, I didn't understand what a normal dog was."

Capitalizing on her sudden fame, Lena set off on a mission to raise awareness. She would spend all day long standing in the main square of San Francisco, in front of city hall, urging people not to remain indifferent and to stand up for the rights of their smaller brethren. She carried a large cardboard sign which listed "The rules of coexistence with animals." It looked like this:

Rule No. 1: Don't ditch your pets.

Rule No. 2: If you're not sure whether or not you're going to ditch them, don't get them in the first place. Buy a cactus instead.

Rule No. 3: If you nonetheless want a pet, take one off the street. It's waiting for you and will love you dearly for your kindness. And what more do you need from a pet than love?

Rule No. 4: If you see someone mistreating an animal, smack them. They won't do anything back because only huge cowards torment animals.

Lena formulated hundreds of similar rules. The most famous one was: Don't assume that saying "Hello" entails more intelligence than saying "Woof."

The residents of San Francisco sympathized with Lena for the most part. They would listen to her and agree that something had to be done. Arguments would nonetheless sometimes erupt. Lena's presence in the main square irritated many. Such people are irritated by lots of stuff, virtually everything actually, but it's important for those kinds of people to have a living and breathing target for their irritation. On the other hand, it was also entirely plausible that the municipal Housing and Community Services Board, which was responsible for the capture of strays and was well compensated for its efforts, had launched a full-on counter-campaign against Lena in an effort to maintain job security.

As an example, skinny old men in newsboy caps, sometimes even in traditional embroidered shirts, would walk up to Lena and say, "What are you messing around here for, child? Do you have nothing better to do? Ukraine's on the brink of ruin. Soon it'll be wiped right off the map. The Communists have made it back into Parliament, and you only have dogs on the brain."

Or, as another example, women past their prime, typically blondes wearing strings of traditional red beads and black boots with spike heels, would walk up to Lena and say, "Have you no shame? There are so many kids in Ukraine living on the street, under bridges, with nothing to eat, sniffing glue, and you're worried about dogs! People deserve a decent life first, and only then animals."

Lena hated it when someone used children to make an argument. She would reply, "There's enough sympathy to go around in Ukraine. Let's make a deal. I'll worry about the dogs, and you worry about the kids."

That kind of response satisfied neither the old men in the newsboy caps nor the women in the strings of beads, and they would continue to hang around Lena and her cardboard signs, coming up with more and more new arguments in support of their moral rectitude. When Lena could no longer stand it, she would yell at them, "What do you want from me? Go your own merry way! Go do something! Protect whatever it is you think needs protecting, and stop waging war on people who are protecting something that's important to them! I couldn't care less about the country! I couldn't care less about kids! Dogs and cats alone I love! I have a right to that."

Lena was bluffing here, of course, because in reality she did care about the country and about kids. But, as she would later say, it's impossible to protect everything all at the same time. You have to start small. And once the small has been saved, it just may turn out that the big won't need protecting because no one is attacking it anymore.

The dogcatchers — there were about a dozen of them on the municipal Housing and Community Services Board's crew — would come see Lena as well. They would try to get to her with pity. They would say, "How are we going to feed our kids if we lose our jobs?"

Since Lena's reaction to the mention of children was always equally negative, the dogcatchers quickly figured out that there would be no convincing her with words.

That was when Lena was beaten up for the first time. One evening, as she was walking back to her dorm, two men dragged her into a dark courtyard, knocked her down and began kicking her in the kidneys. They tore the cardboard sign with "The rules of coexistence with animals" into tiny shreds. The assailants were silent during the educational operation. They just huffed heavily. And at the end, when she was close to passing out, one of the men said, "If you keep it up, we'll put an end to you."

Lena was beaten up a second time after her interview on local radio. It was in late fall, on the eve of the next scheduled HCSB raid. Lena warned about the attack on the radio and called upon the city's residents not to go to bed but to take turns keeping watch in the streets. A surprising number did just that. Lena herself lay in wait for the dogcatchers' van and punctured its tires with a nail.

That time she got beaten not only in the kidneys but everywhere. And not in a deserted courtyard but right in the street, in broad daylight. There were four assailants this time, their faces all hidden by hoods. Not one of the numerous eyewitnesses stepped in to help Lena. People gutlessly averted their gazes and scurried by, all the while likely thinking about those same kids that needed to get fed.

After the bloody brawl, Lena barely succeeded in dragging herself to her dorm and locked herself in the shower room for a long time. She was looking at her black-and-blue body in the mirror and thinking of those who had beaten it up. ("I don't understand," she would later say, "how you can hit another human being just because they're preventing you from killing animals. There's something illogical and wrong about it — beating someone for the opportunity to kill.")

What happened next is not documented anywhere and is based purely on rumor. A reconstruction of the events could have gone as follows.

Late one Friday night, Lena went to the boxing club Chervona Ruta. The club officially belonged to the university, and Lena's classmates from the phys ed department worked out there on Fridays. Unofficially, the club belonged to one of the most notorious criminal bosses in the history of San Francisco, a guy nicknamed Monk.

Lena came in and said to the head coach, "I want to talk to Monk. Where can I find him?"

Only a few people had personally met Monk, but everyone had heard about him and everyone was scared of him. He got his start, as had most of the gangsters in the early '90s, in racketeering and petty theft. Later he gradually brought the bazaars under his "protection," and by the late '90s the entire local alcohol business was under his control.

The word on the street was that Monk was cruel but principled. On the one hand, he supplied San Francisco with adulterated booze, and on the other, he kept drug and human trafficking out of the city. Monk said that booze was an indicator of a society's moral and material conditions. People drank it not because it was available but because nothing else was. They drank it when there was no work, no faith, and no future. If at least one of these three things reappeared, people stopped drinking. That's why Monk didn't consider his professional pursuits a sin, and that's how, as a guardian of the sacred in a dark and soulless inter-time, he got his name. Rumor had it that he had financed the building of a number of churches in the city, which he would visit incognito once in a while to sing in the choir. He liked to sing. Rumor also had it that it wasn't Monk who confessed his sins to the priests but the priests who confessed to him.

Until relatively recently, the local distillery produced a sixty-proof brandy named after Monk. It was chestnut-colored and had a strange pungent smell, possibly of blackthorn. The recipe was kept under lock and key. Production stopped on the day that both Monk and the boxing club Chervona Ruta went flying into the air in an explosion of unidentified origin.

The club's head coach, who was also the head of Monk's security detail, was at first stunned when he heard Lena's request.

"Are you suicidal?" he asked bluntly.

"No. Quite the contrary. I very much want to live." She pulled off her shirt and showed the coach her bruise-covered blue back.

"Whoa, who did *that?*"

"Some nice people. Let me talk to Monk. I need five minutes tops."

"You can talk to me," said the coach. "Monk doesn't accept complaints from the public."

"I'm not going to complain. I have a concern."

"Talk or scram!"

That was when the door to the next room suddenly opened and a hoarse, somewhat creepy voice inside said, "Let her come in."

Monk in fact didn't accept complaints from the public, but once in a while, when he was bored, he would make an exception, attributing it to a good mood and karmic improvement.

Lena entered the secret room. Monk was sitting in a dark corner in the company of four thugs. His face not visible.

When Lena began talking, her voice trembled. "Hello. My name is Lena."

Monk was silent.

"And your name is Monk. I've heard a lot about you. You make people into alcoholics and kill them."

Monk chuckled softly and sprawled out in his chair. His gold teeth flashed in the darkness. These teeth were known throughout the city. People said that he had had his healthy ones pulled to get implants allegedly because he considered his oral nerves superfluous.

Lena went on talking. "And I have nothing against that. Everyone has their own brain and can choose their own path. Maybe they're even born in order to make choices. Then you can see who they really are."

"I like your theory," said Monk.

Lena grew bolder. "I don't believe that there is evil that must be punished, but I do believe that there are unscrupulous people who can be transformed. They're not evil. They just have no conscience. The people who have for whatever reason forgotten that they're mortal are the ones without a conscience. When someone reminds them of this, they can become better people."

"What do you want?"

"I want you to help me."

"My help is expensive. What can you offer me?"

"Nothing," Lena replied honestly. "I don't have anything."

Monk chuckled again. Lena was amusing him. She babbled on. "There are two types of weakness, Mr. Monk: weakness resulting from worthlessness and weakness resulting from innocence. I have no pity for those who are weak because they're worthless. But those who are weak because they're innocent need to be protected. That's my mission… and yours."

"Mine? How do you figure?"

"Because you're just like me. Even though you have a lot, in reality you have nothing. And, just like me, you'll die soon."

Monk grew serious. He could've at this point ordered that Lena be hung from the chandelier by her feet and left dangling there till morning because, as rumor had it, those who got on his nerves often ended up dangling upside down. Lena waited.

"Say what's on your mind," Monk said at last, "but be careful. If I don't like what you have to say, you're going to have problems."

Lena stood straight-backed in the middle of the dark room as if about to recite a poem at a national poetry competition.

"Help me punish the people murdering stray dogs in San Francisco!"

The room fell silent. The thugs were gearing up to remove Lena from Monk's presence. One of them whispered, "Boss, she's... a complete dumb ass."

"No, wait," said the boss. "Let her finish talking."

"You see," Lena mumbled, skipping most of her vowels out of sheer fright, "humans can have three types of relationships. The first is with an equal, for example another human being. The second is with something higher than themselves, for example God. And, well, the third is with something lower than themselves, such as a homeless dog. I believe that all three types of relationships should be equivalent. People should treat a dog the way they would another human, even more than that, the way they would treat God. When a group of people kills hundreds of dogs in the city overnight with official permission and then tosses their carcasses in the city dump, to me this is the equivalent of them killing God and throwing Him out in the trash."

"Boss, she's lost her marbles," the earnest bodyguard again butted in.

Monk plunged into thought. While he pondered, Lena managed to mentally scroll through what she remembered of the Our Father seven times. Then Monk stood up, walked over to the window, looked out it and said, "I don't agree with you. I don't like dogs."

"But this has nothing to do with liking!" Lena cried ardently. "I can dislike a lot of things, but that doesn't mean that I have the right to kill whatever I don't like!"

Monk paused for a moment, as if to intimate, "Shut up and don't ever interrupt me again." Then he proceeded calmly, "I don't like dogs. But that's precisely why I'll help you. Because this is how I see it: Whoever kills a dog is a dog himself. Whoever kills a cockroach is a cockroach himself."

Lena wanted to respond that by such logic you ended

up with: "If you kill a human, then you're human." But she kept her mouth shut. And that was probably the right thing to do.

What was discussed next, or whether anything was discussed at all, is unknown. Lena herself, incidentally, always denied having met Monk. She would maintain that the criminal element had gotten involved in the animal welfare issue independently of her. Reportedly, the dog-catchers had shot up the dogs in one of Monk's bazaars and didn't clean up the carcasses. Monk got really pissed off about that and took care of things in the best way he knew how.

The dogcatchers were abducted from their homes in the middle of the night and kept hung upside down for a few days God knows where. Afterwards they returned home reformed men. They immediately changed professions and happily worked from then on as plumbers. One of them even filed a lawsuit against the city for having been forced to murder animals for many years, demanding compensation for moral damages. He even requested free therapy for his resultant insomnia. Unsurprisingly, the man lost the lawsuit.

The municipal Housing and Community Services Board tried for some time to fill the newly vacated posts, but there were no interested candidates. The head of the HCSB resigned unexpectedly, and his position was filled by a woman who had previously been responsible for landscape maintenance in the city's public spaces. She at once found a location and starter funds for the opening of the long-promised animal shelter. Volunteers materialized.

A movement for the protection of something finds supporters very rapidly, Lena would later say. People naturally like to rally behind a good cause, no matter how hopeless it may be.

A Biography of a Chance Miracle

In all fairness, it should be noted that the shelter was of little help and that the strays didn't begin to magically melt away upon its opening. Cats and dogs went on rummaging in the city dumpsters, people went on hating them as they continued to pull up their shirts for rabies shots, and the Communist Party once more got into Ukraine's Parliament in the next elections.

Lena wasn't disheartened. Undeterred, she went on repeating that in a hopeless battle, the important ones were those who were fighting because they weren't letting time turn them into monsters. You can't win the battle, but you can win your own self.

When Lena was finally issued both her passports, she checked herself out of the university dorm, in which she no longer had the right to live anyway, said goodbye to her parents, who had accepted their daughter's idea to set forth into the world with relative calm, and bought a ticket for the San Francisco-Bratislava bus, which was the cheapest and simplest way to cross the Ukrainian border into the rest of Europe. From there, Lena planned to travel on. The possibilities were endless, and the future that hid behind them at once frightened and enticed her.

The ticket cost 150 hryvnias. The bus departed at 6:15 p.m. from the main terminal. It was scheduled to be in Bratislava the following morning. Lena wrote down the exact same sentence in her journal three times: "I'm not running away; I just want to see the world." Why she felt the need to write this sentence three times is unknown.

But it is reliably known that Lena never did get on the San Francisco-Bratislava bus, which did pull out of the main bus terminal after a ten-minute delay. And she never did cross the international border on it, a fact employees of Ukraine's Border Service later confirmed in writing.

Because here's what happened.

On the day of her departure, Lena held a farewell canine rally in San Francisco's main square. Not many people came. To be honest, no one did. Wet snow was falling. Lena was soaked and numb. Her posters were soggy, like stale bread in milk. Her feet squelched in her boots. Lena was ending her career as an animal rights activist on a lackluster note.

As she was packing up her things to leave, she noticed a roundish little woman, kind of like a doughnut, standing not far away and boring into Lena with an embittered gaze. Her face and her gaze seemed familiar.

"You always have dogs on the brain!" the little woman yelled. "I hope you croak!"

That's when Lena remembered. It was the mom of her classmate Ivanka, the one that Lena had always called Dog.

"Ms. Maria, what's going on? What happened?"

It had been many years since Lena had seen Dog. The last time they had spoken was in the hospital, after Dog's failed marriage and serious illness.

The little woman said nothing more. She turned away and walked off, leaving Lena standing alone in the deserted square, in the wet snow and late autumn gloom. Lena would later write that there was no worse place and no worse time to wish someone that they croak.

Instead of heading to the bus station, Lena set out in search of Dog.

9   THE IMMOBILITY WAR

Ivanka's family lived in a large five-room apartment in the same part of San Francisco in which Lena had once lived with her parents.

As a child, Lena didn't like visiting her friend there. The apartment smelled of poverty and of a heap of people all squatting on top of each other like some primeval tribe. There were twelve of them in all: ten kids, the dough-nut-shaped mom and the one-armed dad. Later they even took in a set of grandparents from the village. And all of them, save Dog, were rude, even downright mean. They would eye Lena warily, the way you would a rival whose mere existence threatens your very own.

There were always mountains of dirty sacks full of po-tatoes lying in the entryway as well as a few of onions and a few of apples. It looked as if the clan subsisted on these three things alone. Dog's mom always looked exhausted and disgruntled. Lena never once saw her laugh. Dog's dad never laughed either. Lena stayed out of his way, thinking that he might suddenly begin beating up everyone — her-self included — for no good reason because when you only have one arm, you may get the urge to employ it to make others show some respect, or at least a little fear.

Lena entered the building and took the elevator up to the sixth floor. Everything looked exactly like before. The door to Dog's apartment was still the same color and still displayed the "Vote for Darmohray" sign scrawled in black magic marker, even though Darmohray had long since lost the city council election and vanished from local high politics ten years before.

She rang the doorbell. No one answered. She waited a long while and rang again. For Dog's family, it had always been customary not to open the door when the doorbell rang because everybody thought that someone else would get it. Lena waited. Finally the door squeaked, and the doughnut-mom, wearing a short nightgown, appeared in the doorway.

"Why are you here?" she asked, no longer so caustic.

"I'm Lena. Ivanka and I used to go to school together," Lena replied for some reason.

"I know who you are. Go, and may I never see you again."

"I'd like to talk to Ivanka. Does she live here?"

Dog's mom reluctantly let Lena into the hallway.

"Careful, the sacks," she said.

Curious faces, none of which Lena recognized, peered out of the neighboring rooms. She took off her shoes.

"Where's Ivanka?"

"Down there, in the back room."

Lena headed down the hall into the depths of the apartment as Dog's mom burst into tears behind her. Lena glanced back, but there was no one there anymore. Four doors simultaneously closed without a sound. The hallway stank of onions and soil.

"Ivanka?" Lena cautiously poked her head into the back room. Dog had once shared this room with her older sister. They were always fighting and arguing. The older sister had become a hairdresser.

"Ivanka?"

Dog was sitting in a chair by the window. She was staring out of it. The window was wide open, and wet snowflakes and street noise were drifting into the room from outside. On the windowsill bloomed the queen of immortal houseplants, a geranium, botanical name *Pelargonium*.

"Hi, Dog," Lena chirped. "Surprised to see me?"

Dog smiled but didn't stand up to greet Lena. She looked even smaller than before, and incredibly thin. Her ash-blond hair was woven into a pathetically thin braid. She was in a turtleneck with a shapeless sweater on top. She had violet-blue bags under her eyes.

"Lena, I'm very glad to see you," said Dog.

"Me too. I'm heading abroad. I want to see the world. I just stopped by to see you before taking off. How are you? Is everything OK with you?"

"I'm fine. I heard about your success in the fight for animal rights. I saw you on TV."

"Yeah," Lena dismissed it with a modest wave. "I had nothing better to do. We managed to get a shelter set up. Shelters are being set up in Lviv and Kyiv too. The important thing is to take the first step."

Lena sat down on the edge of Dog's bed. The stench of soil and onions clung to her nose.

"If you decide to get a dog," she said, then faltered a bit, "you know, or some other kind of pet, stop by the shelter. There's a ton of them there. And cats too. All healthy and sterilized. The vet there's good."

"Thanks. If I want a pet, I'll go to the shelter."

"My bus is actually leaving in half an hour. I don't have much time."

"No worries. Go on. I'm glad that you stopped by."

Lena remained seated.

"You're sure that everything's OK? Maybe you'd like to walk me to the bus station. We could chat a little more along the way?"

"I can't. You go on."

"Do you have something to take care of?"

"I just can't go."

Dog hung her head apologetically. She stared at her legs. That was when Lena noticed that her legs were wrapped in a blanket.

"Dog, what's wrong with your legs? Can't you walk?"

Dog didn't reply.

"What happened, Dog? How did it happen? How long ago?"

"It's been two years already."

"You've been sitting in this room for two years?"

"Yeah, I've been sitting here."

The room melted away into the wet snow. Lena's throat tightened. She would later recommend not to fight the tears when your throat tightened. Otherwise you may choke.

"Don't worry about it," said Dog. "I'm used to it now. It's fine. There's no need to pity me. I'm just unlucky."

"There's no such thing as unlucky people!"

"Yes, there is," Dog countered calmly, her thin fingers fiddling with the hem of the blanket on her immobile lap.

The bus to Bratislava was leaving in fifteen minutes.

"It's my fault," said Lena.

"Nothing's your fault. You yourself said that no one is to blame for anything."

"I was wrong."

The bus to Bratislava was pulling out of San Francisco. Dog was looking at Lena devotedly, her eyes full of hope and gratitude.

"What about seeing the world?"

"I'll find the time. I have my whole life ahead of me."

When people say that they'll find the time, they never manage to find the time. So claimed Lena, who was always rushing everywhere. When people say that their whole life is ahead of them, typically it's behind them already. And so it goes, ad infinitum. When they say that they want to see the world, they forget that they're looking at it right then and there. When they say that they're not running, they are. And when they say they are running toward a specific goal, they are running away from something. In her journals, Lena wrote, "Words are duplicity and self-deception. I don't have time for that kind of crap." She never again returned to her journals. She once again had a clear-cut plan in her head.

"Dog, I'm going to make a person out of you."

First Lena got herself a job as a waitress at The Goldfish and rented a room with a kitchenette in an old house not far from the city park. She was in the twenty-eighth year of her life.

The house was dilapidated, with tall old ash trees growing in the yard. At night, when the wind blew, the trees would creak eerily. The rest of the house was occupied by a single eighty-year-old woman, a former employee of the local ethnography museum. Her previous profession had had a profound influence on her aging mind. The woman had turned her house into a repository for all manner of junk and trash. She would stockpile goods from all the neighboring dumpsters, saying that she'd be thanked for her work in the future when the culture, or rather the lack of culture, of the present day was researched. "I'm laying the groundwork for future archeology," the woman would say. Every now and then she would experience fits of aggression. She would smash bottles, dishes and windows, swearing like a cabbie and stripping naked. Just like that, stark naked, she would run out into the street, amid the cars and stunned pedestrians, looking like a helpless demon that had lost its control over a world from which evil had been permanently erased. When Lena would try to steer the demon back into the house, or at least get some clothes on it, the woman would yell at the top of her lungs, "Leave me alone! Back off! I'm going home! I'm going back *home!*"

On her first day, the museum lady conducted a little interrogation of Lena. "What do your parents do?" she asked.

"My dad's an engineer. My mom's a chocolate maker."

"And what do you do?"

"I'm a valeologist."

The museum lady acted like she understood what that meant.

Lena added, "I make people healthy."

"So you're a doctor?"

"You could say that."

"I don't like doctors. Keep your distance from me."

"Got it."

Then Lena took Dog in. Dog didn't protest and packed up her own things into a little backpack. But the move wasn't that easy.

"Dog, don't you have a stroller? A wheelchair, or whatever it's called? How are we going to get to my place?"

"I don't."

"Fine," Lena said and turned her back to Dog. "Then take a deep breath and climb up. You'll go piggyback. Grab my neck. Just please don't strangle me."

The first attempt to lift Dog failed. As did the second.

"You look skinny, but you're damn heavy. Suck in your stomach!"

Dog's mom was waiting for them in the hallway with her arms crossed on her chest. She was furious. "Where are you taking her?" she yelled. "Ivanka's a cripple. She's supposed to sit at home!"

"Ivanka's going to stay with me for a while. It's no big deal. What difference does it make where she's sitting?"

"I never did like you, Lena," Dog's mom said and moved aside.

Lena carried Dog out of the building like some underdeveloped, overgrown child. The wind kept blowing Dog's scarf in Lena's face, and she kept yelling, "Pull the scarf away, Dog. I can't see anything!"

Dog would pull it away obediently.

"We just need to make it to the trolley stop, a hundred meters or so. It'll be easier from there."

It took them an eternity to conquer those one hundred meters. Dog kept trying to make Lena's job easier by hoisting herself up higher on her shoulders.

"Stop clawing at me, Dog!" Lena was yelling. "You're making it even harder for me! Don't move. Hold on to my neck, but don't strangle me!"

All of the seats on the trolleybus were taken. Refined pensioners were on a free outing to the city park. Other pensioners were headed to the local cemetery. It had recently become a popular meeting place for singles. Widows and widowers would make each other's acquaintance at the graves of their departed husbands and wives.

"Would someone mind giving us a seat?" asked Lena. "This girl can't walk, and I can't carry her anymore!"

In unison, the pensioners pensively turned their heads to the window, recalling at that exact moment the entirety of their war and postwar past devoted to hard labor and heroic self-sacrifice. Lena approached the first old man and said, "If you don't get up right now, I'll plant her on your head, and I highly doubt that your head can handle that kind of load."

The old man and his neighbor simultaneously sprang out of their seats and howled from a safe distance, "Young people these days! They get drunk as swine and then oust an old man from his seat! Let the old man stand. As if he hasn't stood enough in his life! Who raised you to become such brats?"

The other passengers chimed in enthusiastically, and so it went on for the rest of the trip.

One retired lady just couldn't calm down. She felt obliged to initiate a pedagogical discussion. She even went to the trouble of getting up and walking up closer. (She was probably hard of hearing and was afraid of not hearing their answer.) Standing over them, she asked in a sugary voice, "Do tell us, girls, who raised you to become such brats?"

Lena replied, "Why, you did, as a matter of fact."

The retired lady burst into tears while Dog whispered, "You won't leave me here alone now, will you, Lena?" Her face, pale as chalk, beamed with joy, as if she had just returned home after many years of suffering and lonely wandering.

In an interview with a local journalist, Dog later said that she hadn't known Lena's plan and hadn't wanted to know it. "Lena was the only person to ever love me," said Dog. "I trusted her and don't regret it to this day. She was strong and always knew what to do at a time when I was spineless and a coward. I'll be honest. I didn't want that much out of life. I wanted to have a family — just as big as the one I grew up in, only better. But Lena wanted something greater. A small joy wasn't enough for her."

"How did you become crippled?" asked the journalist.
"From the cold," replied Dog.

This journalist — a failed writer unable to make a living off anything other than vapid tabloids — wrote sappy feature stories for the city paper from time to time. Its readers liked that kind of stuff. He was a cynic and a drunk. He would typically mock his own heroes in his stories, but both his heroes and his readers were oblivious to this. His way of writing, which could be described as the "I-can't-help-it-that-I-live-in-an-era-of-mediocrity-and-idiots" style, is still popular among many readers today.

"You got married at fifteen without ever getting a high school diploma, isn't that true?" The journalist asked Dog.
"It's true," replied Dog.
"Your husband was a religious fanatic and abused you, isn't that true?"
"It's true."
"He forbade you to eat, wouldn't talk to you, and would make you hold an old door above your head all night long."
"Yes."
"You began to hemorrhage due to mental stress and spent three months in a hospital, isn't that true?"

"It's true."

"And then you went back to him?"

At that point Dog snapped. "You don't understand. He promised me mountains of gold!"

"And what exactly did these mountains look like?"

"He brought me flowers," Dog was saying through tears. "He bought a cake. He said that he loved me and that we'd start a new life together. And I had nowhere else to go. I probably loved him too. My husband left the church, really, he did. He let me watch TV again. At first things were good. I found a job in a store selling household chemicals. I didn't want that much, just to have a family, have children and live out my life, as it's meant to be. We had a small garden that I planted with tulips. If you had only seen how they bloomed in the spring! It was so beautiful! People came from the city just to have their picture taken in front of them! I brought the tulips to the bazaar for the May holidays and sold every last one. I made three hundred hryvnias. I wanted to go on working with flowers. It would've been a really good business. I figured it all out. You invest, for example, one hundred hryvnias and make three hundred in return. You more than double your investment. Just imagine what a good deal that is. The only thing that matters is that the flowers grow, and mine were growing. I have a green thumb. But the flowers got on my husband's nerves for some reason. He didn't want me to work with flowers. He would get worked up. He would yell. Every day he yelled at me. Well, and then…"

"And then he started beating you?"

"He had never beaten me before, but that was when he started. At first he just beat me a little, as if for kicks. But over time he began beating me more and more, harder and harder. The flowers really got on his nerves. He started beating the crap out of me. He beat my kidneys to a pulp. I'm missing one now. He knocked out two teeth too, two of my front ones. I had some false teeth made. You can't even tell, can you?"

"You can't," said the journalist and inserted a photo of Dog grinning broadly alongside this quote in the article.

"Why didn't you leave him?"

"I had nowhere to go. There was this girl that visited me once. She was making a documentary about domestic violence in Ukraine for a foreign audience. She told me that domestic violence was a serious problem in Ukraine and that I should leave him because sooner or later he'd kill me. That's what all the psychology books said. She gave me an address. It was a kind of shelter for women like me. She claimed I could hide there for a while, in that shelter. I promised to go there. That I'd leave him. When my husband found out about the reporter, he clobbered me so hard that I spent three days passed out on the floor in the foyer. And he did nothing. He didn't even move me to my bed to die in peace. I don't understand how a person can be like that. How can you torture someone like that? As I was lying there on the floor, I kept imagining that I knew kung fu. I was fighting so well, just as well as men, if not better. Men, if you actually look, don't know how to fight for real. They just wave their fists around, hoping that the woman won't fight back. But I would have given him such a good wallop back, no holds barred, right in the balls. Right in the balls!"

"Our newspaper is read by men too," said the journalist.

"I'm sorry. I'm not talking about all men. There are nice ones out there too."

"Where?"

"Don't ask me. I haven't met any. On the third day, I came to and got up off the floor. He was sleeping. I looked in the mirror and didn't recognize myself. My face was bloated, my eyes swollen with black bruises. I looked horrible! You can't even imagine! I found the address that the reporter had given me and set off on foot. It was night. The first snow was on the ground. I don't remember if it was October or November. It snowed early that year. I walked all the way to the shelter, which was about six kilometers. It's out toward Kalush, out in the woods so no one can find it.

"I got there, and it turned out to be an actual shelter.

It smelled like schnitzels. And I was so hungry that my mouth was watering from the smell of those schnitzels. The director let me in and heard me out. I told her, blah-blah-blah, that I had nowhere to go, that I couldn't go to my parents' house because there was a whole shelter full of people there even without me, and yeah, it was embarrassing too... but my husband would kill me at home. We weren't far from that point already. If I went back he'd kill me. I told her that I had a job, I worked in a store and that I'd pay her when I got my paycheck. I wanted to start a new life, a completely new one. Maybe I'd move to another city, to Lviv or even Kyiv, so that he couldn't find me and so that I could put that endless horror behind me.

"The woman politely listened to my story. She kept quiet the entire time. And then she said, 'We don't admit anyone without a referral from a gynecologist.' That was it. Period. But where was I supposed to get a referral? It was the middle of the night. I told her that I could bring it in the morning, but she wouldn't budge: 'Rules are rules. I won't admit you without a referral.'

"So I started saying anything I could think of, pleading with her. I said, 'So where should I go now? What should I do with myself?' And she replied, I'll never forget these words, 'Lady, how in the world should I know? What's with the pity party? Come back with a referral tomorrow, and we'll do everything by the book.' My world turned upside down at that point. I thought to myself, here I am asking for help for once in my life. I won't make it through the night but they can't legally admit me without a referral from a gynecologist. These are dogs, not people. And I'm a dog too. Lena was right about that.

"I asked her if I could wait out the night on the bench there, but the woman said, 'This is no bum hangout! This is a government institution!' I walked out onto the dirt road. It was snowing, a full-on blizzard. There were woods all around me. My legs were buckling. I wandered aimlessly for a while in the woods and finally sat down under a tree. Someone once told me that freezing to death was the most pleasant way to die. It's true, I can confirm that. At first I was cold, but then I began to feel good. Warm, even hot. And this sense of joy came over me. I remember that I was laughing to myself. You could hear my cackling throughout the entire forest. At the time it felt like I could do anything and understand anything and that my problems were small and unimportant. It was as if a veil had been removed from my eyes. And then the woman appeared."

"The one from the shelter?"

"No, a different one. I couldn't see her face well because it was dark. She said to me, 'Give me your hand.' I gave her my hand, and together we flew upward. Like birds. We went soaring across the sky. She held me tight so that I wouldn't fall. Later the doctors told me that stuff like that happens when you're freezing to death. The blood vessels in your brain contract and you slip into euphoria."

"So were you flying or hallucinating?"

"Hallucinating most likely. As if people can fly?"

"Presumably not."

"I don't remember what happened next. I woke up in a hospital. I couldn't move my legs. The doctors said that it was from hypothermia. Something in me that's responsible for walking froze. They could've operated, but it was expensive, so I declined. I was thinking that sooner or later I'd warm up and my legs would start working again, but they didn't. I can feel my pelvis. I can sit on my own, but everything below that is numb. And that's how I live, like half a person."

"And what about your husband?"

"He was very remorseful. He went back to his church. He said that he just couldn't do it without God."

After the interview, the journalist cited the same statistic regarding violence in Ukrainian homes that everyone knows — everyone but the abusers and their victims, that is. The only new detail that he offered was that a thousand Ukrainian women died annually at the hands of their husbands. The journalist also offered data about the number of children that dropped out of school prematurely for various reasons, attributing this phenomenon, of course, to low levels of education among the populace. The final point of his article pertained to the country's disability problem. There were two and a half million disabled people in Ukraine. With one stone, he killed three birds.

"I used to often imagine that we were living together," Dog would say to Lena, "like real sisters."

"Yeah," Lena would reply, "but not having any legs is a real pain."

Dog set herself up in an old easy chair that the previous tenants had left behind. Sometimes she would read books, but mostly she just stared out the open window. Her view consisted of the quiet and deserted Mayakovsky Alley, an old Austrian building that now housed Municipal Dental Clinic No. 5, and the doom-filled people who frequented it for state-subsidized fillings.

"When I watch them," Dog would say, "my own teeth start bothering me. All of them, one after another, even the false ones."

On the surface, her life with Lena was no different from her previous existence. Dog ate little, slept little, and asked for Lena's help three times a day to go to the bathroom. It wasn't a problem in the morning and in the evening, but lunchtime was another story because Lena had to slip out of work.

"We have one long-term goal," Lena would say, "and that's to heal you so that you can walk again. But in the meantime, we need to find you some kind of cart on wheels. I can't drag you around on my back anymore. Once you have a wheelchair, you'll be more independent. You'll be able to walk around… er… roll around on your own. And you'll be able to… go to the bathroom on your own. You just need to buff up your arms a little."

uring out the correct procedure, Lena went to
ment of Social Welfare, a pilgrimage site for
people with limited possibilities. For three hours she waited her turn in line. Dozens of other people were waiting
alongside her in the hallway: blind ones, deaf ones, people
without arms or without legs, people with cerebral palsy or
Down syndrome, the mentally deranged, men and wom-
en, children and adults. Lena had never seen that many
handicapped people all in one spot. Usually they would
sit at home, as marginalized monsters, and only venture
out into God's world in extreme emergencies so as not to
disturb anyone with their presence or tarnish the unconscious full-fledged happiness of full-fledged people.

The cripples were eyeing Lena with suspicion, hostility
even. Maybe they thought that Lena had bought her disability status in order to gain access to one of the numerous benefits.

"Forgive me for being healthy," Lena said to them at last.
The cripples sulked on in silence. They probably didn't forgive her. Lena couldn't blame them.

When Lena finally entered the office, there were only
a few minutes left before the regulation-prescribed lunch
break. The woman behind the desk was shifting restless-
ly in her chair in anticipation of the pork chop she had
brought from home.

"What do you need?" she asked Lena.

"Hello. My name is Lena. I live with a friend of mine
who can't walk. She needs a wheelchair."

"Your paperwork."

Lena readily held out her passport. Without a passport,
she would later say, you're a nobody in this labyrinth of
legalities.

"Not *your* paperwork, the cripple's," said the woman behind the desk.

Lena pulled Dog's passport out of her other pocket and
gave herself a mental pat on the back for thinking to bring
it along. But this passport didn't satisfy the woman behind
the desk either.

"You can't be *that* stupid! Her disability papers! The opinions of the LKK and the MSEC! The rehab program! The pension confirmation!"

"Stop!" Lena cried in bewilderment. "What are the LKK and the MSEC?"

The official looked at Lena as if she had just arrived from another planet. It wasn't clear whether she wanted to laugh at Lena or reward her with an expletive.

"Has your friend been medically examined?"

"Yes, she can't walk."

"Where's the medical opinion confirming that she can't walk? Where's the commission's report confirming that she's disabled? And if she is disabled, then which disability group has she been assigned to?"

"She's disabled," Lena was murmuring. "Trust me. All she's done for two years is sit. I'd bring her here, but she's too heavy for me to lug around. She's small alright but heavy as hell."

"I need the paperwork from the doctors and the MSEC."

"What's the MSEC?" Lena asked plaintively.

"It's the commission that assigns individuals to a particular disability group."

"So once I have the paperwork from the MSEC, my friend can get a wheelchair?"

"Legally, yes."

"So is that a yes or a no?"

"We can only operate within the framework of the law. Goodbye, miss. I'm on my lunch break."

Lena still managed to ask, "And how am I supposed to haul her around to all these commissions? Maybe there's some kind of temporary wheelchair we could borrow? I'll bring it back in a week or two."

But the woman behind the desk was already busy with her pork chop.

The commission with the mysterious name, which Lena would later learn stood for the Medical-Social Expert Commission, met only when all of the requisite documents had been submitted by mail. It took Lena a number of weeks to pull all of them together. Because Dog wasn't mobile, the commission offered to convene at her place of residence.

"We can come," they told Lena, "but in six months at the earliest. We have a waiting list. It'll just be faster if she comes to us."

So Lena put Dog on her back, and they tottered off to confirm Dog's disability. The office was inconveniently located on the fifth floor. There was no elevator or any other way of getting there other than up the stairs. During their conquest of the summit, Dog incessantly apologized, while Lena kept saying, "It's OK. Don't worry about it, Dog. You need this piece of paper. You'll get a wheelchair, a small disability check. You'll be able to use public transportation for free. We'll get through it. Nothing is so bad that it can't be endured."

Here, of course, Lena was mistaken.

The first three times, they didn't get a chance to meet with the commission. They hadn't made it all the way up before the workday ended. They had to go back down those very same stairs and climb back up them a week later.

"But they'll definitely see us next time?" Lena would ask the secretary.

"Lady, how in the world do I know?" she would reply. "Sooner or later they'll see you. Can't you see there's a line? All of them want to be cripples."

A week later the same scenario would repeat itself. The secretary would announce the end of business hours and promise that everyone would have more luck next time.

"Could you at least tell me," Lena would ask, "if there's some other way to get an appointment with the commission? Maybe we should pay something? I'll pay, just tell me how much!"

The secretary would snort indignantly and walk away, probably because Lena was offering her money in a hallway full of witnesses.

When they were finally called in, Lena couldn't even

believe it. The first thing she said as she dragged her friend into the room where the commission met was, "You people are going to make me into a cripple too one of these days."

There were four of them sitting behind the long table, two women and two men. They whispered lethargically among themselves and, with just as much lethargy, gazed at the deformities of the world with weary eyes.

"Name," said one of them.

Dog introduced herself. To play it safe, Lena said, "And my name is Lena."

The people behind the table opened the folder with Dog's documents and rifled through them apathetically.

"Yes, we have your paperwork."

"We spent three weeks collecting it," Lena stressed, be it as a point of pride or as a complaint. But the commission once again declined to grace her with its attention.

One of the men, presumably the chairman, began reading aloud in a patronizing tone, "One kidney missing, severe hypothermia resulting in paralysis of the lower limbs…"

"Is that even possible?" asked the woman sitting to his right.

"I don't know. It could be something neurological. Ma'am," he said, turning to Dog, "your doctor recommended an operation, but you declined it. Why?"

"I didn't have the money," replied Dog.

"As far as I know, medical care is free in Ukraine," the chairman said, without batting an eye.

Dog got a little flustered. "I don't know… The doctor wanted five grand."

"Are you accusing your doctor of being corrupt?"

"Good God, no! I didn't know it was for a bribe."

"The report from the doctor doesn't mention any money. It just says that you declined having an operation. Therefore you knowingly subjected your body to the risk of disability. You alone are to blame here."

"I come from a large family," Dog was mumbling. "My

parents weren't in a position to help me. My dad is a cripple himself, and I have no money."

The chairman of the commission changed the subject.

"Have you worked anywhere?"

"I used to sell household chemicals in the village shop."

"Where's your proof of employment."

"They wouldn't give me any. They said I was working there off the books."

"In other words, you haven't worked anywhere."

"But I have!"

"No proof of employment means you haven't."

The man whispered something to his neighbor. They both tsk-tsked with dissatisfaction.

"Let's go back to your injury. Why is it you can't walk?"

"I don't know why," Dog replied barely audibly. "My legs just won't move."

"That's not a diagnosis. Your medical record indicates that you developed severe hypothermia and lost feeling in your legs as a result."

"That's true. I can't feel my legs."

"How do we know you're not lying to us?"

"Because she hasn't lied a single time in her life!" Lena cried.

"Silence please." The chairman cut her off. "Don't speak unless you're spoken to."

Turning back to Dog, he said, "The doctor noted here that he had never encountered anything like this in all his years of practice. We haven't either. In the case of severe hypothermia, extremities affected by frostbite are as a rule immediately amputated to avoid gangrene. These are called amputation stumps of the lower extremities. In your case, the bone and muscle tissue in your legs wasn't damaged. Therefore, in theory, you should be able to walk."

"But she can't!" Lena cried again. "Get up, Dog, show them that you can't even stand up!"

"We're going to have to ask you to leave in a minute!"

"And that would be fine because I can leave, but she can't!"

"Calm down, ma'am!"

The commission members leaned in and talked something over in a quick whisper. Then the chairman rose from his seat and solemnly announced, "Based on the submitted documents and our personal consideration, we, the commission, comprising the chairman, two deputy chairmen and the commission's official secretary, hereby assign you to the third disability group for a period of no more than one year on account of the likely reversibility of your handicap. At your request, the commission may reevaluate your application for disability status in a year's time. For the duration of the next year, you have the right to claim benefits prescribed to individuals of the third disability group by the laws of Ukraine. Specifically, you are granted free access to public transportation, with the exception of subways and taxis, and once every two years you are entitled to put yourself on a voucher waiting list for recuperative treatment at a medical resort. In the event that you obtain employment, which we strongly encourage you to do, you will be granted twenty-six vacation days."

"What about disability pay and a wheelchair?" asked Lena.

"Disability pay is only granted to the third disability group at full retirement age, and only in the amount of fifty percent of a regular pension. Wheelchairs are only issued to individuals in the first disability group with category A or B handicaps."

"So there isn't going to be any wheelchair?"

"Members of the third disability group aren't provided with wheelchairs. They're not considered essential for this group."

"How is it not essential? Take a look at her! She's been sitting on her butt for two years already!"

"The commission has completed its review of this case. Please leave the room."

"Wait a minute!" Lena was shouting, as Dog softly cried. "So you've come to the conclusion that she isn't even disabled, that she can walk and work? Right?"

The commission chairman, a rather burly man with graying temples, came around from behind the table in order to escort Lena out of the room.

"Please don't start a circus, I beg you! You can resubmit her documents in a year. Now leave the room!"

"I'll go," said Lena. "But she should leave on her own since you've decided she can walk!"

Lena stormed out of the room, leaving Dog sitting on a chair and crying. The commission members went running after her.

"Take her with you! What are we supposed to do with her?"

"Let her go on her own! She can, after all, can't she?" Lena was shouting in response from the stairwell already. "That's what *you* said, not me!"

Later Lena was ashamed of what she had done. She insisted that she had only left Dog to fend for herself in order to teach the barbarians a lesson. She wanted to prove to them that they had been wrong in their decision and should reconsider it. "I reacted impulsively," Lena would say. "I didn't think through how the whole thing would end."

And it ended with the official commission secretary calling a cab and two security guards carrying Dog downstairs in their arms, sticking her in the cab, and ordering the cabbie to drive her to wherever he liked. Naturally, they didn't give him any cab fare. Lena had to pay him since he threatened to help himself to the TV and the hair dryer in their apartment.

For the following few weeks, Dog kept asking for Lena's forgiveness, probably in order to be able to forgive herself. That's easier sometimes, to ask forgiveness in order to forgive yourself.

"We'll find some other way," Lena would reassure both Dog and herself. "We have to fight for justice. Don't worry, Dog. Our little war has yet to begin."

Lena hunted down the doctor that had diagnosed Dog and informed him that she had an important matter to discuss. The doctor was surprisingly polite and even offered her a cup of coffee.

This kind of politeness from employees of public institutions, Lena would later say, was worse than the hissing of a hundred vipers. Where in the world did they pick up such fake smiles and such feigned courteousness? Where in Ukraine did these soulless hypocrites get mass-produced?

"We've met already, haven't we?" the doctor asked Lena with a smile.

"No. We're meeting for the first time. You see…"

"But I'm pretty sure that we've met before."

"You're wrong. You had a patient two years ago, a friend of mine, who lost all feeling in her legs from the cold."

The doctor leaned on the arm of his chair and took a moment to think.

"Hmm… yes… I remember the case," he said. "It was a very strange case. Are you a relative of hers?"

"No, not a relative, but I take care of her."

"And? Is she walking?"

"No. She just sits all the time."

"Well, that happens sometimes."

"That happens sometimes? You wrote in your report that it can't happen."

The doctor gave her a smile again, this time not a polite one but a crafty one.

"It can't happen, but it does. In this world, things often happen that we can't understand."

"You also wrote that you recommended surgery but that the patient declined," Lena continued.

"Yes. That was my recommendation. But surgery wouldn't have helped anyway. In my professional opinion, the girl will never walk again."

"Then why did you recommend it? And why did you

include it in your report? You made it sound like she declined it, so it's her own fault that she can't walk!"

"We have certain rules. We need to present patients with options that may help them, no matter how slim the chances of success."

"Do you have a conscience at all? You wanted five thousand hryvnias for the operation! For an operation that wouldn't have helped!"

"That's a lie. Medical care is free in Ukraine."

"Because of you," said Lena, "the medical commission wouldn't approve her for the first disability group."

The mask of feigned politeness began to slowly slip off the face of the God of Healing.

"Why because of me? Do you know how many people apply for disability? If the commission approved everyone who applied, we would have a whole city full of cripples."

"But she can't walk! She can't go to the bathroom on her own! She spends all day staring out the window and crying! She has no money. Her family couldn't care less about her, and you're going on about a whole city full of cripples?"

"Wait a second. Why'd she have to go wandering in the woods in the winter? Who dragged her there?"

"So you remember her case perfectly well!" Lena erupted. "But you've conveniently forgotten that it was public servants just like you that denied her help when she needed it most and refused her shelter when she had nowhere else to go! She just got tossed out into the woods to freeze to death!"

The doctor interrupted Lena's tirade. "Why'd you come here?"

"I want you to rewrite your report. We're going to appeal the decision."

The doctor smiled yet again. This made Lena leery. The doctor said, "There's no need to appeal. I can take care of everything."

"Really?" For the brief moment between this sentence and the next, a spark of hope rekindled in Lena. Though not for long.

"She'll get assigned into the first group. I'll arrange everything. But it's going to cost a little."

Lena didn't respond.

"You do realize," the doctor was saying, "that nowadays you have to pay for everything. People apply for disability mainly in order to evade taxes, to import cars from abroad duty-free. And that amounts to upward of a few grand on one car alone."

"What are you talking about? What car? I need a chair, a wheelchair, so that my friend can at least be somewhat mobile on her own."

"I said that I'd take care of it, and I'll take care of it. Five thousand hryvnias."

"You have the same flat rate for everything, don't you?"

"It isn't much," he said in an attempt at self-justification. "A year or two of disability pay, and she'll recoup her investment. She'll get a monthly check. OK, two or three years tops. We'll get her registered for lifetime disability. Just imagine how much she'll make! She'll get a wheelchair, medical care, and all kinds of perks. They'll set up a phone line for her for free. She can get treatments in medicinal spas on the Black Sea or at the mineral springs in Slavsk. That's not bad either. She'll get the full workup, so to speak."

"If I had that kind of money, I'd buy her a wheelchair myself."

"If five grand's your limit, you'll be looking for a while. Unless, that is…"

Lena said, "Listen, I'd rather give you my savings so that you can get your own disability status. Your handicap is much more terrible than hers. You've had your heart amputated. Or what is it you would've called it… a stump of the heart?"

"Get out of my office," the doctor hissed like a hundred vipers.

Right after this, while working the nightshift at The Goldfish, Lena wrote her second manifesto. This one was entitled "A Manifesto to Cripples from a Cripple" and began with the observation, "I have no legs, but you have no heart." This text, unlike the first one, was never published anywhere. The literary and art magazine *Thursday* had been discontinued in the interim due to a lack of funding. And the local newspapers all categorically refused to print Lena's manifesto and her two subsequent articles because the topic of disability scared off readers.

"You have to understand where we're coming from," Lena was told in one of the editorial offices. "People are tired and frustrated. They expect positive stories from a newspaper. And there's nothing positive about disability. It's a taboo topic. People are more scared these days of becoming handicapped than they are of dying. And besides, just think about it — why should healthy people read about the sick? Why should they pity anyone? Just so you know, the most common causes of disability these days are car accidents involving drunk driving and failed attempts at diving into water, for example, when someone lands on a rock. It's no one else's fault that these people became cripples. They brought it on themselves. By being stupid."

Cripples don't need pity, Lena would reply. They became crippled be it through stupidity or a simple lack of luck, and that's their personal misfortune and the misfortune of their friends and family. They need to live with this, not you. But they have their own little cripple rights encoded in the great laws of Ukraine, and the only thing that we should be talking about is the implementation of those rights. We shouldn't be talking about pity but about rights/ A society is healthy only when the rights of everyone, even the sick, are being implemented. The disabled don't expect pity and empathy from the civil servants in government offices. They just expect the civil servants to do their jobs, which is the only reason they're sitting in those offices to begin with. The disabled don't expect pity and compassion from their doctors. They just expect them to do their jobs, which is the only reason they're sitting in the hospitals to begin with. The disabled don't expect pity and empathy from people in the street just that people not point at them as if they were lepers. Is that really asking too much?

We don't know, is the reply Lena received in the newspaper's editorial office. You should contact the non-profits.

Lena did just that. She found the one and only non-profit in all of San Francisco. It operated under the somewhat cynical name Life Lies Ahead and had all of a few dozen members.

The head of the organization, Anton, had been bedridden for ten years. Unlike Dog, he couldn't sit or turn his head. He just looked straight ahead, and his hands barely functioned. Only three of the fingers on his left hand could bend. He could use them to hold a cup of tea.

Anton was crippled as a result of one of the two leading causes of disability, drunk driving. He and a friend were heading home from a nightclub. His friend fell asleep at the wheel, and Anton tried to steer the car on a curve. The friend walked away with a few scratches while Anton crashed through the windshield, was flung a few meters, slammed into a tree and broke his neck. He didn't remember his first two years as a cripple. He thought he had died. On two occasions his heart stopped beating.

When Lena visited this Anton to get his advice, he was lying in a bed in the yard of a single-story house. A pretty fortyish-looking nurse was feeding him with a spoon.

"He can eat on his own too," she told Lena for some unknown reason. "Anton has two beds. One is here, in the yard, where he lies in the summer and when it's warm. The other one is in the house. That's where he spends the winter."

"And there's no hope of recovery?" asked Lena. "Oh, forgive me if I…"

"There's always hope," Anton replied amicably. "It's the only thing that distinguishes me from a tree trunk."

"He's so cheery!" the nurse jumped in. "He's always joking. It's never boring around here."

"So how do you make ends meet? Do you get a pension?"

"I do," said Anton. "It just barely covers the Pampers."

The nurse nodded, confirming that, yes, it just covered the Pampers, she could testify to that. Anton went on. "I'm lucky. My parents run a business. They invest all their money in immovable property. Namely me."

"See, I told you he's always joking!" the nurse chimed in. "Invalids like Anton only have one employment option, and that's to work online. I know nothing about computers. But he's a pro."

An opened laptop was lying on the bed next to Anton. With the three working fingers on his left hand, he was able to move the cursor of a virtual mouse.

"I'm not earning much yet. I just started last year, and it takes time. I'm making about fifty bucks a month for now."

"And what is it you do?"

"Well, that's a secret. You're better off not knowing. What I do isn't entirely legal."

"I won't tell anyone," Lena promised.

Anton laughed merrily. "I create, roll out and sell porn sites. When a site has more than ten thousand hits, you can sell it."

"So how do you roll them out?"

"Through other, more popular sites. I put banner ads on them. People click on them and end up on the site I made. When you've reached a certain number of hits, the site is ready to be sold."

"That sounds exhausting," Lena sighed.

"It's hard to come up with new banners each time, ones that people notice and want to click on. It used to be enough to just write "Black Man Messing Around with Two College Girls" or "Lesbians on a Beach" and the site would be swarmed with gawkers. But now I'm having to come up with something newer, harsher. People are no longer intrigued by blacks and lesbians. Sometimes even I get disgusted, to be honest."

Lena wasn't disgusted. She didn't know much at all about the Internet and knew even less about porn.

"It's good that you have someone to take care of you. Your parents hired you a nurse," she said.

"They did. She's been taking care of me for five years. We got married two years ago."

The nurse giggled. "As soon as I met Anton, I realized that we were soul mates. As you can see, he's constantly joking. He's not one to lose heart. We always have a lot to talk about. Even though he's in bed and will remain in bed, he's the best man I've ever met. Being able to walk doesn't make a man. Knowing how to be a man does.

And so the story goes, Lena would later say.

But some stories went altogether differently.

As a general rule, invalids, particularly those who couldn't walk without assistance, would sit for years on end in their apartments, ideally on the sixth or seventh floor, and gaze out the window. They couldn't go out into the street on their own because their wheelchairs, for example, wouldn't fit in the elevator, if there even was an elevator in the building, which wasn't at all guaranteed. If the wheelchair did indeed fit in the elevator, then it could just as well not fit through the narrow front doorway of the building. So someone would need to carry out first the wheelchair, then the cripple. But in some instances — and this was actually the norm rather than the exception — the cripple didn't have anyone to help him, other than maybe a feeble old mother. So, he would have no choice but to sit at home for years on end and wait for someone to take pity on him, to ask a friend or some distant relative or some neighbor to take him out for a walk and bring him back home once he had had his fill of fun.

A Biography of a Chance Miracle

In some instances, the invalid would luck out, and his building would have both a wide elevator door and a wide front door. Then the cripple could go out on his own in his wheelchair. But even these lucky few wouldn't get all that far because within two or three meters an inescapable surprise would be awaiting them in the form of an ordinary curb, sometimes high and other times low, but in either case substantial enough to damage the wheelchair finally obtained after many years and much exasperation. Or at the very least to flip both it and its owner onto the asphalt in one go. With time, some of the adrenaline junkies learned to overcome these obstacles, so unnoticeable to two-legged creatures. Others would wait for a kind pedestrian, whom they would ask to help them onto the curb if they weren't in too much of a rush. But there wasn't much point to this kind of help because within another few meters there would be yet another surprise in the form of yet another curb.

When all was said and done, it was best to just sit at home and gaze out the window.

Some people said that there were no wheelchair ramps in the city because that would make the construction of roads and sidewalks significantly more expensive. Others claimed that their absence was a crafty Soviet strategy to keep cripples off the streets, to keep them sitting at home so that no one would see them, especially not foreign journalists. Because in the Soviet Union, there was no sex and there were no cripples. The proletariat was made up exclusively of physically healthy, asexual people.

It is true that a new social service recently appeared in San Francisco that helps wheelchair users descend from their prisons in the sky, either to go out for a ride, or visit a doctor, or get some tests done, or fulfill one of a million other normal human needs. This service functions a bit like a rescue squad. Four big guys show up at the door. Two of them grab the cripple under the armpits while the other two carry the wheelchair. The service costs half a month's disability pension. Over the course of a month, if you don't eat or spend any money on an apartment or medical care, you can get out of the house exactly twice. And some cripples sacrifice everything for the sake of such a seemingly bizarre treat.

Lena said, "My friend hasn't been able to walk for two years. She needs a wheelchair. In the Department of Social Welfare, they told us that she'd get one but only after she'd been assigned to a disability group. We submitted the paperwork but got a rejection. They said that my friend wasn't at all disabled. We're going to appeal."

"I've been through all of it already," Anton replied, cheery as always. "And here's my advice to you. Pay whatever they want. Otherwise you'll waste time. You'll drive yourself nuts and still won't achieve anything. You're going to end up paying either way. It's not worth fighting them. They won't cave in because if they do, they'll have to cave in to all the other cripples out there too. And that would contradict the fundamental principle of Ukrainian bureaucracy."

"That's not true. I don't agree with you."

"Then good luck."

Anton's wife lit a cigarette for him, and he took it with his three functioning fingers.

You can't even imagine, Lena would later say, how much you can do with them sometimes.

10   A Bit of Theory

Two years ago there was an academic conference of young psychologists at the University of San Francisco, which, frankly, was of no benefit to anyone, including the young psychologists themselves, but which should nonetheless be mentioned.

The student V. Chubenko (age and gender unknown) chose Lena's story as a research topic and presented his conclusion that her behavior was caused by the hero-savior syndrome.

How the student came to know such extensive and cred-ible-sounding details of Lena's life remains unclear. It's possible that one of her relatives works in law enforcement and obtained the information for him. It is also unclear whether the referenced syndrome is actually recognized in the field of psychology, and, if it is, whether it pertains to the phenomenon described by V. Chubenko.

The study was published alongside other studies present-ed at the conference in the university newsletter, *The Path of the Young Scholar* (pg. 55–57). This publication is held in the university library, but as of yet no one has checked it out.

The young scholar V. Chubenko claims that the causes of Lena's questionable behavior can be found in her early childhood, specifically, in her parents' not entirely cor-rect approach to child-rearing. Her parents, whether con-sciously or unconsciously, demanded that Lena earn their love. Such an approach typically results in complete failure because, as the young scholar argues without reference to any primary source, it is impossible to earn love. In always attempting to be the best at everything, Lena very quickly realized that in this world there will always be others better than you. A psyche that exists in a state of perpetual self-comparison with others necessarily finds itself in pure mental hell. Such people are fifty percent more inclined toward suicide in adolescence. Should they nonetheless make it through their teenage years, never having successfully earned anyone's love, their psyche begins to consciously refuse any love whatsoever, while unconsciously continuing to actively seek it, but in a different manner. The psyche becomes socially hyperactive. It responds acutely to the slightest manifestation of injustice and is ready to sacrifice itself in order to eliminate this injustice. Such people formulate their own criteria of injustice. They themselves decide who is an enemy and establish the rules of battle, presumably in order to later become the self-proclaimed hero of this self-proclaimed war, according to the study's author.

Examples of the hero-savior syndrome are widespread and easily identifiable. Such people, for example, often spend years waging war on their local supermarket because they once bought stale bread there. "We're building up civil society," these people will say, but looking at the problem more broadly, you will become convinced that expending years of your life on such trivialities is actually a waste. In the end, the manager of the supermarket will admit, "So it happened once. We sold you stale bread." And what? Did it make you feel any better?

Other people, for example, will just as ardently try to protect three trees in a public park from felling and development. They talk about how they used to relax in the shade and coolness of a particular tree in childhood. They chain themselves to the tree. They don't sleep out of a fear of a night attack, and they hammer nails into the tree trunk hoping to damage the feller's chainsaw. This kind of battle is logical but only partially so because a city cannot remain the city of someone's childhood indefinitely. It expands and changes, and not at all in accordance with the laws of nature. If these three trees don't get chopped down, then ten other ones will. But the other ten trees don't matter to people with the hero-savior syndrome. Trees don't matter to them in general. The battle itself is what matters to them because it is only while in a state of battle that they feel themselves in the center of social history and can comfort themselves with the thought that they're changing this history. In their late years, heroes talk only about their great contributions to history and their great war, just as veterans who have survived a true war talk only about trenches and daring feats. Should you accidentally say to a veteran, "But war is pointless," he'll get angry and offended because that would mean that his trenches and his daring feats were also pointless.

So went the hypothesis of the study's author V. Chubenko.

Lena and her behavior fit very well into his overall theoretical framework. Lena only wanted to be loved, the young psychologist kept repeating. That was precisely why she came up with this whole mess with the homeless dogs and later with the rights of the disabled too.

V. Chubenko even met with Lena's parents in order to expound on the complete erroneousness of the views with which they stuffed their daughter's childhood consciousness, thereby causing such serious deviations in her psyche. The parents, in self-defense, just kept repeating, "We loved her just like other parents love their children. We loved her."

Lena's personal life and her relations with men further corroborated V. Chubenko's thesis. Lena had had only five or six relationships, he pointed out. And none of them had lasted longer than a few months. Men typically went running from Lena because she demanded incessant and irrefutable proof of their love. Lena's partners were expected to assure her, at least three times a day, that they loved her and that they would love her immeasurably till the end of their days. Her former lover and classmate K., the volleyball player from the regional team, spoke on this particular topic. He said, "She completely bowled me over with her love."

"But did you love her?" asked V. Chubenko.

"How should I know?" the athlete replied.

Another of her lovers, a former skier who now works for a small insurance firm, openly admitted that he had never loved Lena because "she's one of those types that can't be loved."

A third asked to remain anonymous. He noted that he had never doubted that Lena "is simply a fool and will come to a fool's end." As he put it, people like her needed to be isolated from society while still in early childhood. Lena's college roommate Vasylyna broke two of his ribs.

Lena lasted the longest with Yogi Paul, whom she met while in search of her great miracle. After their botched first encounter, they crossed paths a second time when Lena was working at The Goldfish. Yogi Paul stopped by one evening and ordered a double shot of vodka and an apple juice. He didn't recognize Lena. But Lena remembered him well. She hollered at him snippily, "Oh no, how is it that a nirvana dweller has sunk to the level of mundane earthly pleasures?"

The yogi sullenly drained his two glasses and left. He returned the following evening and ordered the same thing. No less snippily, he asked, "So, has the mysterious woman who knows how to fly and saves miserable people turned up?"

"It turns out that she doesn't actually exist," Lena grumbled.

"Who knows?" said the yogi.

"Do you know something?"

"No. But she just may exist. Or she just may not exist either."

"I don't understand you!" cried Lena.

"Because you want to understand everything with the mind, but you have to understand with the heart."

"Oh, please!"

Lena would later say that she hated psychobabble as much as she hated injustice because some sort of constant and objective truth did in fact exist. "There's the mind, which understands, and the heart, which feels. Why confuse people by complicating such simple things? How can the heart understand when its nature is to feel? Rabbits don't bark, and a dog won't suddenly start eating cabbage!"

"I like you," Lena said to the yogi, "but I don't like your need to try to find more purpose in your life than it actually has. It is, of course, none of my business, but I find it cowardly."

"So what kind of purpose does your life have? Aren't you doing the same thing? Aren't you trying to give it greater meaning?"

Lena thought back to the great people that were supposed to come crawling out of her, and to the blue Plasticine swan that she had inherited from her preschool teacher, and to the black rider on the black horse that rode around the deserted city during May thunderstorms, and to the rainbow, and the meat grinder.

"I've always thought that my life was special," Lena confessed for the first and last time (V. Chubenko placed particular emphasis on this point). "I thought that I was living for some special and noteworthy purpose. That I was better and smarter than others, that I somehow understood and felt more than they did and could therefore help them. I believed in my own god because my god couldn't be the god of others. My god was smarter than the gods of other people. I had my own viewpoint, which couldn't be the viewpoint of other people because I didn't want to be like them. But the point is that I'm not them after all. I'm just as different as everyone else. Are you following me?"

"Not entirely."

Sooner or later there comes a moment when people with the hero syndrome get disillusioned with their own heroism and lose all faith in it, V. Chubenko insisted in his

his is called "the crash of core illusions." An illu-
h is very dangerous even for a healthy psyche, he
went on. That's why most people try to guard themselves
against such trauma and prefer not to harbor any illusions
at all. In order to avoid failure, people choose to simply do
nothing because you can't lose if you're not playing. Inac-
tion is a commonplace defense mechanism. Certain behav-
ioral norms emerged long ago already in society, outlining
how one should live and what one should want in order to
avoid ending up a loser. You know all of them: being born,
finishing school, working, getting married, bearing children, then having your children produce grandchildren,
and the grandchildren great-grandchildren. Having your
own home, having three friends who don't forget to call
on your birthday, believing what everyone else believes,
loving as everyone else loves, and dying when your time
comes.

Whether or not we like it, such a life model must be
deemed healthy, asserted the young scholar, as usual without reference to a source. Lena strayed from this model
and, after encountering a major disappointment, was left
with virtually no chance of finding her way back. More
simply put, this was the start of her rapid downward spiral.

Yogi Paul was, incidentally, the only man who played by
Lena's rules and professed his love to her three times daily.
One would think that Lena would've been happy. And
she was for some time. (Yogi Paul didn't even swear Lena
off after all that. He insisted that he loved her and always
would. Today he's married, has a son and runs a rather
prestigious and successful school of Eastern practices in
San Francisco. He hides nothing from his wife. She also
studies yoga, spent three years living in Nepal, speaks four
languages and is a mathematician by training.)

"I like you too," Yogi Paul would tell Lena. "I just don't
like your maniacal need to help everyone."

"I haven't helped anyone yet."

"But you want to."

"I just want Dog to get a wheelchair. That's the right of people whose legs don't work."

We forget, V. Chubenko wrote in conclusion, that the concept of "lawful right" is in reality nonsense. There are laws, and there are rights, and often, virtually always, the two contradict each other. Society is not and never has been built in accordance with the principles of equality and justice. There can be no such thing as an ideal society when there are no ideal people. But there does exist an ideal balance. If someone is wiser, then someone else must necessarily be dumber. If someone is fortunate, then someone else must necessarily be unfortunate. If somewhere things are better, then elsewhere they must necessarily be worse. Lena didn't agree with this because heroes by their very nature don't agree with the status quo and work toward its destruction, without proposing any replacement. They fight against things, not for them. If the planet were populated only with heroes, there would be nothing left of the planet but stones and bones.

Lena never read this analysis of her psychological problems. We will never know if her attitude or actions would've changed had she read it. It's possible that Lena knew, or at least suspected, what drove her and what her rebellious spirit yearned for. The single difference between the author of the study and Lena was that V. Chubenko already knew the end of Lena's story, while Lena didn't. She likely gave no thought to how her interminable war with San Francisco's social services would end. Her friend Dog, whom the young psychologist unhesitatingly categorized as having a persistent victim complex, kept asking feebly, "Maybe we should drop it, Lena? I think I'm slowly starting to feel my legs already. I recently dreamed that I was running."

Dog wasn't being entirely honest because she couldn't feel her legs and, incidentally, doesn't feel them to this day.

"There's no way to back down now," Lena would object unequivocally. "We'll win because the truth is on our side.

You can't just say that something's black when it's really white. We'll show those sub-humans what's what."

"I would also like to know what's what," Dog would say.

"And so you'll find out."

In the weeks following the denial of Dog's disability status, she and Lena submitted an appeal contesting the decision of the MSEC. The appeal, however, was unsuccessful. Actually, it wasn't reviewed at all on the grounds of "a lack of all required documentation."

"Those wanting to issue a denial," Lena would later say, "will never have sufficient documentation. In this country it's simply impossible to gather it all. One has to wonder why they don't also require a certificate confirming the death of the applicant, for example. It could read something like this: 'Issued prehumously to so-and-so as official corroboration that the named is actually dead.'"

It furthermore turned out that Lena wasn't authorized to simultaneously work and take care of Dog. Caregivers were only allowed to give care, not engage in other pursuits. The state paid them a monthly assistance stipend of five hryvnias for this kindness.

"How are you supposed to get by on five hryvnias a month?" Lena would marvel. "And how can I be her caregiver if Dog officially isn't disabled?"

Lena's questions went unanswered. They would tell her, "We act only within the framework of the law."

"Your laws are pure obscurantism! They were contrived not to help people but precisely in order to not help them!"

That was when Lena launched her demonstration in front of San Francisco's White House. She called it white because that's what it really was. White. A massive, multi-story, white structure shaped like a crescent. All the local authorities had their offices there. That was why picketing it was very efficient and convenient, particularly since Lena wasn't able to conclusively decide at exactly which government office she should target her frustrations.

She brought Dog to the square before the building, planted her on the pedestal of the monument to the three bandura players, and unrolled a poster that read "THEY CLAIM SHE'S NOT A CRIPPLE."

11   AN EXPLANATORY MEMO

From: Bohdana Ivanivna Bihun
         Director of the Office of Social Policy

To: Taras Mykolayovich Movchan
         Deputy Mayor of San Francisco

         Internal, not for release to the press

July 14, 2006

Dear Sir:

I, Bohdana Ivanivna Bihun, hereby wish to provide you, Taras Mykolayovich, with a written explanation of my position regarding some widely discussed recent events, which have undoubtedly cast a shadow over both my office and my career. Upon reading this account, Taras Mykolayovich, you will clearly see that I am in no way to blame for what transpired. I was only acting in accordance with the Constitution of Ukraine, the laws of Ukraine, the decrees of the president of Ukraine, the resolutions of the Supreme Council of Ukraine, the ordinances of the Cabinet of Ministers of Ukraine, the instructions of the Ministry of Labor and Social Policy of Ukraine, the directions of the head of the Regional State Administration, the instructions of the head of the Central Office for Labor and Social Welfare of the Regional State Administration, the decisions of local government authorities, the directions of the mayor, and the regulations of our department, as well as other legal and administrative provisions.

Taras Mykolayovich, you know me to be an upstanding

and prudent staff member of the city council. My professional performance has never given you cause to call my competence into question. I have been serving the community for more than thirteen years. Over the years, I have seen all kinds of things and dealt with all kinds of people, but, I must confess, it was my first time to face something like *this*.

Our office does everything in its power and within the scope of its abilities to provide all of the residents of San Francisco with the benefits and services which, in accordance with the laws enumerated above, we should provide them. Our primary focus is on underprivileged citizens, who make up thirty-five percent of the city's total population. This is a very high percentage, and you are as familiar with this figure as am I, Mr. Taras. We do all we can to avoid leaving anyone without some form of assistance, but our capacities and resources are not limitless. Although it does not fall within my direct responsibilities, I personally meet with citizens for five hours a day, five times a week, and try to solve their problems right then and there. Just so you know, over my years of service, hundreds, even thousands, of thank-you notes have accumulated in my file cabinet from citizens whom I have helped. But these thank-you notes are not what make me proud. I have worked and will continue to work for the good of the city because that's my job, my life's work.

I would like to bring it to your attention, Mr. Taras, that I crossed paths with Citizen O. (who incidentally always referred to herself as L.) in the past. She came to me regarding the matter of stray animals. My notes on this meeting and its outcome can be found, upon request, in my visitor log. I must admit that even then I had begun to have doubts about her stability. This citizen acted very aggressively, refused to listen to what I was saying, tossed around baseless accusations, spoke incoherently, and likely didn't know herself what exactly she wanted. I nonetheless managed to resolve this conflict, and, as you are most likely aware, the unacceptable abuse of stray dogs, which the citizen brought to our attention, was promptly eliminated. But our office wasn't satisfied with this achievement, and the first shelter in the region for our smaller four-legged brethren was opened in the city last summer. It was then that we demonstrated our sincere commitment to developing urban policies based on the principle of a humane coexistence between man and nature.

However, based on subsequent events, it appears that Citizen L. was just conducting a practice exercise in her canine activities.

You know, Mr. Taras, and please forgive my getting emotional, but I personally take great offense at such unequivocal stances on the part of certain citizens. Namely, that the government is by definition bad because it is the government. That the government only steals and gets rich off its citizens. You and I both know how far from the truth such allegations are.

It was only later that I made inquiries and ascertained that Citizen L. grew up in a dysfunctional home. Her parents are divorced. She experienced a psychological trauma in early childhood when her preschool teacher died tragically before her very eyes. L.'s best friend from school got married at age fifteen! You will likely agree with me that this says a lot about L. herself. She never finished college for unknown reasons, even though she was in a state-funded slot, likely obtained through connections. In a private conversation, the chair of her department informed me that L. was an irresponsible student and that her studies were hindered either by the indifference of today's youth or by a lack of intellectual ability. These are not my words but those of the department chair, a respected and trustworthy man.

And now, more concretely, about the incident in question.

Citizen L. first appeared on the square before city hall sometime in early March of this year and launched her unauthorized one-woman demonstration. She brought along the previously mentioned school friend, the one who got married at age fifteen. As a result of a tragic accident, the girl lost her ability to walk. So Citizen L. brought along her crippled friend (whom she called "Dog," incidentally, just imagine!) and set her right on the cold pedestal of the monument, which is a part of the decorative ensemble of Mykhailo Hrushevsky Square. We don't know whether or not the invalid had consented to such a stunt. It is possible that criminal intent and domestic violence were also at play here. I have already contacted law enforcement to look into the matter. Invalids, being unable to stand up for themselves, are, incidentally, the most frequent victims of domestic violence in our region.

There's only one thing that interests me: Why didn't Citizen L. come to me straight away? Why the need to immediately resort to radical measures by staging a demonstration before city hall without talking to someone about it the day before? I assure you, Mr. Taras, that I would have found a solution to whatever the problem was. My only fault lies in not having had any inkling of Citizen L.'s contentions.

Her poster said, "They claim she's not a cripple."

Who would claim such a thing, Mr. Taras? Anyone can plainly see that Ivanka — that's the disabled girl's real name — isn't able to walk. After having a conversation, we would've found a way to help her at once. However, it's still unclear to me, as an employee of the social service, why, for example, we should have at all engaged with Citizen L. Who is she to the injured party? A godparent? A sibling? An in-law? How are we to know what her personal stake is in the matter? Perhaps L. wanted to use her friend's disability benefits to launch some sort of criminal activity. I'll be honest, in hindsight I don't doubt this.

For several weeks no one paid any attention to Citizen L.'s demonstration. This is, of course, unacceptable. We should respond to such things with lightning speed. Demonstrations discredit the city government and undermine people's confidence in it. I didn't take urgent measures for one reason alone: I was unaware of this demonstration. As you yourself know, when you're buried up to your ears in work from eight in the morning till six in the evening, it's hard to keep an eye on everything.

Journalists played a decisive role in this story. The city had never before witnessed such blatant unprofessionalism! Instead of coming to me, asking me what was going on, hearing both sides of the conflict, and then allowing readers and viewers to draw their own conclusions (such, after all, are the generally accepted rules of journalism in the civilized world!), these people opted to make do with the mendacious statements of an unstable woman and, as a result, turned thousands of city residents against us.

You know how the whole thing started, with that disastrous newspaper article and the front page picture. Two young women are standing under a blanket of wet snow in the deserted square before city hall and are holding a by then completely illegible poster in their frozen hands, while above them a headline reads "THE INDIFFERENCE OF OUR TIMES: DYING IS BETTER THAN SURVIVAL." I have no doubt that it was this photograph that triggered everything. This is a striking example of how the public consciousness can be manipulated. The day after the appearance of the article, people began to gather in the square. That was when I first noticed the demonstration. People were just standing in front of the main entrance to city hall. They weren't holding posters; they weren't shouting; they were simply standing in silence. I'll be honest with you, it was an eerie sight.

That is why I was thrown off and didn't understand what was going on. Please understand, I needed to first ascertain the cause of the public's dissatisfaction in order to determine how to proceed. After thirteen years of experience in my field, I have become one hundred percent convinced that it is impossible to please the public. They always want more. That is why I waited. I thought that the spontaneous rally would dissolve by the following day. But I admit that I was mistaken. The next day, even more people gathered in the square. They were joined by cripples on crutches, wheelchairs, and stretchers, some even in strollers. And all journalists need is the next scandal. They swarmed here like flies to carrion. With cameras, with the newest equipment. My skin still crawls just thinking about it.

And then all of these stories on TV! "San Francisco Rises Against Injustice," "Cripples of San Francisco Declare Hunger Strike," "Wheelchair War Continues." It was horrible. I haven't seen a bigger mob in the city hall square since the days of the Orange Revolution.

That was when I received a direct phone call from Kyiv, from the ministry. In a not entirely courteous manner, I was ordered to break up the rally as quickly as possible. Accompanied by my two deputies, I went out to the demonstrators. I asked, "Ladies and gentlemen, what is it you want? What are your demands?" And the crowd began to hurl insults and outrageous allegations of corruption at me in response. That was the protest showing its true face. The people themselves didn't even know what they wanted. They were just letting off steam. You know how it is: If you haven't gotten anywhere in life, then who's to blame? Right, the government. If something's a little off, who's to blame? The government. The government is always to blame.

I did not succeed in having a sensible conversation with the demonstrators. That's why in the evening, on my personal time, I went to the disabled girl's home, to her registered address. I didn't find her there, so I talked to her parents. They are honest and hardworking people. They have many children and live modestly. They scrape by as best they can in order to raise the children and give them a decent start in life. As do we all.

I spoke primarily with the disabled girl's mother, Mrs. Maria, an industrious and even-tempered woman. I explained to her that everything that had happened to her daughter was the result of a big misunderstanding on both sides, that the state always looked after its citizens, and that we would do everything possible to rectify the situation. I told Mrs. Maria that by law the state could not and should not negotiate with Citizen L., who has no formal relationship with the victim. Ivanka's legal guardians are her parents, her family, namely the people to whom she truly matters. Mrs. Maria was in complete agreement with me. She admitted that she had never liked L. and suspected her of being psychologically disturbed. She was doubtful, as was I, that her daughter had come to Hrushevsky Square of her own volition. Ivanka had simply fallen prey to a con artist. Just think about it: as if it's normal to call a person "Dog"!

During the course of the difficult multi-hour conversation, the victim's mother and I reached a compromise: Ivanka would receive first-group disability status for life, with all the corresponding benefits prescribed to this disability group by Ukrainian law. She could pick up her wheelchair from the Department of Social Welfare the following day. The Office of Social Policy pledged to install a telephone line in the apartment in which the invalid lived within a month, and within three years the invalid's family would receive a car, which is also included in the benefits package for citizens who aren't mobile.

As I was leaving Mrs. Maria's apartment, she squeezed my hand and thanked me warmly.

I resolved the conflict and believe that I handled the matter correctly. I'm even proud of myself. As the saying goes, justice has triumphed.

The parents of the injured party picked up their daughter from the square before city hall, and the demonstration dissipated on its own. Citizen L., incidentally, put up a struggle. She tried to prevent the parents from taking the poor cripple home, yelled all kinds of nonsense, and accused them of all seven deadly sins. I was left with no choice but to involve the police. I reiterate that she had no formal relationship with the victim. In my opinion, L. could've been — and should've been! — brought up on criminal kidnapping charges. Perhaps then the whole mess could've been avoided.

I ask you now, Taras Mykolayovich, as a colleague and as a professional, what did I do wrong?

12   HOW SHE MET THE LAST WOODSMAN

This story is slowly reaching its end.

Dog's parents took their daughter home in blissful anticipation of the government-funded car.

Lena laid down her arms and returned to a conventional life, the kind that entails birth, maturation, procreation and death.

Yogi Paul, on his breaks from yoga exercises and meditations, planned their shared future with zeal uncharacteristic of Eastern teachings.

Lena's parents got remarried.

Lena's college roommate, the discus thrower Vasylyna, spent the next Summer Olympics in the bathroom once again. After the closing ceremony, when her stomach had returned to normal, she said, "I don't give a hoot. So it wasn't meant to be."

The former lit professor Theophilus Bunny self-published a book entitled *Hairy Tortoises from Henan Province or Why It's Imperative to Believe in Everything*. After waiting half a year for a positive or at least some kind of review, he again tried throwing himself under a train, but the suicide attempt was unsuccessful because the trains had been canceled that night due to flooding.

The butcher Misha switched to selling sausages.

The former members of the youth organization Resistance Movement established a radical-right party with Darwin at the helm and made it into the city government on the next election. Their first project was to rename Builders Street Stepan Bandera Street.

A Biography of a Chance Miracle

Lena's acquaintance, the doctor Olha Ivanivna, opened a paramedical practice. Her principal specialties include surgery-free breast enhancements, a ten-kilos-a-day weight loss regimen and cellulite cures. Individual consultations are also available on the following topics: willpower strength-training, self-confidence acquisition, the art of flirting, and self-defense against male betrayal.

The local criminal boss nicknamed Monk was killed in an explosion in the Chervona Ruta boxing club. His remains were identified by his false teeth. They alone survived unscathed.

Seeing all of this, Lena would say that there was nothing more interesting than observing the passage of time. Being a witness to the beginning and subsequent development of stories that appear completely unnoteworthy at first glance. Feeling how memory swells and expands every which way, how it grows bigger and bigger, how it fills your entire body and keeps you from sleeping at night. "Memory is all I have," Lena would say, "memory like an endless database in which every trivial detail is chaotically tied to other equally trivial details. And it's very important to me to keep all of them in sight, to remember everything all at once. That's why I can't sleep at night. As soon as I close my eyes, some sort of recall mechanism starts up. My thoughts skip from one memory to another, and sometimes I worry I'll never come back from that journey."

"Don't worry, you'll come back," Yogi Paul would tell Lena, adding, "You need to learn how to forget. Memories are a tether to the world, and you do realize that the world isn't pleasant enough to warrant remaining in it forever."

"I don't remember the color of your eyes," Lena would reply somewhat disjointedly, "but I do remember the bag that my mom used to take with her to the chocolate factory when I was five. Am I losing it?"

Yogi Paul was in the process of opening his school for Eastern practices then, while Lena was still working at The Goldfish. She used to say that she liked that tipsy aquarium because very interesting specimens would come swimming in once in a while.

Once, for example, she got to know a woodsman there. He lived in the nearby mountains and had come into the city to sell a plot of his land to a health-and-wellness resort for two hundred dollars. He had been celebrating with the money for three days straight. He drank only whiskey.

"Why should I drink cheap crap today?" he would say to Lena, while embracing a bottle of something amber-colored and expensive-looking. "For once in my life, I've earned it. Whiskey — now that's the drink of mountain folks."

"So you're a real woodsman?" Lena would ask.

"They don't get any more real than me! I've been a woodsman for fifty years! I know every tree and every mangy fox!"

"And you've seen pheasants too?"

"And why wouldn't I have? I've seen them. I've seen a whole pheasant family. I'll be honest with you, there's not much to see. The male, yes, he's handsome, with a splendid tail and brilliantly colored, but the female, well, she's pretty much a chicken, a drab brownish-gray with dull little eyes. They sometimes all come out together to graze in the meadows — the male, the female and three little pheasant babies. Not only have I seen them, I've even tasted them!"

And the woodsman would pour some more whiskey into his cognac glass. He was a short man, slight but daring, and bursting with painfully inexhaustible energy. Lena would later describe him as a good-natured gnome that had escaped from a madman's dream.

People called the woodsman Marusechko. Incidentally, there was a write-up about him not long ago in a reputable Kyiv newspaper. The article was entitled "The Last Aurochs Herdsman."

"But forget the pheasants," Marusechko said to Lena that evening. "I've seen aurochs."

"Aurochs?"

"Wild cows."

"I know. I've seen aurochs on TV."

"But I've seen them in person, just like you now! I've herded them, like normal cattle!"

It's still unclear whether Marusechko was lying or telling the truth. His name was known at all the major TV stations and all the national newspapers with a halfway decent circulation. For a decade, the woodsman had bombarded the media and the Ministry of Forests and Wildlife with letters that always began the same way: "There's a crisis! Help! The forests are being chopped down! The animals are being shot up!" Marusechko never received a response to a single letter.

He would say to Lena, "That's OK. Little strokes fell great oaks. We have democracy in our country. I've read the Constitution. I know my rights and obligations. I'm fighting only through legal means! I send letters wherever I can. They know Marusechko everywhere, in all the agencies and departments! I write to journalists so that they come and show people the truth."

"And what, have they come?"

"Not yet. But, you wait, they'll come. Boy, will I tell them a thriller then! I'll tell them everything! How they're cutting down the forests, how they're raking up stones from the rivers for their fortresses, how they're shooting wild animals with their rifles! There used to be a herd of elks in the lowlands here, but now you won't find a single one. Only a handful of bears are left. That's because they catch cubs and keep them in their restaurants, like dogs, on a leash. They're scum, not people! The wolves have retreated far into the mountains. The foxes have grown mangy from fright. And then the creeps come to me with their insolent faces and say, 'Shut up, old man!' But why should I keep quiet? They won't live to see that day! They already 'talked' to me Mafia-style — that's what they call it — and shook me down, for some big bucks! And beat me. And shot at me. But it takes more than that to mess with Marusechko!"

At this point Lena was ready to leave the woodsman alone with his forest lawlessness and his whiskey bottle, but Marusechko grabbed her by the hand, pulled her close and whispered, "I'll tell you a secret. The worst ones are the shooters in uniform."

"Hunters?"

"What hunters? What are you talking about? Like we have hunters around here! These are murderers, animals! They buy themselves rifles for thousands of dollars and come here to *relax!* They shoot whatever they want whenever they want. They would shoot people too but don't dare to yet. They have no conscience and no fear. Red List Species, Green List Species — it's all the same to them! These pigs gorge themselves so full that they can barely stand and then start pulling the trigger. And they're not scared of anyone or anything because they're the ones in uniform. You know what I'm saying?"

"I do."

"Without a uniform they're nobody!" The woodsman ranted and raved. "Just losers on stubby legs! A sagging belly, a bright red face, bloated cheeks. It makes you want to just grab one and pop him with a needle! But in uniform they have power and are scared of nothing. Not of the law, and not of divine wrath. Tell me, please, how can you shoot an aurochs? It's just a cow, standing there staring at you with big trusting eyes!"

The article "The Last Aurochs Herdsman" appeared in newspapers not because of the tenacity of the woodsman Marusechko but as a result of unexpected public interest in the eradication of animals on the Red List of Threatened Species in Ukraine. At the suggestion of Kyiv environmentalists, the entire year was proclaimed the Year of the Aurochs. It was then that an amateur video documenting an illegal hunt was circulated, and it must be said that Marusechko was right: The hunters were completely hammered, while the aurochs, as they were getting shot from a distance of five meters, just stood there and trustingly gazed down the barrel of the gun.

Commenting on the video, government officials insisted at first that it had been doctored and later that the aurochs were being shot in a noble attempt to save Ukraine's agriculture industry (and not because the head of a male brought in tens of thousands of dollars on the black market). And that only sick animals were being shot. The ones that wouldn't survive the winter anyway.

In support of the government's theory that aurochs were harmful, some "farmers" materialized who swore that a herd of aurochs had trampled their entire harvest. "Ordinary peasants" tearfully claimed that aurochs had smashed their barns and fences "literally yesterday."

"These are seriously dangerous animals!" some government official insisted at a press conference. "They shouldn't be roaming around the villages! They belong in a zoo or wildlife preserve!"

In response, journalists began to collect stories about the aurochs, and some of them really do read like thrillers.

There was, for example, a wounded aurochs that by some miracle managed to survive a hunting round and came wandering into a village. The annual harvest festival was taking place just then in the village. In the village center, right next to a monument to the Unknown Soldier, a little stage had been erected, and the village chorus, comprising four old women, was singing Ukrainian folk songs in four-part harmony there all day. In the middle of the action, before the very eyes of the dumbfounded villagers, the wounded aurochs clambered up on the stage and let out a despairing roar. The singers jumped off the stage in fright, one of them almost killing herself in the process. When the village-wide panic had abated, the villagers began to debate what to do with the aurochs. One of them said, "Why, it's just like a cow! And what do you do with a sick cow?"

The men fetched their axes and hacked up the aurochs.

They divided the meat among themselves. And they did this, naturally, in a not very equitable fashion because the one guy that didn't get any meat lodged a complaint with the local branch of the Nature Protection Service. That's how the story became public. The police arrived and questioned the villagers. They even wanted to arrest someone as an example, but in the end they left empty-handed, realizing that the whole village would've had to be locked up. A young conscientious officer later told a journalist how he couldn't talk to the villagers because "their eyes were almost glowing red with some kind of satisfaction, as if they had just tasted human flesh."

There was another story about a little meat-processing plant that was secretly producing canned delicacies out of aurochs meat. The delicacies were called "From the Ivory Tower Bush" and could still be found until quite recently at banquets of high-ranking Kyiv officials.

The article "The Last Aurochs Herdsman" was about a herd of aurochs — the last in the region — and their tragic demise. A total of six animals.

The woodsman Marusechko told the reporter, "I noticed them right away. I saw their tracks in the woods. I was thinking to myself, 'OK, this is bad if they've wandered all the way here. I won't be able to save them.' I tended them every day. I would head out into the woods in the morning, asking myself, 'Well, where are my cows today?' And then I noticed them grazing in a clearing. Such handsome, proud animals. When you get up close to them, you feel their might. It's impressive! Even both Klitschko brothers couldn't lift an aurochs together. It's a beast! I kept my mouth shut, didn't say a word to anyone so that it wouldn't get back to the shooters in uniform.

"In the winter, a small calf appeared. Well, I was thinking, 'Now they'll definitely shoot them up. An adult aurochs's meat isn't good. It's tough, but the calf's meat is tender. They'll come to celebrate New Year's, the vermin.' And sure enough. I remember it like it was yesterday. It was the old New Year, January 14, early morning. Everything was covered in snow. It looked like paradise! 'Where are my cows?' I was thinking. I walked out into the woods and saw them standing in a circle in the clearing, the calf in the middle. That's how they protect their offspring. And then a giant SUV pulled up from the other side. The aurochs were startled and set off in a run. It must be learned behavior because normally they don't run. They just stand around. The aurochs were running along the edge of the forest. I was running through the forest between the trees, and the SUV was crawling through the clearing like a tank, like it was nothing, a piece of cake.

"The aurochs stopped by the river, poor things, not knowing what to do next. The ice wasn't very thick that year. The winter was warm, but there was no other option. The aurochs ran out onto the ice, hoping to scoot over it, but the ice cracked under their weight and they all sank into the water as one. It wasn't until April that I was able to fish out their bodies. I wrote a letter to Kyiv, telling them there used to be aurochs here and now they're gone. I wrote down the SUV's license plate number. I wrote down everything. No response."

The sharp-tongued woodsman concluded his tale like this: "Greetings from the empty woods, you pigs!"

But that evening, long before the appearance of the article, Marusechko smiled at Lena mischievously and pronounced that every bad thing had at least an ounce of good.

"Six of them drowned," he said. "I saw that with my own eyes. But the calf was left on the bank. I thought they would shoot it any minute. And, lo and behold, this fatso rolled out of the SUV, drunk and barely dragging his legs. He pulled out his rifle. I couldn't watch. I just couldn't. But I couldn't do anything either. So I hobbled on home. I'll tell you the truth, Lena, my eyes were flooded with tears. I came home and sat down on my porch.

It was frosty but sunny. Such a nice day, such beauty all around. The snow was glistening in the sun, and I was crying like a child because I felt sorry for those creatures. You understand? My heart was breaking, to tell you the truth. And then it happened! A miracle…"

"A miracle?"

"A miracle. A true miracle. I'm still not sure exactly what it was. You can believe me or not, that's your business. I don't know, maybe I'm messed up in the head. Anything's possible."

"So what happened?"

"I was sitting on the porch when I heard something fluttering through the air, almost like a bird, but humo-o-ongous. I rubbed my eyes and couldn't believe it. And you won't believe it either. There was a woman flying there. I give you my word. A woman, a normal living woman, just as alive as you and me, nothing special about her. But it was as if some kind of force was holding her in the air. And she was holding the baby aurochs in her arms. How she managed to snatch it away from in front of that rifle, I have no idea. And I'll tell you, the calf was very young, but still it must've weighed twenty or thirty kilos. And it was like nothing for her. She placed the calf before me and alighted. I was speechless. I was thinking, 'OK, now I've officially lost it. This is it. It's time to turn myself in to Tsokolivka, the local loony bin.' But she said to me, 'Take the calf, I beg you.' Well, I pulled myself together a bit and replied, 'I'll take it. Why not?' She thanked me and flew away."

Lena also poured herself a whiskey. Her hands were shaking and her heart pounding.

"Do you think I'm nuts?" Marusechko asked.

"No. A lot of people have seen this woman."

"She had a yellow kerchief on her head, with burgundy flowers, I think."

"I'd also like to meet her," Lena said dreamily. "If she really does exist, then this changes a lot of things."

"What the hell, if we're going to drink, then we might as well drink! Pull out a new bottle."

A Biography of a Chance Miracle

Lena didn't get home till the early morning. The last thing that she saw as she drifted off to sleep was an endless field. Giant hairy cows grazed on the field. Smiling elks with ample antlers strolled nearby. Wolves howled magnificently from all four sides of the field. Bears sucked their wild-honey-stained paws. And in the tall flowering grass rustled a family of pheasants, who had nothing to fear because the foxes had long since grown mangy from fright.

13 HOW SHE PEERED INTO THE DARKNESS TO SEE THE LIGHT

Tsokolivka is a large building with a single long, dark corridor. For whoever enters it, there is no road back. That's probably why Tsokolivka is referred to as a quagmire, a marshland, a swamp. It is also said that if you spend a long time peering into the darkness of Tsokolivka's corridor, the darkness will begin peering into you too.

Lena was brought here in the summer of 2006. At night. At first they kept her in a separate room. Later she was transferred to a shared room. That's actually where I met her.

The first things that I recorded about Lena were: "Thin, pale, smokes. Looks normal, but there are a lot of normal people here. What's her secret?"

Only later did I realize that there was no secret. Lena never hid anything. She was exactly the person that she seemed to be. Exactly the same as people thought her to be.

We would talk a lot, and I would meticulously record each of our conversations because it's a habit I have. When I write everything down, I can be calm and not obsess that I'll forget something. The doctors consider this habit to be one of the main symptoms of my disease.

When Lena first arrived, she was constantly crying. She would cry very loudly, wailing really, and her weeping would seamlessly blend into the general audio atmosphere of this place. The people here tend to enjoy a good cry.

They enjoy having a good wail. That's actually the only nice thing about Tsokolivka: You can let yourself do everything in here that you would be embarrassed or scared to do out there. You can cry to your heart's content in here. You can scream like a raving lunatic. You can make faces. You can stroke random people on the cheek. And there's one woman here that does that nonstop. She comes up to you and just strokes, strokes, strokes. In short, everything that is forbidden on the outside is allowed in here. But what's allowed on the outside is forbidden in here. And therein lies the catch.

This is how Lena ended up here. She told the story many times, and it was always exactly the same, so there's no possibility of any inaccuracies or misunderstandings.

One evening Lena's longtime friend Dog called to wish her a happy birthday. Then she said, "Are you mad at me, Lena? I'm sorry that I'm so spineless."

"Dog, I'm not mad at you," Lena replied. "Where'd you get that idea? In fact, I'm proud of you."

"Proud of me?"

"Yes, proud. You're a tough cookie. You've been through so much, and you still haven't given up. You're not spineless, you're strong. You're stronger than I am."

Later on Dog would brag to everyone that Lena had called her stronger than herself.

"How's the new wheelchair?" asked Lena. "Do you go out in it? Now you're almost independent, no?"

"Well…" Dog began to sob into the phone. "I went out once. And, you know, Lena, it was very nice. Very."

"Why only once?"

"Because the wheelchair broke."

"So have them fix it."

"It can't be fixed. I need a new one."

"So have your parents go to the Department of Social Welfare and fill out a form, and you'll get issued a new one."

"They went already, and they filled out the form. Now I have to wait."

"How long?"

Dog let out another sob.

"You understand, Lena, the Department of Social Welfare issues a wheelchair for five years. That's the regulation. If mine breaks before the time's up, then there's nothing that can be done. I have to wait five years or buy one at my own expense."

"But why did your wheelchair break so fast?"

"It was probably my own fault. I was careless."

That was when the earth lurched under Lena's feet. The following day, in a fury, she burst into the office of Bohdana Ivanivna Bihun, the director of San Francisco's Office of Social Policy.

"You filthy liars!" Lena roared. "How can you lie to people like that?"

Bohdana Ivanivna was sitting at her clutter-free desk smiling. She had been eagerly awaiting this meeting.

"Calm down," she said in a honeyed voice. "What happened? It seems we've met before. Your name is Olena, no?"

"Lena! My name is Lena!"

"Well, Lena sounds rather Russian, but you're Ukrainian after all…"

"Her wheelchair broke on her first outing!"

"Whose wheelchair?" Bohdana Ivanivna inquired sweetly.

"You know very well whose. My friend's. Her wheelchair broke. I saw it myself. That thing's not a wheelchair, it's a wheelbarrow! It's a piece of plastic crap from China! You could at most make it from one end of the room to the other in that thing without putting yourself in mortal danger. What if she had broken her neck out in the street?"

"Why don't we lower our voices a bit?"

Lena silently lowered herself into the chair opposite the civil servant.

"The Department of Social Welfare," said Bohdana Ivanivna, "issues the wheelchairs that the government buys. We don't personally choose the wheelchairs ourselves. Whatever kind we receive is the kind that we issue. And, yes, they are from China. At the moment, the government can't afford to purchase wheelchairs from, let's say, Germany. The German ones are of better quality, that's true, but they're considerably more expensive."

"But it's dangerous to move around on the ones that you issue. They break like matchsticks."

"That is not my responsibility, please accept that!"

"So what is my friend supposed to do now? She's immobile yet again."

"Legally, we may only issue a wheelchair once in a five-year period. That's the law. We didn't make that rule. Your friend should've been more careful with the wheelchair. These wheelchairs have undergone government testing. If they're handled with care, they sometimes last even longer than five years."

"Listen," said Lena, "tell me the truth. Don't hide behind the law."

Bohdana Ivanivna flinched. "What truth are you looking to hear? What other truth could there possibly be here?"

"You promised my friend's parents a wheelchair, a phone line and a car but haven't fulfilled any of your promises."

"They got a wheelchair! It's not our fault that your friend is such a klutz. The telephone line will be installed any day now! The phone installer is apparently very sick right now."

"You just wanted to shut them up so that they wouldn't protest anymore."

"And what exactly are you protesting against, Lena, if I may ask?" Bohdana Ivanivna hissed triumphantly.

"She's my friend."

"Well, then go, help your friend! Do something. Buy her a wheelchair. Why are you pestering me?"

"I'm not pestering you. This is your job. Instead of helping the disabled, you're misappropriating the money meant for them. Isn't that true? Don't lie. You order proper wheelchairs but issue cheap crap. Then you divvy up the difference among yourselves."

Lena grew pale. She felt nauseous. Later she would say that it had felt as if she had eaten a bowlful of poisonous mushrooms, or as if a piece of skin from a Spanish tomato had gotten stuck to her stomach lining. That happens to people when they're exposed to a great deal of stress. The body craves cleansing on a physical level.

Bohdana Ivanivna was shrieking. "That's a goddamn lie! I don't need the cripples' money! The wheelchairs went through government testing! They're suitable for use!"

"Show me the paperwork that confirms that."

"You leech! I'm calling the cops! Do you think you can just latch on and suck the blood out of me?"

"Show me the paperwork."

Bohdana Ivanivna turned toward the window to pull herself together. She inhaled and exhaled six times. She inhaled through her right nostril and exhaled through the left. She probably learned this technique in a handbook on "How to Preserve Your Nerves in Conflict Situations." When she turned back to Lena, she was once again composed and her face was steely gray and pale. You could reinforce the skeletons of high-rises with faces like that.

"Get out my office," she said. "I'm under no obligation to talk to you. You're not related to the invalid. You're just a hysterical broad that's underwhelmed by your own life, that's what you are."

"Bohdana Ivanivna." Lena unexpectedly began to plead. "I understand that's how the system works. You can't change it on your own. But you can change yourself. You can at least help someone, at least a little. These people are cripples. Many of them regret that they're still alive. Help them, and you'll see how good it feels to help instead of lying."

Bohdana Ivanivna came up to Lena and leaned in so close that Lena couldn't help but notice the red veins in the whites of her eyes and the way that a gamut of colors had blended to make her irises a single shade of putrid mud.

Bohdana Ivanivna whispered to Lena, "You won't achieve anything, Lena. And your friend will rot in her rank hole before she gets anything from me. You shouldn't have played at 'democracy.' I warned you. He who laughs last, laughs loudest."

At these words, the civil servant began to glow with the murky light of incarnate revenge. Lena gazed into this light and saw nothing. The earth lurched under her feet once more but this time with such force that, as Lena would later describe it, she experienced a brain-quake.

She grabbed Bohdana Ivanivna by the neck and squeezed with all her might. Bohdana Ivanivna began to gurgle and flail. Lena squeezed her neck harder and harder. She saw nothing and heard nothing. The neck reminded her of an old vacuum cleaner hose that had suddenly gone haywire and, instead of sucking crap in, was now spewing it out. Lena had to stop it. She was screaming, "Shut up! Die! I don't believe that you're real! I don't believe that such things happen!"

Bohdana Ivanivna's face turned blue, her lips grew puffy, and her eyes began to bulge out of their sockets. She was trying to wriggle her way out and was clawing and grabbing at Lena's hands around her neck, but Lena's grip was now as fixed and steely as Bohdana Ivanivna's grin had been before. Lena would later say that she had even had a metallic taste in her mouth. Her hands, her muscles and even the blood in her veins had turned steely.

Bohdana Ivanivna's secretary poked her head into the office and sounded the alarm. Her shrieks brought all of the bureaucrats from the entire floor running. They stood helplessly in the doorway and watched the head of the Office of Social Policy being strangled by Lena. One of the witnesses later described how he had been flummoxed and couldn't figure out what to do.

"You don't see that sort of thing every day," he kept repeating. "If you had only seen Bohdana Ivanivna's face, all blue and swollen like a frog's. It's horrible to admit, but I just thought to myself that her true self was emerging. If we're going to be honest, she was a rather contemptible person. There are rumors that she used to organize bloody dog fights in town. They got the dogs from the animal shelter."

Finally two men sprang to their colleague's aid. They later said that prying Lena's hands off was harder than prying open a bull terrier's jowls.

"This girl was a hundred times stronger than the two of us solid men put together. We were convinced that we wouldn't be able to rescue Bohdana Ivanivna. We hit the assailant on the head, but it was as if nothing had happened to her. She had a head like a lead balloon. And then a second later, the girl suddenly went limp and collapsed on the floor."

By the time the security guards pushed into the office, Lena was lying under the desk, not moving. Someone later claimed that she had been foaming at the mouth, but that's not true. There was no foam. Lena just lay there and watched with a blank stare as Bohdana Ivanivna is carried out of the office. And then she watched, with that same stare, as she herself is carried out, as she is taken first to the police station and asked a string of questions, as a few days pass and Lena's parents arrive and cry over her, as some man comes and shines a little flashlight in her eyes and says, "She's ours, we're taking her," as she is again taken somewhere, where she walks down a long corridor, and as the darkness in the corridor peers into her, as if to say, "Welcome, I've been waiting for you for so long."

Bohdana Ivanivna spent a few days in the hospital, recovered and went back to work. That was when she wrote the explanatory memo to her superiors in which she laid out her own take on the circumstances surrounding the tragic incident. A panel that included the mayor and his two deputies met behind closed doors and decided unanimously that there were no grounds for Bohdana Ivanivna's termination. Bohdana Ivanivna got teary-eyed when she appeared before the panel and said, "I appreciate your support! I can't begin to tell to you how stressful this has been for me! You bend over backwards trying to help people, and what do you get in return?" The bruises on her neck were so blue they were almost black.

The court found Lena to be psychologically disabled and ordered compulsory treatment in a mental hospital. Fearing another episode of sudden-onset aggression, Lena was initially kept in a private room, then eventually transferred to a shared one.

The first thing that Lena said to me was, "If Schneider himself were to come from Switzerland now to have a look at his former pupil and patient, then even he would wave his hand dismissively and say, 'Idiot!'"

What that was supposed to mean, I don't know. Presumably it was some quote, but I still haven't been able to figure out from where.

We would talk a lot. I gave Lena a quick overview of the situation. That officially there are a million crazies in Ukraine. But unofficially possibly as many as eight million. The most widespread conditions are alcoholism, schizophrenia and stupidity. I, personally, am a schizophrenic. I have to write down everything that I hear and think. At first I wrote things down on my arms, and then on other parts of my body. I was brought here when I took to writing on my internal organs. Recording things inside myself would be a hundred times more reliable, I figured. Lena agreed with me.

I wasn't able to determine her diagnosis on my own. She seemed to be completely normal once she stopped wailing at night, although she would do strange things sometimes.

Half a year later, for example, she wrote a statement to the chief physician announcing that she wanted to renounce her Ukrainian citizenship and that it was her lawful right to do so. That she was an ethnic Ukrainian by birth but could no longer remain a citizen of Ukraine because she found the laws of the country to be a personal encumbrance. The chief physician added Lena's statement to her medical record.

"I insist on it," she would say to him. "I'm renouncing my citizenship."

The doctor got sick of listening to it and consulted a lawyer he knew. He couldn't care less what kind of citizenship his patients had. But it turned out that Lena couldn't renounce her citizenship because she was serving a sentence for the infringement of Ukrainian laws.

"What a sophisticated Catch-22," Lena said and never revisited the matter again.

The following events were even stranger.

Lena, for example, kept asking the management of Tsokolivka to patch a hole in the wall of our room, though I can assure you that there was no hole in the wall. The plaster had crumbled in a number of places, it's true. Our roommate Yakha, who claimed to be from Chechnya but was in reality from somewhere around Kolomyia, liked to gouge away at the walls with my pencils, but you could hardly call those markings holes. Finally Lena hung a white sheet over the wall and calmed down. Once in a while she would gaze at the sheet as if she could or wanted to see someone there.

And then one night something incredible happened.

Yakha waited till everyone was asleep then stealthily set out to eat the apples that Lena's parents had sent her. Yakha really liked apples, and pears, and plums, and anything edible for that matter. We knew this, which is why we would hide our food parcels under our mattresses or pillows, sometimes even tying a goodie bag around our midriffs. Lena alone never bothered. She wasn't stingy, and Yakha used this to her advantage.

So anyway, Yakha got up quietly and crept over to Lena's bed. There, under the bed, the highly anticipated bag of apples should've been lying in temptingly plain view.

Yakha would later say that she had immediately noticed that something was off. Something about the room was different, but for the life of her she couldn't figure out exactly what. The wan light of the moon was pushing its way in through the room's small grated window. Yakha stood in the center of the room and peered uncertainly into the menacing shadows until she finally registered what was going on. Then she cried, "Get up! Get up! Something awful has happened! She's vanished! She's gone!"

We sluggishly poked our heads out from under our covers.

"Yakha, what vanished? The apples?"

"Lena! Along with her bed! The bed's gone! And Lena's gone!"

All six of us sat up in response to the ruckus.

Yakha wasn't lying.

The spot where Lena's bed had stood in the evening was now empty, save for the bag of apples obediently awaiting its thief. The women, notwithstanding the fact that all of them had lost their sense of reality long ago, all suddenly began to cross themselves.

I glanced upward, and that's when I saw it.

Lena's bed was suspended in the air up against the ceiling as if someone were holding it there with invisible hands. Lena was peacefully asleep in it, curled up in a ball. The women's jaws dropped, and the bed slowly and silently sank back down to the exact spot where it had previously stood. When it landed, Lena drowsily asked, "What is it, girls?"

To be honest, I too made the sign of the cross.

Lena glanced around. We all clustered around her and started groping at the bed, as if wanting to reassure ourselves that it was real and not some figment of our very literally sick imaginations.

The bed seemed normal.

Lena too seemed normal.

The only difference was an inexplicable joy that seemed to be radiating from her face.

"Lena, what was that?" I asked her.

Lena smiled at me as if at that very moment she was experiencing a long-awaited enlightenment, as if she had been granted something for which she wouldn't even have dared to ask. I asked her in a gingerly whisper, "Lena, you can fly?"

She didn't respond. Even if Lena knew the answer to my question, she never did give it to me. She was probably worried that I wouldn't understand her reply.

When it grew warm outside, they began to let us out for a few hours a day to stroll around in the hospital's park. The grounds of Tsokolivka were surrounded by a tall un-traversable brick wall. We would ramble among the old trees, each of us on our own path. On the other side of the brick wall, our fellow sufferers — the drug addicts and al-coholics — were rambling in a similar park among similar trees. Tsokolivka was located right next door to the regional drug rehab clinic. The former lit professor Theophilus Bunny once fed nuts to sly ruddy squirrels there.

When we were being taken out for our first stroll, Yakha kept trying to convince the nurses not to let Lena out of the room. Yakha was yelling, "Don't let her out! She'll run away! Don't let her go!"

The nurses didn't listen to Yakha. They had long since learned to ignore their patients' incessant blathering. Later the nurses were very repentant because their bonuses were docked for negligence.

I would follow Lena around everywhere, recording her every word. I knew that there was little time left. I would ask her, "Lena, who are you?"

And Lena would reply with a laugh, "I'm a specimen of the fifth generation."

"You won't leave me, will you?"

And Lena would reply, "I will. And you'll get along just fine without me."

"I won't!"

"You will."

Yogi Paul stopped by a few times. He and Lena would sit on a little bench in the park outside and hold hands. Yogi Paul had grown sullen and thin. He looked unkempt and neglected.

"You'll get out of here soon," he would say to Lena.

"Mmhm," she would reply.

"You're not crazy. You just had a nervous breakdown. It'll pass. Lots of people have nervous breakdowns."

"Mmhm," Lena would repeat.

"You just need to finally start living for yourself, saving yourself, and not wasting your time on others. Other people don't need help. I've told you that before."

Lena would go on mmhm-ing, and Yogi Paul would leave, his once-toned plastic body hunched to unrecognizability.

On the eve of her disappearance, Lena wrote him a letter in which she asked his forgiveness and wished him all the best. She wrote: "A long, long time ago, I was told that there was good and there was evil. And that an upstanding person should be good. That was their duty. And that's what I resolved to be. Good. And so I waited to prove my goodness, to demonstrate it, to put it to use. But time kept passing, and nothing was happening. I did nothing good. Quite the opposite. In my quest to do something good, I engendered evil. And now I'm wondering, what is good really? We know what evil is, but what is good?"

Yogi Paul showed the letter to no one because he was worried that its contents would jeopardize Lena's discharge from Tsokolivka. He was waiting for her and would have gone on waiting indefinitely had Lena not suddenly vanished without a trace.

When it happened, he came to me to find out the truth. He brought me a lot of new notebooks and pencils. He also brought apples and candy, which Yakha later gobbled up at night.

Yogi Paul was for some reason convinced that Lena had been tortured to death at Tsokolivka and that the crime just had been covered up. That her body had been buried somewhere in the park and all traces of her had been obliterated. He even filed a complaint with the police in which he stressed that the circumstances of Lena's disappearance were very odd and that an investigation should be conducted. Because when people simply vanish from a mental hospital, the conclusion should be obvious. Tsokolivka was actually shrouded in a slew of horrible legends. Patients died frequently and suspiciously, but they never simply vanished, of that I'm sure. And I told him this too: "Lena didn't die, she's alive."

"Where is she?"

Yogi Paul was shaking all over from mental and emotional strain. He himself was one step away from a nervous breakdown. I didn't know if it was worth telling him the full story.

"You see," I said, "Lena made the decision to leave this place. I asked her to stay with us a little longer, but she didn't want to."

"How could she just walk out of here? Tsokolivka has more guards than a prison!"

"She didn't walk out."

Yogi Paul sighed heavily. He was full of despair and grief. He was very tired, and I urged him to go home and get a good night's sleep.

"Tell me," he was begging. "I can't go on like this anymore!"

I felt sorry for him. I decided that it was better to know the implausible truth than to believe a plausible lie. That's why I said, "Lena can fly. She flew out of here."

"Oh, please! Don't bullshit!" He sprang up and headed toward the exit quickly, almost at a run.

I followed him with my gaze. I really did feel very sorry for him.

The hospital staff, and the police officers later too, questioned me many more times. I told all of them the same thing: that I didn't know anything and that I didn't see anything. They needed to close the case. I understand that. But my statement would've hardly helped them. I'm a small person. My job is writing things down, not talking. Everyone has their own job. That's what Lena always said. Everyone has to do their own thing.

When I'm sitting on the little bench in the park among the ruddy-tailed squirrels and gazing into the blue sky, sometimes it seems as if I can see her. As if she's flying, rushing to someone's aid. Often I also imagine her racing through the air, holding the rescued baby aurochs in her arms, and it makes me feel particularly good, probably because animals in distress elicit greater compassion than do people. Lena lays the baby aurochs on the ground before the baffled woodsman and says, "Take the calf, I beg you."
And the woodsman replies, "I'll take it. Why not?"
And I get this wonderful feeling when I imagine this.

Lena left me two mementos of her: a blue Plasticine swan and a yellow kerchief with burgundy flowers, the same kind that her late grandma used to call "American." I'm safeguarding the swan and the kerchief in case Lena wants to have her treasures back someday.

There's still a lot I could write, but in my line of work it's very important to bring things to a full stop at the right point and begin everything anew. I'll wrap things up as Lena would have done, had she not considered words to be a waste of time and intellect:

"And so the story goes. But stories, of course, can go in all kinds of other ways too…"

Contributors

ABOUT THE AUTHOR

Tanja Maljartschuk is one of the most prolific and audacious young authors currently writing in Ukrainian, whose hallmark style blends searing social commentary with heartwarming humor and an appreciation for the human condition. The author of eight books of prose, her work has been translated into ten languages and is widely available in German. Tanja's writing has been supported by various governmental and private fellowships from the Chancellery of Austria, the Academy of the Arts of Berlin, the Polish Ministry of Culture and KulturKontakt Austria, among others. She is a past winner of the Joseph Conrad Korzienowski Literary Prize (Poland-Ukraine) and the Kristal Vilencia Award (Slovenia). *A Biography of a Chance Miracle*, Tanja's first novel and sixth book, was a finalist for the prestigious BBC Book of the Year Award in Ukraine, an award she subsequently won in 2016 for her novel *Forgottenness*. Individual stories of Tanja's are available in English in the anthologies *Best European Fiction, Herstories* and *Women in Times of Change*, as well as in literary magazines such as *World Literature Today* ("The Demon of Hunger"), *Words Without Borders, Belletrista* ("Canis Lupus Famliaris") and *Apofenie* ("Losers Want More"). *A Biography of a Chance Miracle* is Tanja's first book to be made available in English; an English translation of her novel *Forgottenness* is in progress.

ABOUT THE TRANSLATOR

Zenia Tompkins holds graduate degrees from Columbia University and the University of Virginia and began translating after fifteen years in the education and private sectors. She is the founder of The Tompkins Agency for Ukrainian Literature in Translation (TAULT), a nonprofit literary agency and translation house. This, her first translation, won the 2017 Kovaliv Fund Prize, a biennial American award for best translation of a Ukrainian work. Zenia is proficient in eight languages and translates exclusively from Ukrainian. She currently lives in Latin America as the spouse of a U.S. Foreign Service Officer.

A Biography of a Chance Miracle

About the Artist

Joe Reimer, hailing from Alberta, Canada, is a full-time artist, photographer and teacher who works in a variety of styles, mediums and subject matter. Having several artistic passions allows Joe to keep his work fresh and new, while still maintaining a high level of quality and mastery.

Joe is also well known for his abstract portrait portfolio. His philosophy for these striking portraits is to only add detail to the essential components of the face, while completely abstracting the rest of the image. These pieces are full of movement and energy, conveying very strong, powerful emotions. He is drawn to the notion of capturing the messiness of our humanity and finding beauty in places we wouldn't normally think to look for it.

Joe is on Instagram @JoeReimerArt and @JoeReimerPhoto or on Twitter @JoeReimerArt. He may be contacted through JoeReimer.com

CPSIA information can be obtained
at www.ICGtesting.com
Printed in the USA
LVHW101000210123
737671LV00022B/271